FOR EVER SERIES BOOK 1

WAITING *for* EVER

C. M. WYLLIE

Dub Press

www.cmwyllie.com

ISBN: 978-1-959583-07-3 (print)

ISBN: 978-1-959583-08-0 (e-book)

Content Warning

This book is meant for mature audiences and contains content that may be triggering for some readers—including sex, alcohol, drugs, profanity, violence, bullying, verbal and physical abuse, domestic and dating violence, and suicide.

If you or someone you know is contemplating suicide, please call or text the National Suicide Prevention Lifeline at 988 or go online to www.988lifeline.org.

If you're the victim of domestic or dating violence, please reach out to the National Domestic Violence Hotline at 1-800 799-SAFE (7233) or go online to www.thehotline.org.

Playlist

- "Innocent," Taylor Swift (Taylor's version)

- "Hell of High Water," Bailey Zimmerman

- "Hey Ho," Lumineers

- "Speakers," Sam Hunt

- "Can You Die From a Broken Heart," Nate Smith & Avril Lavigne

- "Don't Stop Believin'," Teddy Swims version

- "She Will Be Loved," Maroon 5

- "Patience," Guns N' Roses

- "What I Want," Morgan Wallen & Tate McRae

- "Heaven," Julia Michaels

- "I Can't Make You Love Me," Teddy Swims version

- "Warning," Morgan Wallen

- "In My Blood," Shawn Mendes

- "Worst Way," Riley Green

- "Beautiful Things," Benson Boone

- "Stoned," Parker McCollum

- "So Good," Katemale

- "Somebody's Problem," Morgan Wallen

- "I Quit Drinking," Kelsea Ballerini & LANY

- "The Good Kind," The Wreckers

- "Ends of the Earth," Ty Myers

- "Lose Control," Teddy Swims

- "I Don't Wanna Live Forever," ZAYN & Taylor Swift

- "Take Your Time," Sam Hunt

- "One More Night," Maroon 5

- "Love Somebody," Morgan Wallen

Contents

For the dreamers and romantics who know love is worth the fall.
And that heartbreak only proves how deeply we can love.

Every love story is beautiful, but ours is my favorite.

~Unknown

Prologue

Everly

Everyone knows. I can tell by the way they won't make eye contact as they hurry past me down the hall. The whispers. I want to scream at them that it's all a lie, but I just keep my head down and clean out my locker.

"Miss Davis? You're going to be late to homeroom. You don't want to ruin your perfect attendance this late in the school year, right?" Dr. Nia Franklin's voice, like warm melted butter, created a lump in my throat and pressure behind my eyes.

I try to nod my head in acknowledgment, hoping it sends her on her way.

"Everly, is everything okay?"

Nope. Didn't work. Points for trying. I face her with unshed tears threatening to spill over onto my cheeks.

"Okay, honey, let's go to my office. C'mon. I'll get you a pass for homeroom."

As the late bell rings, I sweep the rest of my stuff into the oversized backpack I brought today and follow her down the now empty hallway to her office—one of my favorite places in this school. It's bright, cheery and ... peaceful. I don't have many—or any—places I feel peace anymore. Did I ever? I can't recall another one right now except maybe my bedroom. I'm going to miss my bedroom. And Dr. Franklin. Not Coach Cruz. I won't have to hear him ask me to join cross-country every day in P.E. class. Organized sports? Not my thing. I just like to run. It quiets the noise in my head. Adding some level of competition to it would defeat its purpose.

"Evvie, what's going on? You know you can talk to me." Dr. Franklin, Oak Valley High's guidance counselor, closes her office door and motions for me to take a seat in one of the two chairs in front of her desk.

I always sit in the one closest to the windows. I like the way the morning sunlight feels on my face from that chair. Even when it's not the morning, I still pick it.

Shrugging the backpack off my shoulder, it sinks to the ground next to me and flops over sideways with the weight of all the crap I accumulated in my locker over most of senior year. I don't know how to answer her question. Just thinking about it exhausts me. I guess that's the biggest thing. I'm tired. Tired of it all. I know I can talk to her and have plenty of times throughout high school. She's been helping me plan my college career since my first day of freshman year. Now, three months before I graduate, I just want to leave and never come back.

"I'm leaving OV." I opt for succinct.

She blinks once, twice, then leans back in her chair, folding her hands and resting them across her stomach.

Keeping my focus on her until one tear slips down my cheek, I lower my gaze to my clenched hands. I really don't want to break down and lose my shit in front of her. After a couple deep breaths, I swipe the wet trail from my face and look at her squarely in hopes of conveying my mind is made up.

"You've got three months left. You've easily secured valedictorian unless Eli Tran has a perfect record for the rest of year and you . . . don't. What's happened that you can't stick it out for three more months?"

She's watching me. I can feel it even though I've lowered my eyes again. I don't want to see the look on her face. Whether it's disappointment, concern, pity, I don't want to know.

How do I tell my favorite adult at this school all the shit that's happened in the last month? Maybe she's heard the rumors herself. She doesn't act like she knows. She seems genuinely surprised by my leaving. Maybe I can tell her the truth. I just don't want to hear her try to talk me out of it. My mind is made up. I don't like school anyway, at least not the people part, especially now. The learning part is easy, effortless, and therefore unstimulating. But the people . . . This is why I prefer losing myself in fictional worlds to connecting with living humans. I wish the real world could be more like my make-believe ones. Full of funny, ride-or-die best friends, swoony boyfriends that give "touch her and die" energy and happily ever afters that make for the sweetest of daydreams. But my world here in Oak Valley has become whatever the opposite of that is. Maybe that's the problem. I project some fairy-tale expectation onto real life, and it doesn't measure up, like my older sister, Olivia, always accuses me of.

"I just need to go. I need a fresh start away from here." Without looking up, I see her nodding. I hold my breath and plead silently with the powers that be she accepts this without debate.

"Okay. Where will you go and how can I help?"

Exhaling a long breath through barely parted lips, I say, "I'm going to stay with my mom's best friend in Blue Lake."

Chapter 1

Everly

So far, starting over sucks. I wish I could see it as an adventure. A blank canvas. A fresh start. Mostly I just feel alone, anxious and kind of sick to my stomach. As lives go, mine before wasn't particularly spectacular, but it was mine. And to protect my family—what's left of it—I moved to Blue Lake. I like the idea of doing it for self-sacrificing reasons, like for my sister, who doesn't deserve the fallout of my drama. But the bigger reason, the hard one to admit, is that I was just done. Done being blamed. Done being bullied. Done looking over my shoulder wondering what the next thing would be and when it's coming. Small towns can be tough. And Oak Valley is no different. The generations of loyalty, however misguided, alternately intrigue and sicken me. It amazes me how the schoolyard antics extend to the adults. Everyone weighs in, and it becomes a frenzied dog fight if you wrong *one of theirs*. Sadly, I thought I was *one* or at least lived on the perimeter of the chosen ones. It doesn't matter now. I crossed a line. Except I didn't. I know I didn't. But it didn't matter. The thing about being a chosen one is you get to tell the story, and no one disputes the telling.

One thing I can say about Blue Lake is it's beautiful and remote, the perfect place to disappear. Okay, that's three things. But I'd love to do just that—disappear. I'd prefer to go back to being the invisible bookworm I've been most of my life, and this town where no one knows me, and I know no one except Allie, might be the perfect place to do it. And the scenery doesn't suck. What does suck is not knowing. Not knowing what to expect, what comes next, where I fit in. I feel calmer when I can plan for every possible scenario. For now, staring out the wall of windows overlooking the glass surface of the lake beyond Allie's backyard is allowing me to breathe. Really breathe. For the first time in months.

I can't remember the last time I didn't wake up and forget for just a second before it all came crashing back through my mind. The weight didn't settle on my chest until I felt like I was suffocating. Here, I can go outside without looking over my shoulder. Although I won't be going back to school, but I was over school anyway. It's not how I envisioned finishing my senior year, but Dr. Franklin made a call. I'll finish my senior year remotely through Blue Lake High School. I think I'll like it—remote learning. My anxiety likes it already. And everyone agrees this is the best option for all of us. All of us being me, my sister and my mom. Even Allie, who's never lived with a kid twenty-four seven, likes the idea of gaining a helper. I decide to be as invisible as possible and as helpful as possible when I'm not invisible. Like now.

I take a deep breath before I head downstairs to greet her and start my first day of work. I take one last look around my new room. Bed made. Clothes picked up. It looks like no one lives here. A perfect military brat. With another deep breath, I step into the hallway and close the door.

***

"Morning, Evvie. How'd you sleep?" Allie leans against the far counter in the kitchen and sips from the steaming mug in her hand. She's what I'd guess regular people call *granola*. Even though she owns and operates the local fitness center, not exactly granola, she's equally committed to the outdoors and the earth. Maybe it's more accurate to say she's a health nut. Whatever the label, she oozes it from every pore. She has that glow people talk about in commercials. Her skin is tan even coming off winter. Her hair shines even twisted into a knot on top of her head. And she looks like someone in her twenties instead of her early forties.

"Great. Thanks. It's so quiet here," I answer with the cheeriest smile plastered on my face. The truth is the quiet is deafening. And because it's so quiet, every little rustle of leaves pierces like thunder. I lay motionless and wide awake most of the night pondering if even turning over in bed might be heard down the hall.

"Are you a coffee drinker? Tea? I know tea is supposed to be the healthier option, but coffee will always be the nectar of the gods." Allie holds up her cup in a salute.

"Uh, coffee would be great, thanks. I can get it, though. Where are the cups?"

She hands me one she's already removed from the cupboard for me and I fill it from the urn on the counter and take a quick sip. The bitterness stings my tongue and throat. I take another.

Allie watches me for a moment like she wants to say something. She doesn't. She simply flows past me and out of the kitchen. At the bottom of the stairs, she turns and says, "We'll be heading to the fitness club in thirty minutes. Meet me back down here then, okay? And there's cream and sugar if you don't like it black."

I don't like it black, but I drink it that way to come off as low maintenance. I wander around the kitchen for a minute getting my bearings. She left some quick-grab breakfast out, beyond healthy no doubt. I peruse my choices suspiciously, opt for just the coffee today and head back upstairs to get my shit together.

Allie is great though, breakfast choices aside. She's like the cool aunt who doesn't treat you like a kid because she never had kids of her own. And she is. Cool, that is. She's my mom's oldest friend and lives in what's known as the foothills below the Sierra Mountains of Northern California, about an hour's drive from Oak Valley, the town I lived in my whole life. She runs a fitness studio and lives in this sprawling house that overlooks Blue Lake. Her whole existence is a chill, Zen state of being. Why she's agreed to take me in is beyond me. Lately, I seem to be a magnet for whatever the opposite of Zen is. But she and my mom are more like sisters than friends, and she considers us family. More so than her own that I've never met and seldom hear her speak of. So maybe that's why. Or maybe she's just that nice. Either way, I'm here, in her space, trying to piece my life back together.

Here goes nothing, Ev. Adulting, here I come.

The thing is, I'm not exactly an adult. Eighteen last month, so technically I guess I'm an adult, but I feel like a kid pretending to be an adult. I wasn't quite ready to strike out on my own. Not exactly on my own here, but not exactly *not* on my own. I've left the only home I've ever known to live in the middle of nowhere, skipped months of my senior year to go remote, and now take a job in my mom's best friend's fitness studio and essentially disappear from my life as I know it. I'm not even sure what the job will entail or what I am even qualified to do, but she agreed to give me one, so I guess I'll be grateful instead of feeling sorry for myself. Besides, I chose this. To disappear and start over. I don't care about all the senior year rituals or all the first *lasts*. Okay, losing the valedictorian thing makes me a little bitter—mostly because that suck-up mathlete, Eli Tran, would get it. Everyone knows math is inferior to literature. His speech will probably suck too. I shake my head at the train of my negative spiral. Eli is a nice guy. I don't begrudge him his glory. I left by choice. And I don't need the coveted valedictorian status anyway with my college plans now up in the air.

Fuck, what is my life right now?

The weight of it all has me feeling like the oldest eighteen-year-old on the planet. And feeling old is not new to me. A new level, sure. But I'm stubbornly ready for it. Proving haters wrong is a great motivator. Though they'll never know if I succeed or not. They'll never see me again, God willing.

An introverted homebody, I've always been an easy target. I tried to bond with girls my age, but it wouldn't be long before I said something that caused the blank stares and eventual ghosting. Dubbed a brainiac since preschool didn't exactly help me blend in. Speaking fluent movie, TV and book quotes since puberty for them to fall on ignorant ears got me mocked and avoided. So I mostly quit trying. I decided that being uninterested in them before they could become uninterested in me felt better. But I wasn't without my uses. Some of the more popular girls my age had been asking me to write poems for their boyfriends since seventh grade when I got called on to read one out loud in English class. They were also willing to pay for it. And . . . my accidental, super-secret Cyrano-esque side hustle was born. Of course, it came with all the threats of *ruining* me if I didn't swear to absolute secrecy. What did I care? Not gonna lie, I low-key ate up the idea of their boyfriends catching feelings over something I wrote. And writing gave *me* all the feels, so win-win.

It's also why the only socializing I engaged in were the occasional invites to hang out with my older sister and her group of friends. They didn't treat me like a subpar human. As the youngest of the group and only a member by sibling proxy, I kept a low profile and tried to fly under the radar. Mostly house parties and usually at Chase and Kendall's, the unofficial leaders of their crew. My sister, Olivia, only recently began inviting me. I guess Via felt sorry for me. Or maybe I was old enough now not to be a burden.

Either way, my sister's crew was different—many of them older siblings of the bitchy girls in my class—and their boyfriends. *Small towns.* They treated me like their mascot, which wasn't as bad as it sounds. They doted on me. Did I get a drink? Did I have enough to eat? Was I having fun? It's like they were all playing adult, and I was their kid. But it was a win-win. They got to feel older and superior, and I got more attention from them than I had my whole life. And for well over a year now, they were "teaching" me how to party. After my first hangover, I decided drinking wasn't my thing, so I slowly sipped one throughout a party and faked the "fun." And it worked. It kept the peer pressure to a minimum. Until it didn't.

I shake my head to physically snap me out of the memory spiral and focus on the passing scenery out the passenger window.

The drive to Fit, as Allie calls it—full name Blue Lake Fitness Club—is quick and Allie explains there's a bike trail I can safely use to ride to work on nice days. I left my car back in Oak Valley. What's left of it anyway. Maybe if I save enough money, I can get another one. But I know that won't be anytime soon. I brought my ebike though, so that could be fun if the weather holds. California is known for its sunny and seventy-five hype, but the Sierra foothills are known for being one of the few places in the state that boasts all four seasons, albeit short snippets of them. The trail looks cool, peaceful, like everything else up here so far. It meanders through the trees and follows the curve of the road to Fit. I make a mental note to check it out on my first day off.

Eucalyptus and mint hit my nose first walking through the doors. It's nothing like I pictured. It's huge. And more like some bougie country club than the small-town gym I envisioned. No wonder Allie oozes serenity. The smell alone embodies health and fitness. Every cell in my body exhales. I feel lighter. She gives me the tour, and I feel a sense of home, but I don't want to trust it just yet. I follow her around as she proudly describes the layout. From the juice bar to the men's and women's locker rooms that each boast a sauna and steam room, my excitement builds. This place is incredible for the small *hillbilly* town it resides in.

"Wow, Allie. Impressive! How many employees do you have?"

"Including you, five. Letty helps me manage the place during the day. Two high schoolers, Lilliana and Noah, share the afternoon and evening hours. And Julian and I share the personal training appointments. He and I also lead special classes. He's trained in kickboxing and personal fitness, and I run Pilates and yoga. On weekends, Fit also features remote access that we enable so members can use an app to unlock the doors during modified business hours. When we activate remote access, we lock access to the saunas and steam rooms."

I nod as she explains. *Cool, so we get days off sometimes.* Not that I'm lazy. I like to be busy. I was just wondering how she worked here every single day without any days off. Tension drains from my shoulders at hearing there's only five new people to deal with. Well, four if I'm the fifth. I can meet four new people. "Our Fit crew is really nice," she adds with a chuckle.

I guess I'm not hiding my apprehension very well.

"C'mon. Let's get you a Sunshine Shot. I noticed you didn't eat any breakfast. And juice shots work great on an empty stomach. Letty is the master behind our shot creations."

We make our way to the juice bar around the corner from the welcome counter. She opens a little fridge and grabs two bright orange containers and hands me one. She slams hers like a shot, so I do the same. *Spicy . . . and delicious.* The tangy sweetness wakes up my taste buds and puckers my lips. After the tour, she asks me to fold towels from the dryer in the back room behind the front desk. It's a small area with a table and chairs, washer, dryer, a folding table and some shelves. I throw in my earbuds and crank my old-school rock playlist as loud as my ears will allow and welcome the mundane task.

Armed with my neat stack of linens, I head to the counter a few minutes later to ask Allie where they belong. Coming out of the back room, partially blinded by the wall of terry, I hit a wall. The towels topple over and puddle at the feet of my *wall*, which isn't a wall at all but might as well be. My eyes track large tanned hands attached to larger toned arms extended out low in a clear stance of *what the hell*. I note a long, wide scar on the inside of one forearm but don't dwell on it. I raise my eyes past the tight-fitting thin, white muscle shirt that showcases a sculpted six-pack and bulging pecs underneath. A tan taut neckline with veins protruding on either side connect to a rigid, chiseled jaw and chin. My scrutiny pauses on a full set of pouty lips slightly agape and quickly continues until I meet eyes of crystal blue under dark slightly raised brows. Brows that are almost hidden by the tufts of equally dark brown hair spilling onto a creased forehead. The messy strands fade into a neater buzz beyond his ears. He's most certainly not the high schooler named Noah. He looks older than a high schooler for one and clearly annoyed. My heartbeat trips on the pure virility oozing from this tower of a guy—like no high schooler I've ever met.

Julian. Great, Ev. Way to make an impression on the first of the four. Pulling out one earbud, I begin to apologize but stammer instead. *Uh, I hate it when I do that.* I quickly shove the earbud into my leggings pocket so I can *pay attention to my surroundings* (I hear my mom's voice in my head) and bend over to grab the towels. I think he grunts (*Really?*) as he steps around me and continues on his way to wherever he was headed.

Allie must've witnessed the collision because she chuckles and she's there instantly helping me pick up the pile. She tells me to divide and stack them on the towel racks in each locker room between the saunas and steam rooms. "Just knock before you head into the men's room. We're the only ones here right now, but it's a good habit to get into. Heading into my eight a.m. hot yoga if you need me."

And just when I thought she ignored the collision, she adds, "Don't mind Julian. He can be . . . moody." With a little giggle, she turns to go—then pivots back. "Evvie, breathe. You've got this. Fresh start, remember? Give it a chance. Blue Lake will steal your heart. Promise."

Sounds nice. But to steal a heart, you've gotta have one, and I'm still not sure mine survived the hit.

Chapter 2

Julian

I almost took out Allie's new *project*. Typical teenager, earbuds in and no clue of their surroundings. I should've helped her with the towels. I should've asked her if she was okay. But one look at the saucer-sized doe eyes . . . and then the stammering. *You were one of those projects once, so don't be such a dick.* But Jesus, she might as well have been screaming "Save me." I had to get the hell out of there. And I usually reserve the sauna for post workouts, but I admit it, I'm hiding. Like a little kid. I've got almost an hour before my first client. I just need five minutes in here to warm up my muscles, then I can hide upstairs with the free weights. Where I don't have to hear the stammering. See the sad, broken eyes. Eyes like ones I haven't seen in almost three years. The color might be different, but that pain looks the same. Most might miss it. For me it might as well have been a neon sign on her forehead.

Fuck, Julian. Get your shit together.

I could feel the fissure in my wall like a physical cut. Three years is a long time to feel nothing. I worked at it, got used to it, counted on it. So how could this girl cause a crack within seconds? The sting, the ache was not only shocking. It was unwelcome.

I take a couple deep breaths and let the dry heat do what it does. As my heart rate slows, I continue to berate myself. Allie would be pissed if she knew I came in here commando, but the towels haven't been restocked yet, and I couldn't exactly wear my clothes in here. Plus, I needed to chill the fuck out. I didn't expect Allie's *project* to affect me like that. Or even make the radar. Beyond wanting to be helpful in a good human kind of way, I've gotten pretty good at turning off my feelings. Why now? Why her? But I'm also good at ignoring anything resembling a feeling, should one arise. It's just been a minute since I've needed to. Because it caught me off-guard, I'm now hiding.

Wait. Why am I hiding? From this girl?

Pissed at myself for acting like a prepubescent boy, I throw the sauna door open to head to the locker area to get dressed. One step out of the sauna, however, I slam into a wall of towels. Again! And send the girl flying. Again. What. The. Fuck.

"What the fuck?" I say it more to myself because how is she here smashing into me again? But there she is, sprawled at my feet. The storm-cloud eyes, deer in headlights, staring up at me with her cheeks flaming. At least the flush makes her look less haunted. But I'm no better. I stand there frozen a second too long.

Realizing she's seeing all my junk, I grab a towel from the floor, wrap it around my lower half and find my voice. "I mean, shit, I'm . . . uh, I'm sorry. Are you alright? I'm not usually in here this early. Can I . . . help you with the towels? Or I can just take them for you. Seriously, are you okay? Uh, Ev . . . Ever . . . ?" Jesus, now I'm stammering. What's her name again? It's not a common one. And she's not offering it up.

This waifish girl is just wide-eyed staring up at me, feet out, knees together, legs in an upside-down *V*, leaning back on her hands. She scoots backward like a scared animal backing down from a predator. Once she's a few feet away, she finds her voice. "I agree. What the fuck? And, yeah, why don't you fold them this time? Since I've already done it twice." She stands as she says it, dusting off her butt. "She told me . . . Allie said no one was in here." And with that, she turned and practically ran out of the locker room.

So much for *scared animal*. Except for the retreating part. I stare at the place she vacated, trying to get my bearings. I may have misjudged the *save me* part too. That sass I just witnessed didn't scream *save me*. But somehow it captivated me more.

Instead of the locker room, I aim for the nearest sink and splash icy cold water on my sauna-heated face. I ignore my shaky hands, yank the towel off my waist and swipe it down my face. This is going to be a problem. She's going to be a problem. Bracing my fists on the edges of the sink, I stare at myself, willing my heartrate to return to normal.

You can't save her, man. Who says she needs saving? I argue with the guy in the mirror.

Didn't all of Allie's projects need saving from something at first, including me? Fighting the urge to smash the reflection, I turn and stalk to the locker to retrieve my clothes and get ready for my first client of the day, Drea. I could always count on Drea for a solid distraction. Most days her neediness and blatant attempts at seduction annoy me. Today I welcome it. I only hope she doesn't bathe in her perfume today. I'm already feeling a little nauseous.

Chapter 3

EVERLY

My first day has me rethinking everything. Why did I run away from my life? And why do I act like a complete idiot around guys? Or just *that* guy? Okay, to be fair, I don't exactly have instances to compare where there were any guys to act any kind of way around. Except the one incident—the big bad—that sufficiently wrecked my life as I knew it. I spent the rest of the day avoiding him and dodging his stare. And I wasn't imagining it. Every time I looked up from whatever I was doing, I'd catch his intense blue eyes piercing me in one of the mirrors. I've never understood the cheesy term "undressing me with his eyes," but I think I'm beginning to. I felt naked, exposed, like he could see right through me. And why was he constantly watching me anyway?

He's probably the most beautiful guy I've ever set eyes on. I'm quite sure he could have any woman he wants and probably does. I'd be lying if I said I didn't like it though. I want to be unaffected by him, but I'm not sure anyone with a pulse could deny his appeal. He obviously works at it. Watching him sweat the day away, showing everyone from geriatrics to desperate housewives how to work out was beyond entertaining. I could tell the moves weren't hard for him, but his skin still glistened with the effort of correcting form and demonstrating equipment.

"So, what are we looking at? Oh, solid choice." The body belonging to the voice sets up close to my ear. "He definitely gives the eyes a workout, as well as the imagination. Am I right?"

My cheeks burn as I turn to the person leaning over my shoulder. "Lilliana, I presume," I say, recalling Allie's earlier overview on Fit and the other employees. I smile, not bothering to defend myself, and offer my hand. Do teenagers shake hands?

She looks down at my extended right hand and clasps it in her left like we're holding hands, not a handshake, squeezes and says, "I like you already," with a little giggle. "Ooh, it's Mrs. Stevens. Or Deena, as she insists we call her. How many times has she needed Julian to demonstrate the squat so far?"

"Twice. Is she new?"

"You'd think, right? Nope. She's been coming to Julian for years. One of his first clients. But she's not as bad as Drea. Her perfume alone is enough to gag on. But the way she throws herself at him is embarrassing."

"Perfume Lady was first thing this morning. I think her scent stayed at least an hour longer than she did."

"Sounds about right. I guess it's kind of petty, but it's entertaining watching the Cougar Club compete for his attention. I've even heard he's hooked up with a few."

"Ewww. I think I just threw up in my mouth," I joke.

But my heart plummets into my shoes. Why am I so devastated to hear that this beautiful man whores around with women twice his age? What do I care? Shuddering, I swivel my head away from the *cougar* competition and focus on Lilly, as "everyone calls me." Because of her, I feel like, for the first time since I arrived, that I might enjoy this place.

She slings her arm over my shoulders, pivots me away from the Julian/cougar spectacle and says, "Let's go get a juice shot."

I guess shots are my new thing. At least these types of shots won't get me canceled and ruin my life.

Lilly made the second half of the day fly by, thankfully. Thankful is an understatement. Her personality is everything. I adore her, but by the end of the shift I was so *bothered* by the Julian gossip and the cougar parade that I didn't even stay to work out myself. Allie insisted I learn my own workout so I could better assist at Fit. I bailed. Lilly tried to convince me to stay and workout with her, but I couldn't wait to be alone and contemplate all I learned on my first day. Now back at Allie's, I decide to head out to the lake path and at least take a brisk walk and get some fresh air.

. Taking her back stairs down to the trail, I stop to stretch and loosen up. Across the cove, the sun glares off the windows of the Blue Brew Café & Marina. Being a seasonal business, it'll still be quiet for a couple more weeks, then the bustle of campers will keep the whole lake humming until August. I decide right then to make this a daily habit and take advantage of the quiet until the tourists descend.

Blue Lake is just that. Beautifully blue and aptly named, reflecting the sky like a mirror. The air and the view are so inspiring I trade the walk for a run. I welcome the burn in my legs and lungs, and by the time I reach the marina, I'm sucking air. I stop and bend at the waist, hands resting on my knees, and gulp deep breaths to slow my heart rate. The air and the terrain are not like running in the city on pavement. Once I steady myself, I sit and watch the sunset. I could take the steps down to the dock and sit on the edge or head up to the patio deck and watch from the outdoor dining area off the café. Both were vacant so I could enjoy it in peace. I opt for the higher vantage point of the patio.

Propping my feet up on the chair across from the one I sit in, I cross my ankles and watch the sun sink, setting the lake on fire with its reflective glow. Despite the nerve-racking day, I begin to relax. I do love this place. My mom would bring me and my sister here when we were little. Allie's family owned most of the lakefront property, the café/marina, all the cabin rentals and, of course, her house and the property it sits on. It's all hers now that her grandma who raised her is gone.

We haven't visited in years. Mom got busier with work, and we got busier being teenagers. Well, my sister did anyway. I stayed the same, consumed with my grades and books and make-believe worlds. The few times I ventured out into my sister's world of general teenage debauchery proved to be well above my pay grade and experience level. I didn't know how to play all those mean girl games and flirt with boys and get wasted. The one and only time I got truly wasted, my life turned upside down and transplanted me to Blue Lake permanently. Or at least for the foreseeable future.

Not that I'm complaining at the moment, enveloped by this fresh air and beauty, silence and solitude. Most people don't like being alone. I find it soothing and simple.

Exactly one year after the first party my sister's crew invited me to when I learned hangovers weren't my thing, I broke my rule and had more than one. The peer pressure was at an all-time high that night, and since I was feeling particularly ostracized that day at school and like the most boring eighteen-year-old on the planet, the crew convinced me to hop off that wagon and try it again. Using my newly turned legal status as the excuse to coax me to "live a little for once." There's some clichéd saying in there about fooling me twice, but since both times were my choice, I'm not entirely sure it applies. And I don't know any famous quotes or clichés about being stupid twice—even with my vast memory bank of quotes. But it was stupid for a smart girl like me. Because deciding to cut loose that night and later blacking out caused a ripple effect none of us could've imagined.

As if the universe hears me relishing in the peace and quiet and knows I don't deserve it, a voice from behind me pierces the stillness. "Brew isn't open to the public yet."

I turn ready to explain I'm allowed to be here, but freeze, mouth agape, seeing Julian—again.

"Oh, it's you. Um, Ev . . . er . . . , it's fine. You're fine. You can stay here."

"I know. But thanks. And it's Everly . . . Julie, is it?" I know I'm being a bitch, as he's clearly not trying to be an asshole. He just gets under my skin. Between crashing into him—twice—the rumor of him sleeping with older women (*Gag)* and him being . . . *everywhere* I am, I can't seem to help myself. And why do I give a shit who he sleeps with? Not my circus, not my monkeys.

He smirks at my intentionally mistaking his name and seems to find his confidence and maybe a touch of irritation at my flippancy. "Oh, well, Ever-ly, I didn't mean to disturb you. I didn't know it was *you*. Sometimes, we get kids up here trashing the place with their litter. And I have to be the asshole and run them off. Also . . . I kind of like *Ever*. It suits you."

Frowning, I return my face to the almost sunken sun and answer under my breath, "And I kind of like Julie. It suits *you*."

His "hmph" of a chuckle echoes as he turns and walks back inside.

What is he doing in here anyway? Brew's closed. The back of his shirt displays the Blue Brew logo, an employee shirt. Apparently, we'll be working together here too. The idea of seeing him more made my heart race . . . from dread, I lie.

Guys don't make my heart race. Okay, that's a lie too. But the ones that do are fictional. On pages in books. Or in my dreams—of fictional guys on pages in books. My sister always said I set myself up for failure with my "book boyfriends" because no guy would ever measure up in real life. But that's not entirely true. Chase did. Until he didn't. But I didn't exactly crush on him. I crushed on *them*. He and Kendall were the couple goals of my dreams. And then they weren't. In fact, they ruined my life. Although they like to say I ruined theirs. And by *they*, I mean Kendall.

In the end I guess she got what she wanted. She got to blame me for everything that went wrong and got an entire community to believe it too. Of course, no one thinks Kendall is behind any of it. She never is. That's the mean girl shit I'd never understand or aspire to master. The sneaky super bitch masquerading as the town sweetheart.

I mentally shake my head to clear the image and reminder of it all. I don't need to prove myself to anyone, and I don't have to see them ever again. Seeing the glimmer of doubt in my sister's eyes was enough to bring me here. If she doesn't believe me, then I have no one in OV anymore. I'm not mad at her for it. Weirdly, I understand where she's coming from. I question myself and how I got here. Everyday. Maybe my sister, Olivia, is right. I set myself up for disappointment and failure with my make-believe worlds. The real world so far hasn't come close. Maybe I'm delusional that true love and genuine hearts exists. Chase and Kendall sure fell way short of what they appeared to be—at least in my eyes. Olivia and her boyfriend, Ryan, seem unsure about what to believe. And my sister's doubt in me is more than I can stand. She deserves a break from the drama and essentially raising me the last few years. That was when I came up with moving to Blue Lake—the only place I could remember where I only ever felt happy. I hold no bad memories of this place. And more and more, OV only held the bad.

Chapter 4

EVERLY

Three months ago

His lips on my neck are as soft as I imagined. *How is this my life right now?* His breath warms my skin, cool from the wet trail his kisses leave below my ear. Hearing him whisper my name is like the gift I never knew I wanted. But why me? This doesn't make sense. It can't be real. *He* isn't real. Mitchell Owens, my current *book boyfriend,* has consumed my thoughts since I first cracked the pages. I lift my arm to stroke his cheek. It's almost too heavy to lift and feels thick, like my head, but his face is smooth at the top and rough with whiskers at the bottom. I curve my fingers into the scruff. My arm flops to the bed like it's weighted. I want to keep touching him, but I can't make my arm cooperate.

It takes effort to part my lips and say his name. "Chase," I sigh. *Chase? Not Chase. Mitch! Mitch Owens, my book boyfriend from Sun-*

set Creek. Again, I call his name, louder this time. "Chase?" Why Chase anyway? He's with Kendall.

Chase and Kendall are *the* couple. The super couple. The cutest couple. The couple goals of OV. Everyone wants to be them, even me sometimes. They've been together since before any of the crew started dating—right around their freshman year at OVH, when I was still a kid. Almost every one of the crew is coupled up now. But those two set the bar. They were the first to make it official. The first to go all the way. And now, as college seniors, the first to move in together. All stories I've heard from my older sister, Olivia, one of their best friends. If they're the perfect couple, why me? And why now? Why would Chase ruin everything he has with Kendall to make out with me? My brain knows something is off. But I can't sort it out. My head feels muddy, murky, like pond water.

"Chase," I whine. *Whine?* I don't whine.

"Chase," I repeat more forcefully. "Chase!" I'm yelling now. Why am I yelling at him?

"What are you doing? WHAT THE FUCK ARE YOU DOING?"

I open my eyes, not realizing they were closed in the first place, and see light coming from a gap in the door. The hall light. Chase and Kendall's hallway light. I'm in their room. I'm in their bed. The party. The shots. My buzz. Then everything got spinny. Kendall. Kendall helped me walk to the bathroom. She helped me lie down on her bed. Their bed! That's the last thing I remember until now. Am I dreaming? Am I yelling at Chase? No! *Kendall* was yelling at Chase. And she still is. More like an angry whisper. I can't make out the words. I struggle to sit up as my head swirls. As soon as I move, the whispers stop. A shadow approaches me in the backdrop of the hallway light. As it moves closer, I can see it's Kendall.

"You need to get up." Kendall grabs my arm and yanks me to my feet.

I sway for a second before my equilibrium catches up and steadies me.

"This is how you repay my kindness? Trying to hook up with Chase? Get out, Evvie. We're done. You're done." She's half dragging half walking me toward the door and the lighted hallway.

The house is quiet now. The party must be over.

I hear her words, and I understand them perfectly. They just don't make sense. I hooked up with Chase? I would never hook up with Chase. I would never betray Kendall like that. I've never even kissed a guy. I certainly wouldn't go after someone else's and wouldn't even consider one almost three years older than me. I try to piece it all together as Kendall marches me through their house, grabbing my shoes and bag and thrusting them into my chest. I wrap my arm around them so they don't tumble to the floor. Once we reach the front door, she opens it and pushes me over the threshold and onto the porch.

The cool night air hits my face like a splash of ice water and the frigid wood of the porch stings my bare feet. Both wake me up enough to grasp my situation. I turn ready to explain myself to Kendall, to get her to understand, to understand it myself, but the door slams in my face.

With the cold seeping into my bones now, I dash across the wet grass to my car and climb into the driver's seat. I don't know how long I sit there watching my breath vaporize in front of me, trying to make sense of the last few minutes and piece together the hours leading up to it.

I jump at the tap on my window. Chase is bent over waving at me, his breath heavy and fogging up the window between our faces. I press the start button to unlock the window and roll it down. He nervously smiles at me. It registers through my fuzzy brain that I've never seen him look timid before.

"I'm going to make this right, Evvie. I promise. She'll calm down once I explain." He smiles reassuringly, like he just solved everything with those three sentences.

"Explain what? What the hell happened? Why is she so pissed? I wasn't even that drunk. And I'd never try to hook up with you." I recall snippets of Kendall encouraging me to sleep off my slurred state so I could drive home later. Beyond that, it's fuzzy. Like an out of focus picture. I could almost see it, make out what it is, but I'm not quite sure. The only thing I am sure of—I didn't come on to Chase. That's just not who I am, drunk or not.

Chapter 5

Everly

Present Day

It's been a week. I've been living in one of Allie's spare rooms on Blue Lake and working at Fit for seven days now. And soon I'll start helping at Brew. Online school is even easier than public school. I haven't turned in any assignments yet, but I'm getting them done effortlessly and catching up quickly. I'll have to work out how I'll get myself to and from school when I need to check in and turn in work. A problem for another day.

Via has only called me once since I've been gone. If I'm being honest, that call felt obligatory. I don't call her because I never know who else is around. I mean, she could just not answer my call if she weren't alone, but I don't even want my name popping up on her screen in mixed company. We agreed not to tell anyone (except her boyfriend, Ryan) where I am—just that our mom decided it was best if I left. As far as anyone in OV is concerned, I'm a ghost. Ideally, they'll all forget I even exist. Not likely. But if there's one thing I know about small towns, it's that a new scandal will give said town something else to talk about if you just give it time.

I realize I've traded one small town for another, but I plan to fly under the radar as long as I'm here.

Lilly, I've decided, is my favorite part of Blue Lake so far. She and her boyfriend, Noah, the other Fit employee, are seniors at Blue Lake High, where I'll report once a week to drop off my assignments and finish my senior year. Lilly is a magnet. She pulled me in immediately and radiates this authentic simplicity unlike anyone I've ever met. No agenda, no hidden aggression, or mean girl antics, she is equal parts bubbly sarcasm and laid-back chill. She doesn't waste her words and is a gifted and animated storyteller, which she attributes to her Native American roots—healers and medicine men, she calls them. Her stories appeal to my bookworm nature, and I hang on every word. Especially (selfishly) the tidbits she drops about Julian. Cougars aside, I'm insatiably curious about him. The ripped muscles, chiseled physique, sculpted face, and endless pools of deep blue eyes captivate me. The man could be a model. But his patience with his older clients and quiet reserve captivate me more and frankly don't track with the cougar bait he's rumored to be. I tether between whether he rates as a favorite or someone to avoid at all costs.

According to recent tea from Lilly, he may be a bit of both. She gives me a comically vivid rundown on everyone we encounter throughout the workdays, including Julian—the little she knows. Like that he showed up in Blue Lake three years or so ago and began shadowing Allie, learning to be a personal trainer. Lilly had only worked for Allie the last two years, so it was before her time. I appreciate her commitment to offering me a roadmap to my new life. It makes me adore her more—that she seems to genuinely care if I fit in here, for which I am endlessly grateful. Julian did not. But I'm still intrigued—maybe more in his seeming disinterest. I low-key hate that typical drama-girl response.

Oh, he's not interested in me, okay now I'm interested.

I'm smarter than that, and if my recent past has taught me anything, it's to avoid drama. Over the last week, he's kept his distance, but I would still catch him watching me in the mirrors that litter the walls. Maybe because I'm watching him too. I don't know much or anything about him except that he takes excellent care of his body, works hard at whatever he does, doesn't seem to have much of a sense of humor, attracts older women like a moth to flame and apparently hates old-school rock.

Yesterday, I came into Fit and of course he beat me there, even though I was a half hour early for my shift. Some weird unspoken competition between us, at least for me. I dropped my stuff on the shelf in the back room and flicked the switch for the studio music. Axl Rose was singing "I need you." "Patience" is just one of those songs I can't not love. Old-school rock reminds me of my parents and being young, before life got sad and complicated. It's hard and loud with deliciously long guitar riffs, and it soothes me. This Guns N' Roses song reminds me of my dad. Feeling nostalgic, I turned it up. Not exactly a workout song, but a vibe that makes me sing along and whistle if you know it like I do. As I came around the corner from the office area behind the counter, Julian slammed his weight down with a crash and stormed to the receiver and flipped the switch off, turned and proceeded to storm back to his weights.

"What the hell, *Julie*? Good morning to you too."

He stopped mid storm and, with his back to me, his shoulders rose with the deep breath he took. He turned and focused his eyes somewhere just above my head. "Look, can we not do the sappy old-school rock? It's not really workout music anyway. Cool?" He lowered his eyes to mine and waited.

I gave him half-hearted *whatever* hands as I nodded, shrugged and said, "Sure."

He gave me one nod and turned to go, more calmly, but like it took effort.

Moody much? I wondered for a second if the guy took steroids but dismissed it just as quickly. He takes impeccable care of his body, maniacally reads ingredients labels and is quick to tell Allie if some drink, protein bar or snack she stocks isn't up to his standards. It doesn't happen often because Allie is just as particular as he is. I'm learning a lot about whole body health from them and I'm here for it. I want to roll my eyes sometimes at their overly obsessive ways, but I find it all too fascinating to mock.

Since coming here, my nervous system is the calmest it's ever been, and considering the train wreck that is my life, that's saying something. Overthinking the puzzle of this man doesn't stress me out like it should. It makes my heart race, but in the best way. I find I'm less interested in my latest book boyfriend because it seems I have a real one to obsess over. A guy. Not a boyfriend. Something tells me Julian doesn't do the boyfriend thing. And I am not ready to admit that I care why.

I could never imagine myself with any *real* guy before. Real guys never measured up to the fictional ones. Again, Via might be right (although I'll never admit it to her) and my obsession with fictional characters might've ruined me for real life experiences. Until now. And with everything I've been accused of back home, you'd think I'd be steering clear of all guys. But I can't help it with Julian. He makes me feel things. Want things. Damn the books. I'm creating my own forbidden love interest. He's too old for me. He's seen more life than twenty-one years (according to Lilly) should allow. You could tell. It's in the eyes.

Poetry aside, they really are windows to the soul, and his scream tortured. And if any of the rumors are true, Allie found him on the street and took him in a few years ago. And while I feel like the oldest eighteen-year-old I know—coming here by myself and starting a new life goes a long way in making me feel like an adult—inside, I'm still the virginal, awkward high school senior who's never even kissed a guy. Which makes the rumors in Oak Valley even more ridiculous, although utterly life ruining, at least for me. Everyone else involved seems to be doing just fine with me as enemy number one and the cause of the whole mess. If they only knew how far from a home-wrecker I really am, they'd feel stupid and maybe even guilty.

I still haven't filled in all the blind spots in my memory of that night. My sister got more details after visiting the hospital the next day, but the version of events she was told didn't add up. Kendall found me and Chase in their bed together and threw me out of their house. And after that, she apparently took a bunch of pills and tried to kill herself—the richest, most popular girl in town, who seemed to have everything going for her. It didn't make sense. I don't remember the drive back home. But I woke up in my own bed with the clothes I wore the night before, clearly untouched sexually speaking. I've had snippets of Chase's hands on me, like it was a dream. I did recall Via and Ryan leaving early while Chase and Kendall, their best friends and my surrogate older siblings, assured them they'd look out for me and told them to "let the birthday girl have some fun for once." But is that what I remember or what they filled in for me? Did I come on to Chase in a drunken state?

Somehow, I know I would never do that. But alcohol makes people do things they wouldn't normally do, lowers inhibitions. Still, I didn't want Chase like that. I admit, I am a little obsessed with the idealistic nature of their life together. I envisioned having something like it someday. So maybe I did crush on Chase in some indirect way. I didn't think I did, though. Again, is this just what people are telling me so I'm adopting it as truth? And I could've asked Chase point-blank if I'd had the chance. But I never did. And I didn't dare call or text him for fear I would give them evidence of my "misdeeds." The biggest question of all though was why Chase didn't clear it up. Because it made him look guilty? But still, was he so afraid of Kendall he'd let a whole town vilify and cancel me? Is he that much of a coward? I mean, I wouldn't call him a humanitarian or anything, but I'd not personally seen this self-serving side of him before. And since there was no way to prove my virginity, I sat in silence while they shamed, smeared and bullied me.

I guess it doesn't even matter now. I left town and my life as I knew it, hoping to diffuse the situation. It wasn't fair to Olivia to have her life turned upside down because of me. She practically raised me the last few years while our mom traveled for work. Not that I needed raising exactly. I'm pretty self-sufficient and have been since I turned twelve. But Mom needed to work. I was glad she found an exciting job to keep her busy, if not happy. Losing our dad in Afghanistan when I was twelve threatened to destroy us all. But it didn't. He was a soldier since before I was born. He was deployed somewhere almost all my life. Most of our quality time with him existed through a screen. When we got *the visit*, it shook us, but the daily trajectory of our lives didn't change much—or at all. At least for me. I lost myself in books and school even more than I did before and tried hard not to need anyone. Via lost herself in Ryan and Mom traded in her regular flight attendant job for a VIP one. She's at the beck and call of some of the richest people in the world, traveling to the coolest places, and she loves it. She can't even tell us who she works for most of the time. My propensity for perfectionism grew exponentially after that so my mom wouldn't feel guilty for all the time she spent away. I kept overachieving so Mom had nothing to worry about.

Olivia and I both did our best not to need her. And truly we didn't. The bills were paid automatically, and Ryan happily did some of the *boy* jobs around the house, like mowing the lawn. He and my sister behaved like an old married couple almost since they began dating. Old souls, everyone says. Eventually Mom made enough money to just hire a gardener to come every two weeks. Our house is modest compared to our friends' but nice. It has a built-in pool and each of the three bedrooms is a master suite, so we all have our own bathrooms. Well . . . had. I liked my life there, even though it was boring by most teenage standards. But after that night—*The Night*—I had a social hit out on me and Via started to become collateral damage. I got bullied on social media, including online death threats, until I deleted it all. Harassed wherever I went, the final straw was my car getting vandalized. That was when Via called Allie. Not Mom. Allie.

Today, I'm scheduled to meet Julian at Brew, the seasonal café/marina, to learn the lay of the land. Spring break is coming, then summer, and I'll need to know it all so I can keep up with the diners, campers, boaters and day trippers. This is the first time I'll be on the other side of the crowd. And I'm honestly looking forward to it. Staying busy means less time to overthink and analyze my life. I'm not ready to address whether my new work buddy has anything—or everything—to do with my excitement. But I know it does. At times I think he's intrigued by me too. Other times, he seems utterly annoyed with my mere existence.

I leave early enough so I can walk the short distance around the edge of the lake to Brew. The air is brisk, but spring is making its appearance. The ground is a blanket of green velvet, sparkling in the morning dew, winking at me like stars at night. The air is so clean and crisp it almost hurts my lungs but in a good way. Healing indeed.

As the lakeside of Brew comes into view, I see him sitting on the patio, gripping a steaming mug in one hand, not using the handle. His feet are propped up on the chair in front of the one he's seated on—much like I was the other day. My steps falter and I stop to take in the picture of him. I'm still a good twenty-five yards away, but my presence must disturb his peace and quiet because he doesn't turn but says, "Morning, Ever." Almost as if he were talking to himself, except he says my name.

"Hey, Julie. Beautiful morning. This place . . ." My words crash into the tranquility. I trail off and take another deep breath.

I see his crooked half smile, even in profile—at my use of the nickname. He stands, tosses the last of the liquid from his cup over the railing, and reaches his arms to the sky while still holding the mug in one hand. I hold my breath and watch. His legs are spread slightly as he tilts from one side to the other. His muscles, clearly defined through the thin fabric of his shirt, ripple across his back with the small movements. I swallow, my mouth suddenly desert dry. Rolling his neck, he turns to face me fully as I continue up the stairs to the patio. His eyes land on mine and I see the shutters come down.

All business, Julian smiles at me politely, nodding. "You ready for the day? Gonna be a long one."

"Yep. Got any more coffee?"

That lazy half smile beams again. "Yeah, I just made it." I follow him inside.

***

L earning the routine of the café and marina wasn't as overwhelming as I thought. Julian is a good teacher, patient and straightforward. He also has a knack for short-routing things to get them done in the quickest, most efficient manner possible. I respect this. It appeals to my super-secret deep-seated impatience and gives me another reason to admire this guy and look forward to the time we spend together, even if it's just for work and strictly professional. And I think he feels the same way. Throughout the day, he would give me a hard time, playfully. And he still "messes up" my name, calling me Ever. No one has ever called me that before. I was always Ev, Evvie or Everly. And secretly, I love it. But I pretend I don't. In retaliation, I call him Julie, arguably a girl's name, when he is anything but girly.

The highlight of the day is when he tells me we should meet here every day for the next two weeks to make sure we're prepared for the early spring break campers. Spring break typically falls sometime in April. Blue Brew boasts five cabins and ten tent sites that stay booked solid through spring and summer. The first campers are arriving mid-April.

Blue Lake is a small lake that doesn't allow motorized watercraft. Paddleboards, paddle boats, kayaks and canoes were allowed, and the marina even offered a few that campers could check out for day use on a first-come, first-served basis. It'll be our job to make sure the cabins and tent sites are rent-ready and the water equipment is inspected and safe to use. It sounds like a lot of work for two people, but I'm not about to complain and let Julian—or Allie—think I can't handle it. I've handled a lot worse. And I sense Julian knows I have too. He gave protective vibes throughout the day. Especially when he reveals the first campers of the season are from Oak Valley, reserved under Young, and they'd be here in just two weeks. I feel the color drain from my face, and I sway.

He must see it too. He grabs my arms and pulls me to him, staring down at me. "Whoa, Ever, easy. You okay?"

"Yeah, yeah, I just got dizzy for a second. Probably just need to drink more water." I know that's a sure way to distract him. He and Allie are always harping on about hydration and water intake.

Mission accomplished. He sits me down on the nearest chair and disappears into the kitchen for a glass of water. I hate that I played that weakling card, but I need a minute to get a grip. Young is a common name. It can't be Chase and the crew. Although they have been known to camp up here occasionally on school breaks, there are plenty of other campsites besides Allie's. If it is Chase, he isn't coming here for me. It's a coincidence. A shitty, unfortunate one. Maybe I could just hide out at Fit and take those shifts while Lilly, Noah and Julian take care of the campers. Besides, it probably isn't even him. If it is his crew, that would likely include Ryan and possibly Via if the girlfriends are joining. And Via would've mentioned it to me or Allie or both. Right?

As if on cue, Allie walks in at that moment. She always looks like she's just stepped out of a spa session, quite literally flawless. "Hey, Evvie, how's it going in here?"

"Great. Just taking a quick water break." She opens her mouth to no doubt question where the water part of that break is when Julian walks out of the kitchen with two glasses. She pauses, then says, "Oh good, you're both here. I've got some . . . uh . . . unexpected news." She hesitates with a nervous smile, uncharacteristic, which gets my full attention, my heart jumping in my chest. "I got accepted to this certification/retreat program. It was full when I applied but they had a cancellation in the session coming up. Bad part is the timing. I'd leave this week and be gone for three weeks.

"Noah and Lilly said they could pitch in and take extra shifts during spring break. And Letty already agreed to man the office part of Fit. I know clients will miss not having my classes and training sessions, but I've only taken time off three times in ten years. And only for some training or certification to improve the club. This training would be another great addition. I'd also be networking with some of the top trainers from all over California." When she realizes she's rambling, she trails off and just stands there like she's asking our permission.

I selfishly think, *There goes my plan to hide out at Fit.*

Julian is the first to speak. "Of course. Of course, Allie. Whatever you need. I know the ins and outs of both places. You know that. Do it. Don't worry about a thing. We can handle it. And we've got Pete to man the grill. Shelley to wait tables. If it gets too crazy, we'll hit up Lilly's and Noah's younger sisters to buss and wash dishes. Right, Ever? Uh, Everly?"

What did I stumble into? Both Allie and Julian appear to be chomping at the bit to make everything okay for the other. I look back and forth between them like I'm watching a tennis match, then chime in. "Yeah, totally. I just learned the ropes. It all seems straightforward enough. And it's early in the season. Seems like it'll be slow for a bit, which gives me time to get into the groove before campers."

Allie stays silent for a moment, watching us, considering. "We could do holiday hours at Fit, activate the key app entry and give limited access—equipment area only. Or . . . we could close it for the weeks I'm gone."

"No," we both say at once.

"Allie, we can do this. And more importantly, you should do this," I say with growing confidence. "You said it could really help the club. And that you never take time away like this."

"There's one more thing," Allie looks back and forth like she's at the tennis match now. "I worry about leaving you alone when you just got here, Evvie. This isn't Oak Valley. There is some crazy country shit that happens up here. Not dangerous exactly but stuff you might not be equipped to deal with. I mean, if Julian could maybe . . . check in on you . . ." She trails off and stares at the far wall contemplatively. "This is probably . . . I just need to wait for the next one." She looks like she's holding her breath.

I look from Allie to Julian, who's looking down at his hands still holding the two glasses of water. He looks up as he hands me a glass and says in a subdued tone, "Of course, Allie, whatever you need. I've . . . we've got this."

I take the glass from him and meet his eyes; he clinks his glass to mine and downs his water in one gulp. I raise my glass to my lips as I watch his throat move with the effort. My throat desert dry again, I down mine. I don't look at Allie. Every nerve ending is tingling at the idea of Julian "checking in on me" for three weeks, and I'm afraid it shows. Part of me wants to be insulted. The other part of me has sweat gathering in my pits imagining what "crazy country shit" entails. Maybe I'm sweating about Julian. Maybe he *is* the crazy country shit.

Allie looks relieved. "Ev, Julian is probably the person I trust most in this town. He knows the ins and outs of both businesses. He knows this area and all the CCS."

"CCS?"

"Crazy Country Shit," they say in unison.

"Snakes, raccoons, weather, fire, whatever," Julian clarifies. "Don't worry. It's not as crazy as it sounds."

"Right. Well, thanks, I guess, for handling the . . . CCS portion of the program." I put up my finger quotes as I say it, hopefully conveying calm assuredness to them that I don't totally feel.

Chapter 6

JULIAN

I pull my Jeep into Allie's driveway. What did I agree to? But, really, how could I not? Allie has given me . . . everything. I'm not sure I'd even be here if it weren't for her and her saving ways. And if anyone deserves a retreat, it's her.

And if Ever stops looking at me with those *save me* eyes, I can do this. I'm not sure she's even aware she does it, which makes it worse. *It's just house-sitting*, I repeat to myself. And I don't have to house-sit, per se. I just need to be available, in case. Ever and I don't even have to see each other. Except we do. All day every day at work. Allie did amend the hours at the club and implemented the app access, so Lilly and Noah have more freedom to help us at Brew for the evening shifts and closing. Those two are golden and beyond helpful. I have no doubt we can handle all of this without missing a beat. So why am I hiding in my Jeep like a nervous kid?

Allie left early this morning for the airport. The training program even sent a car to take her to the airport. No wonder she didn't want to miss this opportunity. It appeared to be first-class all the way. It's just Ever inside now. That's why I'm out here. Why does this girl scare me so much? She's here on her own—not quite the damsel in distress she seemed to be that first day. I admit it though: She scares me. She makes me feel things I haven't felt in three years. That's not to say I've been a monk. It's hard to say no when women, beautiful women, throw themselves at you—with no strings attached. Mostly the bored and Botoxed type, older than me and essentially living at the gym to stave off the certainty of aging. The best part is, they only want one thing from me. No feelings involved and they don't want anyone to know. Although in a town this size, that's not possible. I've even heard the rumors, and I don't care. Or I didn't until now. The cougars, as they're known, don't care. I sometimes wonder if they start the rumors themselves to make them feel better about getting older. Either way it has worked well for me, as much as that makes me feel like a little bit of an asshole. I don't do strings, but I'm human. I'd say we use each other. No one is getting hurt, so what does it matter? I've perfected the art of not feeling things.

Until now. Until Ever. And therein lies the fear. The ethereal, haunted gray eyes always watching me, the innocent face, the delicate, graceful frame, the full pouty lips. My body reacting to my train of thoughts makes my point for me. I adjust myself in my joggers to relieve the strain of the fabric and absently rub the tattooed spot on my chest. It doesn't help that Allie told me she's heard Ever having nightmares. I'm not supposed to know that. I'm supposed to be here helping her *manage the house*. Which is a thin excuse at best. Ever is an adult—*ish*. She can house-sit by herself for a few weeks. For God's sake, she's moved here to this town where she knows no one except Allie to start over for some reason. She can house-sit alone. Which means I better be good at selling why I'm here—which is *not* to babysit Ever. I know her mom is largely absent from her life and that she lost her dad in the service when she was young. Allie told me that. That might be why she's having the nightmares; Allie didn't elaborate if she does know.

No matter what this damaged girl is dealing with, catching feelings might mean a walk down memory lane for me. Too many parallels. Summoning memories I've buried. Memories I've worked hard to bury. I decide right there in the driveway. No feelings. I rub the spot on my chest where my heart is supposed to be—the one that got ripped out three years ago. I subconsciously rub the small tattoo there. An outline of a heart, a reminder that mine isn't there anymore, and why. *Nope, Julian, we're not catching feelings, my man.* Business. It's just business, and a favor to Allie because I owe her.

I take a deep breath. Then another. I swipe the back of my hand across my upper lip where beads of sweat form despite the chill in the air. I loosen my grip on the steering wheel and open the door.

Chapter 7
EVERLY

I hear Julian's vehicle pull into the driveway. You can hear everything out here. It's so quiet. I keep waiting for the doorbell to chime or the door to open—if he's house-sitting, he's got a key. After about five minutes, I peek through the window on the upstairs landing. He's just sitting in his Jeep. Of course he drives a Jeep. I noticed it in the Fit parking lot the first day I got here and deduced it was his. I've just never seen him in it because he always beats me to work. Always.

Why is he just sitting there? When Allie first said he'd be staying here with me while she's gone, I wanted to be insulted, but the blood rush of spending three weeks alone with him quickly drowned out the insult. I have no business catching feelings for any guy if the last three months taught me anything. My brain knows it, but my body didn't get the memo.

Where would he sleep? The extra room connected to mine by a bathroom seems the logical choice. Staying in Allie's room would be weird. We'd most likely be sharing a bathroom. My heart drops at the image of Julian in a towel and what I know hides under it. *God, stop already. No guys! Go read a book. Book boyfriends only.* I turn toward my room as the front door opens. Like a little kid I hurry the rest of the way into my room and silently close the door and lean against it to catch my breath.

Instead of losing myself in a book, I sit down on the edge of the bed and take out the new journal I bought for my new life. I haven't written in it yet, nor have I written *anything* in three months. Like I've been hiding from myself, but I don't have to anymore. No one here knows what I supposedly did or hates me for it. If nothing else, journaling again could distract me from the footsteps on the stairs. And the door opening right down the hall. The rustling movements of the most beautiful man I've ever seen in real life just on the other side of the Jack and Jill bathroom separating us and our beds, where we'll both be sleeping for the next three weeks.

STOP, Everly! Just write . . . something.

As I begin to write, I hear Julian move into the bathroom. My brain is tired though from little sleep the night before. Nervous energy about my new roommate? Perhaps. My lids droop, but I put the pencil to paper, willing myself to write, to distract me from my thoughts. I don't even get one sentence on the page before my eyelids drop.

His touch is softer than I expect. His hands and arms, muscled, promise rough but lie. It's smooth, gentle. His fingertips feather light as they trail down my cheek, tuck my hair behind my ear. He leans in so I feel his breath on my skin where his fingers used to be. As his lips reach my ear he sighs my name. "Ever." Only he calls me that. I can't help the shiver it gives me or the goose bumps that rise on my skin. I like the way he says it. I want him to say it again. He does. "Ever?" A question this time. What does he want? I'm right here. I'm already his. I lift my eyes to meet his. To understand what he wants.

"Oh, shit. My bad, I didn't know you were still sleeping."

I blink to focus my eyes. Julian fills the doorway of the adjoining bathroom, our bathroom. He turns to go. I rush to sit up—to stop him. I rub my face with both hands to shake off the grogginess and say, "No, no, I wasn't. I mean, I didn't sleep well last night so I guess . . . I guess . . . I dozed off for a second. Sorry."

That half smile I like so much. "You're sorry for sleeping?"

I feel my face heat up and know I'm blushing. I hate that my face gives me away, because I've honed my acting skills—like pretending I'm fine and I don't need anyone's help. If my flushing cheeks would stop giving me away. I respond in a way I hope sounds unflustered. Something tells me Julian isn't that easily fooled.

Chapter 8

JULIAN

She's apologizing for sleeping? Even in sleep this girl is screaming "save me." Allie is lucky I owe her, or I wouldn't be here, I lie to myself. If Allie didn't ask, I'd have found a way to check up on her. I wouldn't be able to help myself, as much as I wish that weren't true.

"You're sorry for sleeping?" I try to tease, but I hate that she feels the need to apologize . . . for anything.

"No, no. I just meant you don't have to go. Did you need something?"

"I thought we could take advantage of the day off." I hope I say it casually. "Did Allie tell you she closed Fit for the day so we could get settled? It's officially *Inventory Day*." The last part I say with air quotes. "Maybe I could show you around . . . places besides Fit and Brew."

"Yeah, yeah, okay. Uh, give me a minute. I'll meet you downstairs." She's already hopping off her bed, looking around like she's trying to get her bearings.

I back out of the doorway and close the bathroom door. Standing in the middle of my temporary room, I pat my chest with both hands and look around. My palms stick to the pale blue cotton of my T-shirt. My heart pounds against my ribs. I grab my keys and sunglasses and bound down the stairs to grab a couple ball caps, water bottles and towels. I haven't felt this . . . excited in a long time. Weird. And terrifying. I want Ever to love Blue Lake like I do. Like Allie does. Maybe she already does. Maybe she already knows the best spots. Allie said her family came here when she was a kid. I ignore my racing thoughts—and heart—and lie to myself that it's all just a favor to Allie.

It's not like this is the first time I've been attracted to a girl since Taya. But it doesn't usually stick. There's always a red flag that sends me running. Weirdly enough, Ever is nothing but red flags—young, seemingly innocent, broken and hurting—and yet I'm not running. I want her.

Wait! What? Dude, collect yourself.

I head back to the stairs to cancel right as she steps off the last step into the foyer. Her smile is unnaturally bright. Forced?

"Ready?" I hear myself ask instead as she simultaneously echoes me.

"Ready."

Mine a question. Hers a statement.

Chapter 9

EVERLY

I can't trust my dreams anymore. Maybe that's why I don't sleep very well. Oak Valley ruined sleep for me. And dreams. Maybe I ruined them for me. I woke up thinking Julian was touching me, then he was there in the doorway. Was it a dream? The last time I thought I had a dream like that, it wasn't. It was a nightmare. Except it happened. Just not how everyone said it happened. I don't care what anyone says. I would not have come on to Chase. I may never be able to prove it, but I know what I know. Now that I'm gone, they can find someone else to torture and accuse of ruining their privileged, plastic lives. I know me. I know who I am. And drunk or not, I would have never done that to anyone, but especially not to someone I called a friend. I deserve to have this day, with this beautiful guy. In this beautiful place.

I quickly stash my journal with the hastily scribbled entry into the nightstand drawer next to my bed, bounce up and head to the bathroom to splash water on my face. I drag a brush through my hair, pinch my cheeks and head back into my room, grab a hoodie and sneakers and head downstairs. I tell myself I'm only getting the lay of the land for my future job of managing visitors and campers. I might even already know the places he plans to show me. I ignore my racing heart, my dry mouth and the slight tremor in my hands. At the bottom of the stairs, I look up and come face to face with the one that's wrecking my nervous system.

"Ready," we say in unison. Mine a statement, his a question. We both chuckle, again in unison, then smile and . . . blush? I know I do because my face feels hot. But to see the flush on Julian's face gives me pause. It's equal parts sweet and empowering. To know I have that effect on him makes my palms sweat.

I giggle and refrain from saying 'jinx' and sounding young. "So, what's the plan? Where do we start?" I say it with a confidence I don't feel.

"I want to show you my favorite place. But promise you won't tell the campers?"

"Oh, easiest promise to keep. Should we pack anything? Water, uh . . . anything?"

"I grabbed a few things. We should be good. We'll head to the café after, and I'll make us some food."

What is he doing to me? He's going to show me his favorite place *and* make me food? So far, he really is as good as a book boyfriend. *He's not your boyfriend.*

Instead of taking the trail, he takes the top off his Jeep and opens the passenger door for me. He hands me a hat and says it'll keep my hair from tangling and keep the sun off my face. I'm not used to people looking out for me, but I think I love it. At least when Julian does it. After the bullshit of the last three months—or let's face it, five years—this protective vibe is piercing my heart. Someone looking out for me or giving a shit at all is melting me. But who am I kidding? It's *this* specific someone behind the piercing and melting. The butterflies in my stomach can attest.

His radio plays country rock low in the background. He drops his ball cap on his head backward like an afterthought and backs down the driveway. With his hand on my seat, he looks over his right shoulder. His scent coils around me—clean, earthy and a little sweet. I fight the urge to close my eyes and inhale. Instead, I snag my own ball cap off my lap and flip down the sun visor. Using the mirror inside it, I pull a few strands of hair down in front and snug the hat down behind my ears. I dig for my sunglasses in my mini backpack, glad I threw them in at the last minute. I'm not sure how long I'll be able to hide his effect on me. He's worked his way into my subconscious already.

Maybe you don't have to hide it. You can be the girl you think you are with him. He doesn't know you or your past.

I close the visor as he shifts into drive on the road. Before he returns his gaze forward, he smiles at me, his dimple winking at me from his right cheek, so close to his lips I can't help but stare for a second. That full bottom lip has my tongue pushing its way past my own lips to moisten them. With a half smile, I break our gaze, grateful for the barrier of the mirrored sunglasses, and reach into my bag for the lip balm I always keep on hand. I slide it quickly across both lips and drop it back in my bag as he proceeds down the road and around to the café. The drive takes less than five minutes, and I don't question why we drive instead of walk. I like riding in his Jeep. It smells like him—sandalwood, maybe. The urge to lean in and inhale the place on his neck right behind his ear has my fingers curling into my palms hard enough to leave indents. I feel like one of the female main characters in my books, getting swept off her feet by some broody thirst trap of a man.

Life isn't like make believe, Ev. The girl doesn't always get the boy. Breathe, babe!

". . . I want you to . . ."

"What?!" I gasp as Julian opens the passenger door and offers me his hand. I realize too late that I've cut him off mid-sentence.

He half laughs and repeats, "I want you to . . . see the other half of the trail. It leads right to my favorite spot."

"Ohhh, yeah, can't wait." I take his hand because it seems rude not to. It's warm, like his smell. And soft, which I didn't expect from all the dumbbell lifting he does. But it's smooth as it envelopes mine. I don't want to let go. *Down, girl. Just stop, Ev!*

"Stop, Ever."

Huh?

He pulls on my hand to halt my steps toward the trail, then drops it as I stop and turn to face him. "I want to run inside and grab my sunglasses too."

"Uh, sure. Where exactly are you grabbing them from?"

"My apartment," he replies, pointing toward the building next to the café. "It's above the garage that stores all the equipment in the off season. It's not much, but it's perfect for me and convenient to both jobs. And it's a steal because I'm the unofficial property manager when we're shut down." Grinning proudly, he turns and says, "I'll be right back."

Taking the stairs on the side of the building two at a time, he disappears. I knew there was a second story above the garage, but I didn't know it was an apartment. Or that Julian lives there. I want to follow him, to see where he lives. My curiosity grows by the second. I bet it smells like him. I take an involuntary step to follow him in my fascination but stop short. He did not invite me, and his apartment is none of my business. *He* is none of my business.

God, Ev, collect yourself.

I walk to the edge of the trail and decide to stretch a bit while I wait. And breathe like Allie is always harping on. Maybe the deep breaths will rein in my hormones. Or whatever this is.

Chapter 10

JULIAN

Stepping off the last stair, I stop short. Ever is bent over stretching, giving me a perfect view of her ass. Her hands are flat on the ground, her legs spread slightly apart and she's lunging from side to side. She stands up as I remain frozen in place and reaches above her head, first one arm, then the other. Her top rises with each flex, exposing the skin on the small of her back.

Swallowing, I shove the glasses onto my face, thanking my forethought in retrieving them before heading to the cliffs. Pretty soon the cliffs will be littered with locals and occasional campers jumping off into the blue, daring each other with flips and dives. I've jumped plenty of times, not on a dare, but because I like the rush and the chilly plunge. But mostly I prefer the view from the top, sitting above this place I've come to love so much. It grounds me like nothing can or has in the last three years. Lifting weights distracts me and allows me to release anger and frustration, like kickboxing. But the cliffs settle me. And if Ever keeps stretching in front of me like this, I'll need that settling more than I care to admit.

Clearing my throat, I ask, "Ready?" for the second time in fifteen minutes.

She turns, nods and walks toward the trail.

It still amazes me that I live right here with a lake that boasts breathtaking views and a trail that begins in my backyard. We don't talk as we work through the flats.

"I haven't been on this side of the trail in years." Ever, keeping perfect pace with me as the trail begins its incline, is barely breathing heavy and holding down a conversation. I'm impressed. "When did you first move to Blue Lake, or did you grow up here?"

"I've been here almost three years now. I grew up across the lake in South Point. Came here after high school, met Allie, got into fitness and . . . I don't know . . . just never left."

"Oh my God, this view!" Abandoning our conversation, she rushes to the edge of the path to peek between the trees and brush at the view beyond and below us.

My lips curve up at her excitement. I love that she gets as excited by the view as I do. It's spectacular. Until she leans over the edge. "EVER!" I jerk her back from the edge by her shoulders, pinning her back to my chest, curling one arm across her chest.

Her heart drums against my wrist through the thin fabric of her top. She tilts her head up to look at me, her gray eyes wide.

I loosen my grip on her as she pivots to face me. But I don't release her.

"Wha—what just happened? What *was* that?" Her puffs of breath hit my neck just above my collar.

I want to lower my face and feel those puffs on my lips. "You . . . I . . . you just scared me for a sec. A little too close to the edge for me I guess." Like a gravitational pull, I dip my chin, aligning my lips perfectly with hers. And know without knowing they'll be satin soft. Another inch and I'll know for sure.

"Ayo, my dudes. What's good?"

We turn at the sound of Lilly calling out to us. We step back from each other in sync. Still, instinct pushes me to grasp her arm and stop Ever from getting too close to the edge again.

"Lilly. Noah. Hey." I smile and raise my hand in a saluting wave. "What's good with you?"

Noah chimes in. "Taking advantage of the day off to hang at the cliffs before the hoolies take over. Right, baby?"

Giggling, she tosses back, "You're a hoolie, Noah," and punches him playfully.

"You're more hoolie than I am, Southy. At least I was born here. You're from across the lake." He traps the hand she swings at him, pulls her in and smacks her lips loudly with a kiss. "You guys heading up?" he calls and continues up the trail holding Lilly's hand.

The moment is long gone now, which I tell myself is a good thing. I toss my head toward the couple to say *let's go* to Ever.

She falls into step without missing a beat and asks me in a mock whisper, "If Lilly is more *hoolie* than Noah, what the hell does that make us?"

She rallies from our almost kiss like a pro. She's either completely unfazed by it—*and me*—or a pro at compartmentalizing. Something tells me she's had her share of experience in the need to do so, which does nothing to lessen my desire to protect her. Matching her energy, I answer back playfully, "I don't think we want to know."

By the time we catch up to them at the top of the cliff, they're both sitting on the ledge of the jutting rocks looking out over Blue Lake. They make a portrait with their silhouettes against the majestic backdrop. I jar to a stop, seeing them like that, clearly well-matched and in love. It transports me back in time to when I made picturesque moments like that with someone I loved.

Ever collides with my back, snapping me out of my trance. With a giggle and a sidestep, she pulls her phone from her pack and snaps a few pictures of them before they realize we've caught up. If she noticed my reaction, she doesn't let on. Stuffing her phone back in her bag, she spreads her arms wide and turns a full circle. "The air smells cleaner up here, if that's possible," she says to no one particular.

"Yeah, it's why we don't let the hoolies come up here," Noah responds.

"Really? It's off limits?" she asks it with a laugh.

"If only," Lilly cries. "But we post signs and strongly encourage they don't veer from the open trail."

Noah chimes in, "Yeah, she likes to tell the visitors about mountain lions and rattlesnakes to scare them off."

"I prefer telling the ones with little dogs about the owls and hawks, and to keep an eye on their *fur babies*," I add with a wicked grin.

"Wow, you guys really can't stand the . . . *hoolies*." Ever laughs. The sound has me absently rubbing the tattoo on my chest. "I better watch my ass," she adds.

I laugh at her sass and ignore the flip my stomach does.

"Eh, you're in because . . . Allie." Lilly flicks her hand like *duh*. "She's a G. Values this area and protects it as much as she can, without being totally annoying about it." Lilly pauses for half a second like she's waiting for permission, then keeps going. "She gets it. How fast places like this are disappearing. And, well, you're like her family, right? So . . ." She shrugs and stops talking.

"So, you're saying I'm not a hoolie?" Ever winks at Lilly, teasing. "What the hell is a hoolie anyway?"

My mouth turns to sandpaper as I stare at her unobserved, her attention on Lilly. She looks so young and innocent, but she talks with such wit and intelligence. She enchants me. Turning my head away to break the spell, I see Noah watching me, now standing on the edge of the cliff, one eyebrow arched. I arch mine right back in challenge.

With a half laugh, he tosses his head toward the lake. "Too cold for you still, J Mac?"

"Too cold for what? A dive? Eh, maybe." I shrug and glance at Ever to weigh her reaction. Will she think I'm a pussy for not wanting to jump? That I care is the disturbing part.

"Yeah, no, it's too cold," Lilly scoffs. "Are you crazy? That lake is not swimmable for a couple more weeks at least. Don't do it, Noah. We'll all do it the day before we open for campers. One last hurrah. Just wait! Okay? Will you guys do it with us then?" She aims her question at me and Ever.

"I, uh . . . sure. If Ever . . . ly wants to, I'm in." I turn my head to wait for Ever's reply.

She's looking from me to Lilly to Noah to the cliffs and now back to me. "Umm, yeah, okay, I'm in. But none of you get to call me a hoolie ever again if I do it."

"Deal," we all say in unison, then laugh at our timing.

Lilly adds, "And hoolie is just a hooligan. My grams used to call the campers that. Any outsiders really. And I guess I tried to say it when I was a baby, and it came out 'hoolie.' After that, it just stuck."

"Yeah, and now she's got half the town saying it," Noah chimes in.

"So, you're a local trendsetter," I tease.

She rolls her eyes.

"Influencer?" I wink at her again.

She just rolls her eyes again in response.

We spend another hour at the cliffs listening to Lilly talk about Blue Lake and growing up on the other side in South Point, where I grew up too, a few years before her, and Noah filling Ever in on going to school here. She isn't really going to attend, she explains, only turn in her assignments at the high school, through the remote learning program they offer.

I have so many questions. But she isn't offering any explanations, so I decide to save them for another time. Maybe when we're alone she'll want to tell me more about why she left her life to move up here in the middle of nowhere without her family. I know her mom and Allie go way back and are like family. So I get why she would be a good surrogate. But why did she need one? Why is she finishing her senior year up here away from everyone she grew up with and her sister? I mean, I get needing a fresh start away from reminders of a life that became a shit show. When Lilly talked about growing up in South Point, I kept my head down waiting to see if she knew me from there. I didn't figure she would because of our age difference, but I held my breath anyway. I know firsthand how Blue Lake can save someone's soul just by being here. I'm living proof of it. And I see that Ever needs saving as clearly as if she'd said it out loud. Despite my efforts not to care, I can't help my curiosity.

But that doesn't mean you need to save her. Reel it in, man.

Walking back, I trail behind the other three just enough to not be observed. I feel like a creeper—an enchanted creeper. I can't take my eyes off Ever. She walks gracefully on long legs, muscles flexing with the effort. I like that she's taller than most girls but sort of waiflike. Probably hated by girls her age because she's effortlessly thin.

I bet she'd build muscle fast.

My stomach flutters with the train of my thoughts. Ever at the gym, lifting weights, breathing heavily with exertion, sweating. I could see her simulating fighting in a kickboxing class. Watching someone get strong hypes me. Watching someone as beautiful as Ever . . . I adjust my shorts and tell myself to knock it off.

Why now, why this girl? What is she doing to me?

I lie to myself that I just like to help people get strong and feel confident, which is why I later suggest that she let me train her in our downtime.

We decide to complete the rare day off with a cheat meal and order pizza from town and have it delivered to Allie's for the two of us. Lilly and Noah have dinner plans with her family in South Point, so I'm happy to have Ever all to myself. When the pizza arrives, loaded with vegetables—our nod to healthy—she's reaching for plates when I blurt out, "Let me train you." Her shirt riding up just enough for me to glimpse the outline of her ribs as she stretches to pull down the plates has my fingers itching to touch that peek of skin.

"What?" She pauses with one hand on the cabinet door and the plates in the other and looks over her shoulder, pinning me with her smoky eyes. "You want to train me? Like at the gym?"

I swallow and nod. "I do."

"Okay." She hands me the plates and gives me a shy smile.

"Okay." I smile back.

"I don't have to join the Cougar Club, do I?" she teases.

"There's an age limit. You're too young," I throw right back.

"Oh, thank god. I didn't have the right perfume for it anyway." She crosses to the fridge and fills two glasses of water for us.

Our banter makes me way too happy. Happy feels strange. And scary. But so so good.

Dude, reel it in.

Chapter 11
EVERLY

Tonight is one of the best nights I've ever had. Embarrassingly so. By most girls' standards, I'm quite sure it would be considered straight-up boring. But for me it's perfect. After pizza, he pulls out his laptop and walks me through a training plan he personalized for me on the spot. He explains how I'd need to lift weights and not just do cardio. I'm more a fan of the treadmill or elliptical, mostly because I can read while I do it, but I don't admit that to him. Non-bookish people don't get it—the total immersion into a fictional world. I don't even know if he is a non-reader, but most guys I know aren't into reading.

Ironically, I don't think about my current book boyfriend once. During most social activities, it doesn't take long for me to wish it's over so I can go home and read my book. But after the workout planning sesh, we pop popcorn and watch a movie. By the time we decide to go to bed, I'm too tired to even want to read or think about reading. And I've had the best night's sleep I can remember in . . . I don't even know how long.

At one point during the movie, he snags the blanket off the back of the couch and spreads it out so we can share it. We aren't sitting close enough to touch each other. He keeps a polite distance. But sharing the blanket feels weirdly intimate. I hold my breath until he finishes spreading it across my legs. It seems like he was being careful not to touch me. And I wish he would. Touch me, that is. I imagine what his fingers would feel like tracing up my legs, then pulling me to him until they drape across his lap. My fingers itch to push back the wave of hair dipping down over his left eyebrow, almost long enough on top to fall into his eyes. My mouth waters wondering if he tastes as good as he smells. I decide in that moment that I read too many romance novels. I should mix in a thriller or mystery and give the hormones a break.

Once he settles back into his spot next to me, I inhale silently before his scent wafts away. His fingers thread through the hair on his forehead, pushing it back into its messy place on top, just like I wanted to do. Swallowing, I force my eyes back to the screen and tuck my hands under my thighs.

"Are you cold? You want another blanket?" he asks, mistaking me tucking my hands as a sign I'm cold.

He's way more thoughtful and considerate than I gave him credit for that first day. In my defense, he was a dick to me about accidentally crashing into him—twice. In his defense, I guess colliding with a klutzy newbie, once while naked, would irritate even the nicest of guys. Speaking of . . . Julian naked is one of those things I'll never be able to unsee, even if I wanted to, which I don't. God, he's beautiful. And attentive. My book boyfriends have nothing on this guy. Leave it to me to romanticize the situation. I thought I'd have dreamed of him last night, but I slept a sound, dreamless sleep. Until Maroon 5 woke me up at five a.m. wanting "One More Night."

How appropriate.

I immediately zero in on the sound of Julian moving around in the bathroom as I tap my phone to cut off Adam Levine. Is my music library for real right now? And how is Julian always one step ahead of me? Does he even sleep? I find I'm not groggy today but excited. Like a kid on Christmas, I can't wait to get up and see what being trained by Julian entails. I hope it means he'll put his hands on me. I ignore the voice in the back of my mind calling me a slut for my train of thought and instead remind myself that virgins can't be sluts and liking boys is normal. But Julian is not a boy. Even if he weren't a whole ass adult, his intensity tells me he's seen more than most twenty-one-year-olds. I only know he is twenty-one because Lilly told me so. Maybe a little too old for me. For sure more experienced than me. But I don't care. I can't help it. Everything about him fascinates me. And I want to fascinate him too. Something tells me I do. I feel it when he looks at me, the way he speaks to me. I can't wait to get up and . . . workout. I bounce out of bed and catch my flushed reflection in the dresser mirror.

Whoa, girl! Who are you and what have you done with Everly?

Just as I pull a pair of leggings and a sports bra out, I hear the latch of the bathroom door—our signal that the bathroom is free. A little detail we worked out last night before we turned in. We'd lock it when using it and make sure to unlock it when we finished. If the door is unlocked, the bathroom is unoccupied. I wait a full minute before opening the door to make sure he's gone. When I open the door, his scent hits me first. Clean, yes, but warm and slightly sweet. I think it's sandalwood. I know it's more effective than coffee. By the time I head downstairs, just ten minutes later, I all but skip.

Julian leans against the counter sipping from a mug much like Allie was that first day. When he sees me, his eyes crinkle at the corners in a genuine smile.

I smile back with my whole face. I feel it in my cheekbones. God, I need to check myself. But it's not all me.

His eyes travel down my body and then quickly jump back up to my face like he forgot I could see him. Clearing his throat, he asks, "Coffee?"

"Thanks, I got it." I smile politely and reach into the cupboard, pull down a mug and pour from the carafe on the counter. "How'd you sleep?"

"Great. Like a rock. You?" His eyes track me as he answers.

"Best night's sleep since I got here." I nod my head earnestly. Taking a sip of coffee, I catch the frown Julian makes as I glance over the top of my mug. If I wasn't watching, I'd have missed it.

He turns to the sink, rinses his mug and places it in the dishwasher. "Great. I'm going to warm up the Jeep. We can ride together." With that, he leaves the kitchen.

What just happened? I'm getting whiplash from his mood swings. But he's a puzzle I want to figure out. Maybe seeing him in trainer mode, up close and personal, will give me some answers.

***

At Fit, I watch him morph into Business Julian. We start on the treadmill, my warm-up cardio. He asked me to choose—elliptical, treadmill or stationary bike. I chose the treadmill thinking we'd be able to talk. And he did talk, but only about my workout. How he divided it up into three sections—PPL (push-pull-legs), he called it. We started with legs because he said Leg Day was the most dreaded workout day, even by the diehards. Allie has already shown me the machines. Julian demonstrates some free weight exercises. I feel self-conscious, but I like that he spots me to help me keep proper form. I prefer the machines for a quicker workout, but sweating with this beautiful man, just the two of us in the gym, is something I wouldn't trade right now. Who knew working out could be so hot? If everyone had a Julian at the gym, I'd venture a guess no one would skip their workouts. I'm sure that's why we have such loyal and steadfast female clientele here at Fit.

While I finish my workout with a few cool down minutes of cardio, my *trainer* insisted on it, he takes a quick shower in the men's locker room. I didn't bring a change of clothes, not knowing what to expect. Julian apologized for not suggesting it. Afterwards, he drops me at Allie's to shower and change for a full day at the café.

"I'll get things opened up and see you there," he tells me as I hop out of the passenger seat.

I tell him I'll be there in fifteen. I envision a quick sprint to Brew, but as I shower, dress and wolf a quick breakfast, my leg muscles get tighter and tighter. I expected to be sore. I didn't expect my legs to shake just trying to sit down on the toilet. I ride my ebike to Brew instead, grateful it does the heavy lifting for me. Another reason to research getting my own car again as soon as possible. I just don't know how I'll afford it. A problem for another day.

Julian is outside when I get there, taking out patio furniture, cushions and umbrellas from the storage garage. I park my bike near the café door and trek over to help on ever stiffening legs. I force myself to walk normally even though it costs me. Hiding my grimace, I toss my chin up and lift one hand over my head in greeting.

"I got a lot of the furniture set up already." He motions to the array of tables, chairs and loungers. "If you want, you can take the cushions and set them up as I place the seats. We'll do the umbrellas last."

I jump at the chance to do the light lifting. After a few hours of setting up, I can't hide my limping anymore. I've been up and down the stairs more times than I can count, so both legs are so tight, I can barely walk without wincing. As I lift the last umbrella to place it in the holder in the center of the table, Julian appears and takes it from my hands.

"Let's call it good for today. I have a couple loads of sand coming for the beach area tomorrow morning at seven a.m. We can finish up the rest then. Now tell me about the legs."

"Legs?"

"Yeah. You're limping. Did we go too hard at the gym? Too heavy? Break it down for me." He holds up his hand palm out as I start to shake my head. "If I'm going to train you, I've got to know how it's really going, so I can adjust as needed. In case you planned to play tough and lie to me." The last was said with a wink that made my heart flutter and my cheeks flush.

"Ummm, okay they hurt. Like hell. It didn't feel like too much or too heavy at the time, so I don't know what to adjust. But if I weren't too proud, I'd cry. Is that truthful enough for you? I see why people hate their trainers."

His dimples pop out with my last words. "It's probably just a flexibility thing. Meaning we need to have you stretch more. What if we laid off the weights and did more kickboxing and movement type stuff? And don't worry, I've got a good trick for sore muscles. Also, how much water have you had to drink today?"

I feel like a little kid caught breaking the rules, especially when I see him roll his eyes at my answer. "I, uh, left my water bottle on the counter at home. Full." I hold my hands out to my sides, palms up. "I had good intentions." The last I say like I'm pleading my case to get out of trouble, and I hate that it comes out like that.

He turns and lifts his water bottle off the table and hands it to me. "Finish this and follow me. We'll get you some immediate relief. Tonight, you can take a salt bath at Allie's. It'll make you feel like a new person by tomorrow. For now, let's get you walking without limping." He tosses his head toward the stairs leading to his place, turns and heads that way.

I follow along, dreading another round of stairs. Within three steps, my right calf seizes up. I cry out involuntarily and almost drop to my knees.

Julian already started up the stairs and stops abruptly. Turning, he stalks toward me without a word and scoops me up into his arms. Effortlessly, I might add. I open my mouth to protest, but he cuts me off. "Hydration 101, Ever. You've got a muscle cramp, right?" he scolds gently.

I clamp my lips shut and nod, silently cursing my life and the indignity. The excruciating pain trumps my humiliation. At the top of the stairs, he doesn't put me down as I expect and instead continues past what I assume is his front door and the bay window next to it.

He dips around the corner, which reveals a wraparound porch, two separate tubs side by side and a small enclosed structure I deduce is a sauna that stands along the outer wall of his apartment, just beyond French doors that open onto that part of the deck. It's so enchanting and unexpected. Totally hidden from the public but still boasting views of the lake and sunset. In fact, it looks like he quite possibly sees the sunrise from the other side of the deck beyond the two tubs.

Caught up in the quaintness, I didn't let go of his neck even though he set me on my feet.

His voice brings me back from my gawking. "I was thinking you could take a dip in the hot tub here and loosen up your muscles while I lock everything up. Then we can head back to Allie's. Should take me about twenty minutes or so, which would be a perfect soak to get you . . . walking without a limp." He chuckles on the last part. He must read the denial on my face, because he continues before I can speak up and says, "Let me grab you a towel and a robe," turns and disappears . . . to go get them I assume, before I utter a word.

I stand there dumbfounded looking down at my cutoff denim shorts and T-shirt. He can't expect me to wear these in the hot tub, right? As if summoned by my thoughts, he appears with a towel and robe and hangs them on the towel rack that stands between both tubs.

"I, uh . . . don't . . . uh . . ."

"Just go in your underwear." He notes my expression and holds up his hands in mock surrender. "I won't look. I'll be downstairs locking up. And you can just go commando under your clothes back to Allie's. It will be our secret." There was that wink again. He turns to go like none of this is a big deal.

I feel like I'm giving awkward junior high locker room energy—the last thing I want to look or feel like in front of Julian. Stamping down my insecurity, I swipe my T-shirt over my head, glance behind me to make sure he's gone and start to unzip my shorts.

"Hey, Ever?"

I freeze. Julian calls out from around the corner, which I realize for what it is—a polite heads up.

"I forgot to lift the lid on the hot tub. If you're still dressed, I can come do it."

"Uh, yeah, sure," I return loud enough to be heard around the corner. I jerk the towel off the rack and press it to my chest. I have on a sports bra, but I still feel naked.

Julian jogs around the corner, not looking at me, and rushes to the tub closest to the railing. As he lifts the lid, clouds of steam float toward the sky.

Not that it's a good time for conversation, but curiosity has me asking, "Why two tubs?"

"Oh, the other is a cold one," he answers like that explains everything.

Standing with the towel clenched to my chest, I can't help myself. "Cold? For what purpose?"

"Ahh . . ." He holds his hands out to his sides and tilts his head slightly. "So many things," he claims proudly. "More than we have time to get into right now. One, though, is for sore muscles, if you care to try it out." He raises one eyebrow in challenge, looking me in the eye now.

"I think I'll stick with the hot one for now." I don't appreciate the knowing smirk on his face. But just like long explanations, this isn't the time for my sarcastic retorts.

"Fair enough. Hop in. Use the jets if you want or just soak. I'll be back in twenty. And Ever? Finish the damn water in my bottle. Okay?"

As he disappears around the corner again, I hastily shimmy out of my shorts and throw the towel back onto the rack and ease into the steaming water. I think I hear my legs whimper in relief. I tell myself that's why I tolerated the indignance of it all. The relief. My legs hurt like they've never hurt before. I used to run regularly at home, so I've had muscle cramps before, but combined with the soreness of the leg day, maybe I unlocked a new level of pain. And because I want relief as soon as possible, I yank his bottle off the edge of the tub, unscrew the cap and guzzle. Not because he told me to, I remind myself childishly. Since my dad died and my mom got busier, I've developed issues with people telling me what to do. I've been making most of my own decisions since I was twelve, but I'm also smart enough to admit when some *instructions* just make common sense.

Chapter 12

Julian

Ever is already walking better from the quick dip in the hot tub. The guilt of possibly pushing her too hard on her first day of lifting has me mentally kicking myself. I got too excited at the idea of working out with her. I lose my perspective easily with her, I remind myself. Why now? Why this girl? Is it the mirror of brokenness in her eyes? The reminder of another set of broken eyes that broke me too? Or is it the way her stormy grays seem to look right through me? Maybe it's simply that she's drop-dead gorgeous with her long limbs, wavy chestnut hair and pouty lips that beg to be kissed. Or the sassy wit I can't get enough of. *Or all of it.*

"What?" Ever is standing in Allie's kitchen behind me, freshly changed into sweats, her hair still wet from her shower.

My hand freezes on the cutting board where I'm chopping vegetables for dinner. "Hmm," I answer back. *Did I just say that out loud?* Holding my breath, I wait for her reply.

"All of what?"

Shit! "I . . . uh . . . I guess I was thinking out loud. How embarrassing."

"Ooh, yeah, talking to yourself." She tsks. "Certifiable. Kiddinggg." She singsongs it and adds, "I talk to myself too. Maybe it's because we need expert advice." She giggles at her own joke.

"Right." I smirk and continue chopping vegetables, holding my breath and pleading with the gods that she won't ask me about it again. After a pause, she offers to help instead, showing again her maturity that belies her age. And I take the bone she offers, relieved.

"So, what are we eating tonight, Chef Julie? Can I help?" She bounces up to my side and peeps over my shoulder.

Her shampoo or soap or lotion or whatever fills my nostrils and stirs my blood. It's giving sunshine and summer air, and I love it. "Well, I thought we'd go for some pasta with vegetables. It should help with the leg cramps and dehydration. Grilled chicken for protein."

"The legs are much better now. And I'm hydrating, I promise. What can I do to help?"

"Wanna grate cheese? There's a block in the drawer in the fridge. Allie must have a grater in here somewhere."

"I'm on it."

I continue to slice and chop while she opens and closes cabinets behind me, her smell floating through the kitchen, intoxicating me. I try to focus on the sharp knife in my hand and the task before me while this enchanting young woman has me spinning and feeling clumsy. And talking to myself apparently.

Chapter 13

EVERLY

Embarrassment is a new one for Julian. I've never seen him act anything but confident, even when he stuttered on my name that first day. He rallied quickly and dubbed me Ever, which I love more than I want to admit. It's like a special thing that's all ours. Or maybe I just hope it is. Walking in on him talking to himself might be the cutest thing ever. Maybe it was seeing him act like a regular guy that did it. He's always so perfect. Impeccable body, work ethic, gorgeous. It is . . . weirdly comforting to see him awkward and mumbling, but I can tell it's new for him. Or at least not his norm. I decide to cut him some slack and change the subject. Although asking to help him cook may not be the best move. He's a master chef by my standards. All I've mastered in the kitchen is PB&J, scrambled eggs and some other simple basics.

After dinner, I don't want the night to end so I ask if he wants to watch a movie again. He hesitates for a moment, then agrees, but says he has some work to do on his laptop while we watch. There's that perfect Julian energy again—super serious, multi-tasking professional.

I pick an action movie I figure he'll like, but even those have an element of romance in them. Points for trying.

As Julian types away on his laptop, I absently rub my calf that begins to throb again.

He abruptly pushes the laptop closed, sets it on the coffee table, gets up and throws over his shoulder, "I'll be right back."

"Want me to pause the movie?"

"Nope, I'll just be a sec."

And true to his word, he flies up and down the stairs in a flash and plops back down closer to me than before.

"Here, give me your leg. This will help the cramping." I must look surprised because he adds, "It doesn't hurt, I promise. Scoot over here."

I inch closer so that we're almost touching. He lifts my leg, draws it across his lap and pushes the fabric of my sweats up over my knee. I've never been so relieved I thought to shave. He begins moving his fingers along my calf, then unscrews the lid on the jar he brought down. He rubs the cream from the jar in his hands before placing them gently on my calf. He squeezes and tightens his grip as he moves his hands up and down my calf. The icy warmth heats and soothes the ache almost immediately, but I'm convinced the relief has way more to do with the hands applying it. I close my eyes and must've made an involuntary sound of relief because his movements falter for a moment. I open my eyes to find his penetrating blue orbs watching me. How long is too long to stare at each other without breathing?

I break the spell because I need to. Either that or I'm going to completely leave my body and kiss him. "Uh, thanks, that feels better."

I pull my leg back, which makes him pull his hands back. "That stuff works fast."

"Yeah, Allie and I made it."

"Wait. You made it?"

Chuckling, he nods. "I'll be right back." The deep sound of his voice settles in my stomach, warming it like the balm warms my calf.

I watch as he washes his hands at the kitchen sink and decide to take my shot to feed my curiosity. "How'd you meet Allie and get into . . . all of this?"

"Ahhh, that's a long story." He rubs his palm over his chest as he makes his way back to the living room.

Nervous tic? My intrigue is growing. "Well, I don't have any place to be. Do you?"

He sits down in his original spot, not as close. "Maybe we should just watch the movie."

I swallow my disappointment at his seat choice and double down on my inquiry. "Why don't you want to answer the question?" I challenge. My curiosity and interest in this thirst trap of a man outweighs my introverted nature. I don't recognize this bold girl, but I think I like her. I hold my breath and wait for his reply.

"Why are you here?" he counters. "With Allie? Away from your home, your family, alone?"

"Fair. But I asked you first."

I watch him as he turns his face toward the screen. The movie is still playing, but I've turned the sound down. With a heavy exhale, he reaches out and squeezes my foot, his hand swallowing it. I swallow hard at the intimacy of it—not sexual, but it sends a heat wave to my lower region.

"Are we really going to do this, Ever?"

I blink once, twice, wrapping my brain around his words. "Do what?" My brain catches up and smacks my libido back to reality. "Get to know each other? I mean, we work together every day. We'll be sharing the same living space for three weeks. And now you're training me. Wouldn't it be weird not to?"

"Fair," he repeats back to me. "I've just never told anyone before. Except Allie, who I think missed her calling as a therapist, by the way. But even she only got the highlights."

"Hmm." I consider his response and choose the benign part to reply to. "But, right? She's always been that person you can confide in, even when you didn't think you wanted to. How long have you known her? How did you meet?"

"Man, this conversation is making me want a drink. And I don't really drink that much anymore."

"Me neither. Did you used to?"

He exhales again, his cheeks puffing up, lips forming an O. He squeezes my foot he's still holding and turns his face to mine. What I see in his crystal blue eyes breaks my heart. I echo his exhale and keep my eyes locked on his and wait for him to speak.

Chapter 14

Julian

Her eyes look dark gray right now, locked on mine, like storm clouds that perfectly mirror my thoughts. The memories crash through my mind and settle in my chest. I haven't spoken about this to anyone, not in any real detail. Not even to Allie, although she knows more than anyone. She's so easy to talk to and she saved my life, but some of the darkest memories I keep to myself. I'm not sure this girl—or anyone—can handle hearing any of it, let alone the dark parts. I can barely handle the memory of it myself—which is why I try not to remember it at all. But I want to tell her. I want to let her in. Which fucks with my head, because I haven't wanted to let anyone in before. If I tell her, will she look at me the same after? Like I'm some storybook hero sent here specially for her? That might be what captures me most. The way she looks at me like I'm somebody. It transports me back in time to the only other person to look at me that way—make me feel that way. Like someone who matters. And that look lied to me that I could have a do-over. I know I can't turn back time and I know I can't bring her back. Not that kind of do-over. A do-over where I matter to someone again and let them matter to me. Rubbing that place on my chest, the empty heart tattoo, I decide to rip the bandage off. I'll either send her running for the hills or plunge us both over the edge of the cliff. God knows I can't offer her the knight in shining armor she seems to think I am or could be. But damn if I don't want to be.

How did I get here? Am I really going to let this girl in?

I'm clenching her foot in my hands like a lifeline. "I did a lot, right after . . ." I pause, seeing it . . . her . . . again in my mind for the first time in years. "Drinking helped me go numb, try to forget." I watch my hands clasp and unclasp her foot. I swallow, my mouth dry. "When I was eighteen, my high school girlfriend died." I pause, swallow again, my mouth filling with saliva now, my stomach churning. "She didn't just die. She killed herself. And it was my fault." I stop, turn my head, lock eyes with her and wait for the horrified expression I was sure would come, the judgment.

Instead, her stormy eyes go opaque and fill with unshed tears.

I turn my gaze back to her foot in my stilled hands. I don't want to see the pity I know comes next. I start to move my hands from her foot, to leave.

She reaches out and grabs one of my hands in hers. "I'm so sorry that happened." I lift my eyes back to hers and watch one tear spill and race down her cheek. I absently reach out to catch it and she leans into my hand. She closes her eyes at my touch, causing more tears to fall.

What is this girl doing to me?

"Ever . . . don't cry." I can't stop myself. I reach for her and pull her slight frame onto my lap and wrap my arms around her—to comfort her, I tell myself, but the feel of her body in my lap, in my arms, comforts me. I bury my face in her neck and inhale deeply.

She does the same to me. Like mimes, we mimic each other's moves. My hand slides up her back to tangle in her hair. Hers grabs the back of my neck to keep me there. Her body curves around mine. Like a yin and yang symbol, we meld together. And I feel her lips lightly press against the pulse in my neck, almost like she's trying it out. I hear the low *mmm* from her throat as I feel the vibration in her lips. My body instantly reacts. And strangely, instead of fanning the flame, it douses it. I move my hands to her shoulders and, squeezing, I gently move her off my lap and away from me.

"I . . . I'm . . . was that not okay?" She looks confused and embarrassed.

I fucking hate that I put that look there. With my head in my hands, elbows on my knees, I answer, "No. Ever, it's not that. Look, we just . . . we can't do this. I can't do this. I can't be *that* guy. I'm not that guy. Okay?" I can't admit it to her, but I can admit it to myself. I'm scared. Scared of what I feel. Scared of what I want. And scared of how I'll manage to keep my distance for the next three weeks.

Chapter 15

Everly

Without waiting for an answer, Julian gets up and takes the stairs two at a time and disappears into his room. I hear the doors close, first his bedroom door then his bathroom door, moments before I hear the water from the shower turn on.

I sit frozen for a few more minutes, swallowing my embarrassment. Did I really try to kiss him? I have no idea why I went there, like my lips had a mind of their own. *Who are you and what have you done with Everly?* Obviously, I have no clue what I'm doing, and it showed. Was he completely turned off by my efforts? I didn't get that vibe from him. But if the tea is accurate, he's used to much more "mature" attention.

Stick to the book boyfriends of your dreams. You're much smoother in make-believe worlds.

I turn off the TV, casting the living room into darkness, and trudge to the kitchen to clean up any remnants of dinner before making my way up to my room, to lose myself in my current book and attempt to forget about the "boy next door."

By the time I get upstairs, it's quiet on the other side of the bath-room door. I tentatively check to find it unlocked and move toward the sink to brush my teeth. The air is post-shower steamy and filled with his scent. I brush my teeth quickly and retreat to my own room. Intending to read, I flip the light switch off, slide my sweats down my legs and leave them on the floor where they drop, crawl under the covers and take my Kindle from the nightstand.

I awake to his smell, his hands shaking my shoulders and my name on his lips. "Ever, hey, wake up. It's okay. You're dreaming. Hey, it's Julian."

"I know. I can smell you." His chuckle, a deep rumble, is his reply. I love that sound. Then . . .

"I think you're still asleep. You okay?"

Scrubbing my hands over my face, causing his hand to slip from my shoulder, I answer back. "Yeah, I am. I think. Sorry. Did I wake you?" Flashes of the dream come back, and I shudder involuntarily at the images.

"Hey, shhhh. Take a breath. I'm right here. You're safe."

I feel the bed dip where he sits down, and I drop my hands from my face to focus on him. His face is a shadow, backlit by the hall light in my doorway. He came through the hall, my mind registers. Not the bathroom. "I . . . I just have these . . . I remember some of the stuff and it . . . I'm okay now. I didn't mean to wake you."

"You didn't. I was finishing some work. I heard you. Tried to check on you but the bathroom door was locked. So I came through the hall. Listen, I can stay. If you want . . ."

"No." Cutting him off, I scoot up so I'm leaning against the head-board. "I'm good."

"You're shaking. And sweating. Let me get you a cold washcloth. Hold on."

Within moments he's back, rubbing a cool cloth along the back of my neck. Then he blows on the dampened spot of skin.

I feel the pressure behind my eyes before the tears gather. I lean my head forward, intending to hide my face in my hands but end up resting my forehead on his chest instead because it's right there. I want to leave it there, but I don't. I lift my hands to his bare chest and try to push him back.

He's solid and doesn't move an inch.

"Julian, stop. You're confusing me. Why are you being so nice to me?"

I hear his exhale and feel it on my cheek before answers. "I don't know, Ever. When I hear you calling out in your sleep like you're scared, in pain, I can't help it. I want to protect you. Make it stop. I can't leave you alone."

"Then don't. Leave me alone. Stay. Please."

With a groan, he scoops me off the bed and trades places with me. With no effort he sits leaning against the headboard and deposits me snugly in his lap. The soft cotton of his pajama bottoms caresses my bare legs. I remember I'm only wearing a T-shirt and underwear, but I don't care. Shivering at his closeness and his arms wrapping around me, he mistakenly thinks I'm cold. His body is a furnace and I'm still clammy from the dream, but he reaches for the comforter and pulls it up around my shoulders, wrapping his arms back around me on top of the blanket. He rests his chin on top of my head, and sighs as he rubs his hands up and down my arms. I don't know how long we stay like this. I fit perfectly in his lap, like a glove on a hand. Every part of me relaxes into him. The rhythm of his breathing soothes me, lulls me, and I must eventually fall back to sleep.

The next thing I know I wake up lying next to him, his arms still around me, his body stretched out facing me. Mine mirrors his. We both must've shifted in our sleep, but we're still curled into each other, touching forehead to almost toes. I can feel every inch of him like a fever on my body. Heat emanates off him and sets me on fire. I want to move to cool down, but I don't want to wake him. I don't want him to leave. My heart begins a loud racing thud in my chest. I have no idea how long we've been asleep, but it's still dark outside.

His arms tighten around me, his hips pressing against me.

My breath hitches. Is he awake? I don't want to open my eyes and give myself away or break the spell. My arms are curled between us, resting on his chest. I feel his heartbeat speed up. I flatten my hands against his chest and raise my head slowly to sneak a look at his face.

Chapter 16

JULIAN

I didn't think I'd sleep. Not with this waifish beauty curled up on top of me. Her scent alone intoxicates me. But when I wake up, I find her stretched out beside me, our bodies perfectly aligned. Her hands splayed against my chest. I tighten my arms involuntarily, subconsciously wanting to keep her there forever. It's still dark, but I can tell the moment she wakes up. Her heart rate speeds up, and the pulse in her wrists taps against my chest. My body betrays me, and my hips press into her. That's when I feel her move.

She raises her head to look at me.

Adjusted to the darkness, I can see the outline of her face, the flutter of her lashes as she lifts her eyes to mine. Her mouth so close I can feel her soft puffs of breath, sweet and warm on my throat. I tilt my head down to align my lips perfectly with hers. A fraction of an inch and our lips would fuse. My tongue would caress the velvet of hers. Her sigh is an unspoken invitation to do just that. My fingers dig into her hips. She pushes hers forward to meet mine, innocently, involuntary. Like she has no idea what she's doing. I'm sure of it. Or what she's doing to me, which makes it even hotter. There's something more beautiful about someone who doesn't know the allure they carry. I need to taste her. Her lips are as soft as I imagined. Her tongue, velvet and sweet.

Shy at first, she keeps hers in her mouth. Then she seems to come alive. She slides her tongue into my mouth, then back out. I let her set the pace but match her stroke for stroke. Every brush confesses the ache we can't hide.

"Julie," she breathes.

"Yeah, Ever. I know." Pressing my hips into hers, I pull back to look into her eyes, unfocused, a little crazed with desire.

"Mmm . . . please," she whispers.

"Please what, Ever? Tell me." My voice is hoarse with longing.

"Hmm." Her half sigh, half moan is her only response.

I groan. "I know, sweet girl. Me too." I don't want to rush this. I don't want to rush her. I'm shaking with the force of my restraint. This girl is perfect. Her lips. Her body. The way it fits against mine. Like she was sent here just for me. I don't deserve her, but, god, I want to. *Let me have her*, I pray to some god I'm not even sure exists. *Please let me have this one good thing. I will work to deserve her if you just let me have her. I'll protect her this time.* Stuck in my head, I realize I've stopped moving, frozen with this feeling that I've stolen a piece of heaven that isn't mine.

"Julian, don't stop. Please. I want . . . mmm." She trails off on a breathless sigh, grinding against me.

"Yes, Ever. Tell me what you want." Bunching the hem of her T-shirt in my fingers, I push it up and graze her flat stomach.

With a low moan, I capture her lips and tongue again as my hand dances along her ribs until it meets her bra. Her breast fills my hand as she arches into it. My other hand slides up her thigh and stops where it meets the leg of her panties. Sliding my hand under the delicate fabric, I wrap my palm around her naked hip and lift her leg to drape it over mine. I want every inch of this girl right now. It's getting harder and harder to restrain myself. I want to go slow, take my time, but I also know I don't deserve the magic of this moment. She's beautiful, perfect even, and so, so sweet. She tastes so goddamn good. I'm fighting to control myself.

"Tell me what you want, Ever. Say it," I beg.

"You, Julie. Please. I want your hands . . . touch me." Her lower half squirms with her request.

"Are you sure? Tell me to stop and I will."

Grasping my wrist, she tugs it to the vee where her thighs meet.

It's all I need. My green light. I couldn't stop myself if I tried. I pull the soft cotton of her panties to the side and feel her silky heat, wet and slippery already. I circle the hard bud a few times, making her squirm more, while my other hand leaves her breast to snake around her and pull her tighter to me.

A tiny whine, like a plea, escapes her lips a second before I slide my finger into her.

My lips find the pulse at her neck and rain kisses on her heated skin. The sound she makes spurs me on. Half cry, half moan. I plunge a little farther, harder. In. Out. Again and again while I suck on the sensitive spot behind her ear. I could almost come just from this—her response to me. My thumb makes slow circles above my finger that continues its rhythm in and out.

She grips my shoulders, digging her nails in and begins to shudder. She's going to come. The tension builds in her whole body. Her leg muscles tense, her thighs tightening against my forearm. Her stomach taut. She's panting and swivels her head from side to side. As she squeezes her eyes shut, a tear leaks from each corner.

My hand freezes, finger and thumb stilled.

She releases one of my shoulders and grips my wrist, pulling it against her, urging me to keep going. "Please, Julie," she cries.

And I oblige. She is a captivating puddle in my hands. As she comes undone before me, I watch as tear after tear slowly trails down her cheeks while she soaks my hand with her orgasm. I don't know what to make of the tears or my reaction to them. She's not upset or sad, just flooded. I use my lips to mop the trails on her cheeks. Between kisses I whisper to her, not sure what I'm even saying. I just want to savor this, *her*. "Easy, Ever. I got you."

As she settles down, she curls into me like she can't get close enough. Like she wants to crawl into my skin and be a part of me.

I move my hand from between her legs and wrap both arms around her. Cradling her, I bring her as close to me as possible and wonder for a moment how I'll release my pent-up tension. I've never wanted to be inside someone as much as I do right now. I ignore it the best I can, but my body's reaction can't be ignored. She must feel it too, being in my lap.

I know the moment she comes back to reality. She dips her head and nestles her face shyly into my neck. Taking my hand off the back of her neck, I graze my index finger up and down her cheek, coaxing her to look at me.

Beneath shuttered lashes, she peers up into my eyes and lowers her gaze with a half-smile.

"Hi," I brush my finger down her cheek and lift her chin to kiss her lips softly.

"Hi," she says softly.

"You're beautiful," I say to reassure her, and I mean it. I've never been more captivated.

"You're beautiful," she replies, and I feel her smile.

"Hmf." My half laugh vibrates my chest. "Sweet girl, what are you doing to me?" Tightening my grip, I hug her before I release her, then race my hands up and down her back and pull her even closer as she softly giggles.

"Nothing yet. But I think I'd like to."

With a deep groan, I roll her onto her back and nestle my body between her legs. I can't help but grind into her when her thighs part and rise to accommodate me and her long legs twine around me like a vise. Again, I'm struck by the way our bodies meld, like we're made to fit together. "I'm all ears. Please tell me." I kiss the corner of her lips. "Tell me what you'd like to do to me," I all but beg.

Shy again, she dips her head.

I use my hand to lift her chin and force her to meet my eyes.

Half closing her eyes in a last-ditch protest to facing me, she looks up from under her lashes again and gives me that half smile.

I begin to wonder if she's teasing me, playing coy.

"I . . . I don't . . . Would you show me . . ." she trails off.

I freeze. "Ever, have you never . . . Are you a virgin?"

She nods against me.

"Ahhh . . . Are you . . . Did I hurt you? Why didn't you tell me?"

"You didn't ask." Her reply is instant, though still timid. "And no, you didn't." Her fingernail traces the hollow heart tattoo on my chest as she adds, "In fact, I kind of liked it and can't wait to do it again."

My stomach flips at her words. The ice around my heart all but melted now. I reach my hands under her ass and squeeze playfully as I roll onto my back and take her with me so she's straddling me.

She grinds into me, innocently I now know. Her body knows what it wants even if she's never experienced it.

It's almost my undoing. I pull her hips down to grind on me even more. I've never wanted anything or anyone more in my life. More like a need than a simple want, my desire almost painful.

"I want to make you feel how you make me feel," she says earnestly.

"Ever girl, if you only knew."

"Show me then," she repeats.

And I do, because I'm selfish and I want her. And I'm going to have her. Even if I don't deserve her.

As if the gods agree I don't deserve her, the phone on her nightstand lights up and dings in that instance.

"Shit, I forgot to put it on *do not disturb* before I crashed." She crawls off me and reaches for it.

I selfishly want to throw it across the room, but texts at two a.m. aren't random. I'm sure she realizes that too. Deciding not to pout like an asshole, I put my arm behind my head and wait for her to read it.

Her face pales in the light of the screen as the phone slips from her hand and falls to the floor. Her hands cover her mouth, and she starts shaking her head from side to side.

I sit up and grasp her wrists, imploring her to look at me.

And she does. She turns that haunted gray stare on me and I feel my heart sink. Terror oozes from her pores. I press her into my chest with one arm and reach for the fallen phone with the other.

There's no contact name on the text. Just a number.

Three texts in a row:
Evvie, I'm sorry.
Let me make it up to you.
I still think about you.

"What is this? *Who* is this?" When she just continues to press herself into my chest and say nothing, I lean back to try to look at her.

She curls her nails into my skin and looks up at me through her lashes but doesn't answer.

"Hey. Tell me what's going on. I'm here. I won't let anyone hurt you. Talk to me."

Chapter 17

Everly

Three-ish Months Ago

"Evvie, what did you do? Tell me it's not true. You slept with Chase?"

This is the second time in less than eight hours I've been awakened by crazy accusations and wondered how they could be referring to me. Me, who's never even kissed a guy. At least the grogginess is gone now, replaced by the most incredible headache I've ever experienced.

Pressing the palm of one hand to my forehead, I use the other to push myself up in my bed. *My bed. How'd I get home to my bed?*

My sister, Via, is standing over me, hands on hips looking more like my mom than I dare tell her. "What the hell happened after we left?" She watches me struggle to get my bearings, waiting for my answer.

She and Ryan left the party before anyone else. I remember that clearly. I remember them asking if I wanted to stay. Kendall and Chase telling them to let me have some fun for once. Everything else is foggy at best.

Her question hits like coffee to my veins. "What? No! How can you ask me that? Who said that? How'd I get in my bed? How'd I get home? Fuck, my head hurts." Squeezing my palms to both sides of my temples, willing the pounding to stop, I try to piece together the blank spots of the previous night.

Her face falls. "Oh, Ev, I knew we should've taken you home with us. Okay, first things first. Let's get you some water and Advil and then we'll get into what the hell happened." As she starts to leave the room, her phone rings. Looking at the display, she swipes to answer it.

"Hey, babe. Ev is—WHAT? When? No, I'll meet you there. Yeah, I will. You too."

Hanging up, she turns to face me, sheet white. "Ev, that was Ryan. I . . . I need to meet him at the hospital. Kendall, umm, Kendall tried to . . ." Tears well up in her eyes. "She took some pills. She's going to be okay, but she tried to . . . she . . ." One tear spills. "I guess she tried to kill herself last night. I've gotta meet Ryan at the hospital. Chase called him."

My stomach revolts at the mention of Chase or that Kendall tried to kill herself, I'm not sure. Both? I start fast swallowing to keep any contents down.

"I need to go. Are you gonna be okay?" Sliding her phone into her back pocket, she tracks my expression. "I could stay. I mean, do you need me to stay?" Sighing, she adds, "Evvie, what the hell happened last night?"

I shake my head, still holding it with both hands, struggling to stand up as if to go with her.

"No. Just sit down." She stops my momentum, placing her hands on my shoulders. "We'll figure this out. I'll . . . I'll be back as soon as I can. Okay?"

I think I nod. She doesn't wait for an answer. It's just as well. I don't have one. I can't make complete thoughts. I just need a minute to think. Kendall tried to kill herself? The bile threatens to come up again. How were these two the ultimate couple goals less than twenty-four hours ago and now I'm being accused of sleeping with Chase and Kendall is in the hospital for an apparent . . . suicide attempt? Nothing makes sense.

I stand up too quickly, intending to get the water and Advil Via suggested. I sway, my room going dark at the corners and closing in. I reach back and steady myself on the edge of the bed. Run my hand down my chest to my stomach as it protests and threatens to empty itself on the floor at my feet.

I look down at the T-shirt and jeans I still have on from last night. Flashes of Chase's hand moving up the hem of my shirt, his hand on my stomach. The more I push my mind to grasp the details, the further away the snippets drift until they evaporate completely. The harder I try to hang onto them, the fuzzier they seem. I need to fill in the blanks.

Someone has to know what happened, but my answers will have to wait. First things first, this headache and the desert that is my throat. A tall glass of water will surely unstick my tongue from the roof of my mouth and unpeel the inside of my upper lip from my teeth. I stagger to the kitchen, thankful for once that my mom isn't here. I spot my purse and keys on the entryway table, triggering a flash of Chase setting them there . . . last night? Chase was here last night. Did Chase drive me home? Is that when Kendall took the pills? What the actual fuck happened last night? And why does *anyone* think I'd sleep with Chase? And why isn't Chase telling them we didn't?

Chapter 18

Everly

Still clutching Julian's biceps in my clenched fists, I take a deep breath and blow it out on a shaky exhale. I press my forehead to his chest again. I don't want to look at him. I don't want him to look at me differently. What if he blames me like everyone in Oak Valley? What if it happens again and everyone here turns their backs on me? Where will I go then?

"Is that your boyfriend?"

I shake my head vehemently.

"Okay." He nods slowly.

I'm gulping air, trying to catch my breath. I know I have to say it. More shallow breaths.

"A girl back home, a friend—I thought she was my friend, accused me of sleeping with her boyfriend . . ." More gulps of air. "Then tried to kill herself." More gulps. "Then took a social hit out on me." I can't get enough air. "It's him." I'm clawing at my shirt now. I need more air. "I changed my number. No one has it. Only my sister. Olivia." I'm rambling and panting. Sweat runs down my spine. "But they're all friends. Maybe he found it on her phone." I shake my head. "This can't be happening again." My breath hitches. "I left. I disappeared. I left my whole life so they'd all leave me alone. I can't . . ." I can't breathe. My chest feels tight.

The room starts to go dark at the edges, my fingertips tingle.

Julian stands up with me still wrapped around him and swivels, sits me down on the edge of the bed and kneels in front of me. "Ever." He sounds mad. *At me?* "Hey, look at me." His hands shake my legs to jar my stare into nothingness to his eyes. "Deep breath. In one, two, three, four; out one, two, three, four. Again. In. Count with me in your head. Out one, two, three, four. You're about to hyperventilate. Keep breathing and counting. Nothing else matters. Just breathe and count with me, okay?"

The edges of the room come back into focus along with his eyes. *I love his eyes.* The tightness in my chest eases.

Julian puts his hands on my cheeks and pulls my face to his. Then he kisses me so softly I almost can't feel his lips. He moves his hands down my neck, arms, then clasps my hands. "C'mon, let's go downstairs and make some tea." He stands up and pulls me up with him.

I follow numbly. I know I have to tell him all of it now. Will he believe me? I don't want to go back there, even to tell it. I keep breathing and counting as I retrieve my sweats from the floor where I dropped them earlier this evening. Why does that feel so long ago?

***

S teaming mug in hand, I face him across the breakfast bar. "I can't say for sure what happened. All I know is I didn't sleep with him or anyone. I've never even kissed a guy, I . . ." I stop abruptly, realizing what I've just admitted to this man in front of me, who gave me my first kiss and a mind-numbing orgasm less than an hour ago upstairs.

Judging by the expression on his face, he realizes it too.

My face flames with the inadvertent admission.

He clears his throat and takes a sip of tea, sufficiently hiding behind his mug. Swallowing visibly, he asks, voice raspy, "Then why is everyone convinced you slept with him?"

"My sister went to see Kendall in the hospital the next day. She claims she found us in their bed together. And when he left to drive me home, she took a bunch of pills. Kendall admitted she made herself throw them up right after but went to the hospital just in case. Chase told everyone he just went in to use the bathroom and I came on to him. I don't remember anything except waking up in their bed and being thrown out of their house. I remember drinking too much at their party.

"Not something I usually do," I add when I see Julian raise his eyebrow. My heart begins hammering in my chest, tracking the judgment that I inevitably see on every face of anyone that hears about that night. "Anyway, Kendall's dad pretty much runs Oak Valley, so by proxy Kendall does too. I became a pariah overnight. But that wasn't enough for Kendall's friends. I got death threats, bullied online, my car vandalized. That's when I came here—when they destroyed my car. I couldn't subject my sister to it any longer. Kendall and her posse are my sister's best friends. Chase is Ryan's best friend. And of course, none of it could be traced back to Kendall or Chase. And maybe it wasn't them. Just their loyal self-appointed minions. We may never know. It just got to be too much and . . ." I shrug and let my sentence trail off as I stare at the cooling tea in my mug.

"And Allie to the rescue," he finishes for me.

"Yeah, well, I didn't ask her to rescue me," I retort, suddenly pissed.

"No one asks. It's just what she does." He stands to take his mug to the sink. "Ever, I'm not judging you. From the little I know about you, I'd bet money you didn't make a move on him, even drunk off your ass. It doesn't track for me. Maybe getting some time and distance from it will bring back that night. Maybe it won't. But this isn't Oak Valley, and I'm not those people. I'm not judging you," he repeats and takes the mug out of my hand and places it in the sink. "Come on, let's try to get some sleep before the alarm. Kickboxing tomorrow . . . or today technically."

Upstairs, he follows me into my room and waits for me to get into bed. He surprises me by sitting down in the chair next to the bed. "Just till you fall asleep," he explains.

"Somehow I think you being right there will do the opposite." I see his half smile in the diffused moonlight.

"Just close your eyes. Count your breaths."

I roll over so my back is to him and pull the covers around my shoulders, my eyelids already drooping. I wish he were next to me, but I don't know how to ask. And my brain is too exhausted to figure it out. Before I drift off, I call out softly, "Julie?"

"Yeah?"

"Thanks."

"For what?"

"Believing me."

"Night, Ever."

***

The next time I open my eyes, the room is bright, telling me it's later than normal wake-up time. I roll over to sit up and see Julian slumped in the chair, arms folded over his chest that rises and falls with his slow, even breaths. I quietly push back the covers and swing my legs over the side of the bed. Pushing off the mattress with my hands, I stand and look back at him.

Clear, hungry blue eyes meet mine a second before the shutters come down. "Hi—" He clears his throat and tries again. "Hi," he repeats, his voice even deeper than usual from sleep.

"Hi."

"Sleep okay?" He yawns the question.

"Better than I expected." I grip the edge of the mattress and hold my breath. I don't know what to make of waking up with a beautiful man in my room. Or in my life. I hold my breath.

He pouts his lips at my reply.

I change the subject. "What time is it?" I ask, reaching for my phone. "My alarm never went off," I say, looking at the screen.

"It did. I turned it off. Sleep seemed like the priority." He shrugs as he stands and rolls his neck. Several cracks pierce the quiet room.

"Didn't you have sand coming to the beach . . . an hour ago?" I ask, looking at the time again.

"Yeah, Pete and his three boys are out there right now. They'll handle it." He pauses, then, "So . . . kickboxing?" This he says as he reaches out and tucks a strand of hair behind my ear.

As much as I want to revel in that sweet gesture, I'm suddenly furious. Maybe it was him babysitting me in a chair all night instead of lying next to me, or him deciding to shut off my alarm, or changing the schedule without asking me, or Chase's texts last night, or all of it. But shortly after my dad died, I became hyper independent. I don't like people telling me what to do. Especially a guy I'm interested in. Granted, I don't have any previous frame of reference, but him taking care of me is one thing. Him *handling* me is another altogether. Maybe it's just the OV stuff coming up last night weighing on me, but none of those people are here right now. Julian is. *Lucky him.* I take it all out on him, deserved or not.

"Look, I've been making my own decisions for a while now. I don't need a dad. I don't need a babysitter. And I don't need someone making decisions for me. And yeah. Kicking the shit out of something sounds pretty good right now. See you downstairs in fifteen." I say all of this as I stand up and face him. When I'm done, I pivot and storm into the bathroom, my shoulder bumping his chest on my way. I slam the bathroom door and immediately regret it, because it's giving unhinged soap opera energy which is very not me.

When I get downstairs fourteen minutes later, Julian is dressed, his hair damp, his clothes fresh. He's a statue in front of the kitchen slider, with the morning sun beaming on him. I know he hears me; I wasn't quiet coming down the stairs. I wait for him to turn.

He doesn't turn but says to the glass door, "Want to ride to Fit together? There's coffee if you want some." He's choosing his words carefully.

I'm an asshole. "Uh, yeah, thanks. I'll grab a travel mug and take it with me."

He nods once and heads toward the door without looking at me. "I'll go warm up the Jeep. Take your time."

Fuck. I'm such a jerk. Maybe this hillbilly air isn't working its magic on me after all. Rolling my eyes, I begin digging through cabinets for a travel mug.

Chapter 19

Julian

I know this drill. Walk softly and give *it* a wide berth—like encountering a wild animal. I've had lots of practice. It's just been a hot minute since I've seen it up close and personal. Doesn't matter how long it's been. It all comes screaming back in full color. Ever doesn't radiate violence though, just coiled wire ready to snap. And like me, kicking the shit out of something is her remedy of choice.

I keep my mouth shut on the way to Fit and while unlocking the place. Once inside, I turn to gauge her mood. She won't make eye contact but heads to the kickboxing room. I clear my throat and prepare myself for the sass. I ignore the tingle in my gut because it's not helping that I like her sass. The nostalgia it brings equally haunts and enchants me. She doesn't look like her at all, but the familiarity is tangible. It's an essence that I can't ignore.

"Uh, Ever?" She stops but doesn't turn, so I continue. "We need to warm up first. Cardio or stretching. You choose."

"Stretching," she replies without hesitation. "My legs will thank me."

"Okay, kickboxing room then."

She resumes walking as if I hadn't spoken.

I follow behind her with a smirk.

Wait till she realizes we'll be touching each other for the warmup. The tingle intensifies. Adjusting the crotch of my sweats, I follow her.

Inside the room, I start with downward dog and move into some side lunges. She mimics me without looking at me directly but at my reflection in the wall of mirrors. When I sit down on the floor and spread my legs in a vee, she watches me, waiting for instructions.

"Mirror me here," I say, motioning to the space in front of me. She does, still looking every bit as sulky as she did back at the house. I hold my hands out to her.

Without breaking eye contact, she places her hands in mine.

I push the soles of my sock-clad feet against hers and take her hands. I pull her forward, slowly, until I meet resistance. As I release the tension and center again, she follows suit and pulls me toward her, never once breaking eye contact. The room, cool at first, feels warm now. This warmup feels like the start of a hot yoga class—emphasis on hot.

My eyes are drinking in every detail of her face as we move in sync. I note the dampness on her upper lip. She feels the heat too. Although, she's not the one hiding from this magnetism. She's been so open, even as she experienced big firsts last night, unbeknown to me. I marvel at how I didn't suspect it. Yeah, she felt deliciously tight, but I sensed no inexperience. No awkwardness. Maybe a shyness at first, but it was quickly drowned by the hunger and willingness and sweet surrender. Now that I know, though, I can see the shyness for what it is. I need to back up, rewind and slow the fuck down. It's why I didn't sleep next to her last night. I want to take this slow for her. I want these firsts to be amazing for her. I thought I was doing the right thing. The respectful thing. I knew if she was lying next to me, wanting me, I wouldn't be able to not give her what she wants, because I want it too. I want to give her every first.

God, how has she never been kissed? She's fucking gorgeous. Maybe her hometown is full of hideous douchebags. *Lucky me.* But in trying to do the right thing—staying out of her bed, turning off her alarm to give her more sleep—I've completely pissed her off. I wanna make it right. I'm not sure how when she's so mad. And I know this makes me a dick, but damn she's hot when she's pissed. Hotter, I mean.

Standing, I pull her up with me. "Ready to hit some shit?" This I ask with a wink, testing the current fury level.

"Yeah. You offering to be my punching bag?" She challenges, one eyebrow raised.

Okay, still at DEFCON 1. *Noted.* "Let's start with the bag. If that doesn't work, I'll volunteer as tribute." I wink again. I can't help playing with fire. If she knew how much her sass turned me on, she really would punch me right now. "But let's get a few moves down first and practice your form."

She's determined, learns quickly, and her form is impressive. She's told me repeatedly she's not an athlete but a bookworm. But I imagine if she tried . . . anything, she'd be a force. She's coordinated, fluid and frankly . . . breathtaking. Her body is perfect—lithe, graceful, soft but toned. Once we move to the bag, I call out moves from my beginner routine and quickly switch to intermediate to keep her challenged.

I see the change in her stance and strikes within minutes. Her moves become intense, the strikes harder, angrier. She stops listening to the moves I call out, so I stop calling them out. She's fighting an invisible demon. Her breathing becomes pants as sweat runs down her temples. The hair on the nape of her neck curls with perspiration. Her panting breaths turn to grunts, then groans, then sobs.

I watch, knowing she needs it, until I can't stand it anymore. Watching the heartbreak that so closely mirrored my own in unspoken ways tears at me. I step between her and the bag as she swings. Catching her fist in my hand, I grab her bicep in my other hand with a little shake.

Storm-cloud gray eyes pin mine. She blinks once, twice, then opens the fist I hold and laces her fingers through mine, gripping until her knuckles go white.

I pull her toward me with the other hand, releasing her arm.

Her chest heaves out and in against mine, her eyes threaten to spill over. She takes a step back as if to pull away from me—the opposite of what her body silently screams.

"Ever—" I start.

"Don't, Julie. Don't say anything. And don't you dare wink at me again, or I *will* punch you."

I pull her toward me, wrapping my free arm around her neck, tucking our still clenched hands between us. She releases her death grip on my hand and snakes her arm around my back. With her forehead against my chest, her pants of breath heat my skin through my shirt and the tears dampen the thin fabric as her shoulders began to shake. I'm losing the battle of staying immune to this passionate girl in my arms. How can I? Her pain is speaking to mine. The tears soaking my shirt are melting the block of ice that stands between her and my heart.

For the first time in three years, I'm scared. Resting my chin on her head, I hold on to her. For her sake, I tell myself. One thing I perfected in the last three years is lying to myself. And since I'm a liar now, I decide to keep breaking the rules. "Come on. Let's go be rebels and share a sauna before heading to Brew."

That does it. Her face softens. The idea of us teaming up to break the rules tucks the last of her anger away.

"Men's or ladies' locker room?" I ask before she changes her mind. She looks at me blankly. "Tick tock, Davis. Before the place opens to the public."

"Uh . . . women's?"

"Figures." I roll my eyes teasingly, grab her hand and lead the way.

Chapter 20
Everly

Whether it was beating the shit out of the punching bag, the ugly cry, the comfort of this drop-dead green flag or all three, I feel lighter than I have since arriving in Blue Lake. Or in the last three months. Or, full disclosure, since my dad died six years ago. Sitting across from Julian in the ladies' locker room sauna, I tell him so.

After thanking him for . . . everything and after the release of my pent-up emotions, I feel emboldened. Maybe it's the heat or the intimacy of the confined space or that we're *commando* (other than our towels) in the sauna, but I look him square in the eye and let out more than my emotions.

"One more thing. Don't make decisions for me without asking. I've been taking care of myself for a long time now and I don't appreciate the babying—especially from you. You can't kiss me like you did and do . . . what we did and then not treat me like an equal. Fair?"

He has the integrity to look guilty at my mini lecture. And he concedes, sort of. "Fair. And I'm sorry. I really am. I mistakenly thought

I was acting in your best interest. Out of concern. Not in a degrading way. I promise." He locks eyes with me as he apologizes.

Green flag still soaring. I smile and nod my acceptance. But he wasn't done.

"But, Ever?" He says my name like a question; the name he calls me that I love more than he knows.

I arch one eyebrow expectantly and wait.

"How have you never been kissed? You certainly don't act . . ." When my eyebrow goes up another notch, he clears his throat and searches for the right words. "Look, you threw that out like no big deal. I would not have guessed you'd never been touched. You . . . well, you don't . . . act inexperienced. And I'm not just talking about the physical stuff. When you confessed that so casually, it . . . Can I be honest?"

"Please." I hold my hands out like I'm serving something, then add, "Always."

Nodding, he leans forward and rests his forearms on his thighs and says, "That's a lot of pressure on a guy. At least one who gives a shit. And, Ever, I give a shit, okay? More than you know."

I can't help the smile that spreads across my face. Book boyfriend energy for sure.

When I don't speak, he adds, "And it's been a hot minute since I gave a shit. But also, how is it that you've never . . . That no guy has ever tried to . . . I just . . . Look, I was taken aback that I was the first . . . anything." He holds up his hands, as if to surrender. "Not in the way that sounded. I'm just surprised, and I guess I wanted to protect you or shelter you or . . . hide you from the shit of this world. I didn't mean to overstep."

A lone tear slips out and rolls down my cheek. *How do I have any tears left?*

"Thank you, Julie." I swipe the dampness off my cheek with the back of my hand, place my palms on my knees and lean my face forward toward his. "And to answer your question, no one's ever made me want to kiss them before. Until now. So maybe we should get out of here and go to work before it gets any hotter. Or before I want to kiss you again." Then I wink just like he did earlier.

Chuckling and shaking his head, he stands and holds out his hand to me as he says, "Where the hell did you come from, Everly Davis, and what in the world am I gonna do with you?" I open my mouth, intending some pithy comeback, but he snatches the hand I reach out to him, pulls me to his chest and cuts me off, tapping his other index finger on the tip of my nose, dragging it softly down my lips and chin. "Don't. Let's just go get dressed before the cougars show up."

"Wait, you call them cougars too?"

"That's a conversation for another day." He's not giving dismissive vibes because he smirks as he says it. It's more like self-deprecation, which is cute for this smoking specimen.

In less than five minutes we're heading out the door, with Julian clasping my hand in his, intertwining our fingers. As he opens the door, letting me precede him, Sylvie Dixon, arguably the hottest cougar of the group, comes around the corner, almost bumping into me as she looks down while digging through her bag. Julian drops my hand before she even looks up.

She lifts her head, and her automatic smile of greeting disintegrates as she swings her eyes from me to Julian.

"Julian." She doesn't bother to greet me but plasters the lipsticked smile back on her face as she gives him her full attention, followed by an exaggerated pout. "We've been missing you at kickboxing and of course our personal sessions. Cheryl is doing okay running the classes, but we all miss youuuu." Her voice is whiny while trying to sound seductive. And she's perfectly coiffed from head to toe, including a full face of makeup. Her pink-nailed hand reaches out to rub his arm as she says the last part.

I keep walking toward the Jeep, slowly hoping Julian will catch up so I'm not standing there waiting. I don't hear his reply or her pouty response, just their voices. But he does catch up to me right as I reach out for the door handle, and he puts his hand over mine and opens it for me. On the short drive back to Allie's, he doesn't bring up the cougar sighting, so neither do I.

We work all day at Brew with everyone pitching in wherever it's needed to get ready for the season. Seeing things from this side gives me an even greater appreciation for Allie and all she brings to Blue Lake. It feels good to contribute to it. At the end of the day, my body is sweaty, dirty and sore, but the good kind. The labor-intensive work cleared my head as much as, if not more than, the workout did that morning. But I'm exhausted, physically and mentally.

Julian drops me at Allie's when we finish, saying he needs to catch up on some stuff at his house and he'd be back later. I shower, eat and decide to read in bed. I awake sometime later, my room now dark, my book open beside me on the bed. I sit up trying to figure out what woke me. *Julian*. It sounds like he's talking in his room. I can make out the low rumble of his voice but not the words he's saying. His voice gets louder, then he's clearly shouting *no* over and over.

Springing from my bed, I rush through the bathroom into his room and stop short. The room is dark except for a dim moonlight glow from the slider. My eyes zero in on the outline of Julian in his bed, tossing back and forth, the sheet falling off his torso, hugging his hips and tangling in his legs. I approach the bed silently and see his fists clenching the bottom sheet. I reach out to touch his flexed arm. His skin is hot and clammy. I open my mouth to say his name, to wake him from his turmoil.

When my hand meets his skin, he grabs it with his other hand and his voice, raspy, says, "Tay, don't go, please. Stay with me." He puts my hand to his face and kisses my palm.

My stomach drops. I can't let him think I'm someone else. "Julian," I whisper-shout.

He moves my hand from his lips and presses it to his cheek. His eyelids flutter open as his eyes try to focus in the dark. "Ever." He sighs my name and my heart speeds up, thumps so loud I think he'll hear it. "Stay with me." He tugs on my hand now, pulling me down, and I let him.

I sink to the edge of the mattress.

He wraps his arms around my torso as he backs up to make room and drags me down to lie beside him, drawing my back to his chest. He laces his fingers with mine, his palm covering the back of my hand. His other arm is tucked under the pillow we're now sharing as he nuzzles my ear with his nose, inhales and sighs. "Ever. Mmmm." He's instantly asleep again.

Chapter 21

JULIAN

Sunshine. Her shampoo smells like sunshine and breaks through my consciousness. My body responds to her presence before my brain realizes she's there. My raging hard-on grinds into her sweet ass before I can stop myself, which wakes me up completely. How am I lucky enough to find this treasure in my bed, her body touching mine from neck to toes? I inhale deeply. I can tell she's awake by her breathing, even though she doesn't turn or even stir. My hand goes to her hip, and I control the urge to press into her again. But she backs herself into me and reaches her hand up to cup my neck, stretching hers to invite access. I gladly accommodate. I can't help myself, especially when she's all but asking. I nuzzle into her perfect neck and kiss the soft spot behind her ear.

"Hi, Ever," I whisper into her ear.

"Hi, Julie," she breathes.

I roll her onto her back and straddle her, planking my arms on either side of her head. "And what did I do to deserve waking up to you in my bed?"

She lowers her lashes shyly and I'm quickly reminded of how innocent she is.

That splash of reality drowns the moment. I roll off her and lie on my side watching her, my palm resting on the flat of her stomach. "Bad dream?" I ask, hoping maybe she needed me in the middle of night, and in my sleep, I obliged.

"I guess. I woke up to you calling out in your sleep, so I came to check on you," she replies softly.

"Wait. I did?" My chest tightens.

"Yeah," she answers, not looking up.

I reach out to tilt her chin to look at me. "What'd I say?"

"You mostly said 'no.'"

"I . . . I don't remember." I rub the scruff on my jaw. "Thank you for . . . Thank you."

She nods slowly, her eyes tracking mine.

I comb my fingers through the hair on my forehead, pushing it back off my face. "I haven't had a bad dream in a long time. Thought maybe I was cured," I say with a grim smile.

She attempts a smile back but pinches her lips together instead.

"Hey. What's up? What'd I say?"

She looks up at me, eyes round and the lightest shade of gray I've ever seen, and answers. "You were asking Taya not to leave. Then you sort of woke up and pulled me down next to you and fell back to sleep. I mean, you called me by my name before you did though. I didn't want to wake you, so I stayed. I hope that's okay."

She sounds dejected, and I hate myself right now.

"Of course it's okay. More than okay. Listen, Ever, I don't know what I did to deserve someone like you. I should leave you alone. You're too good for me."

"Not according to everyone in Oak Valley." Her face falls with that revelation.

"Well, they're all idiots." I reach out and stroke her face, and my touch causes her cheeks to flush. I prefer the flush to the sadness and place a soft kiss on her cheek.

Shyly, she looks up through her lashes and asks, "What if I don't want you to?"

"To what?"

"Leave me alone?"

With a groan, I roll onto my back and exhale at the ceiling. "Ever, what are you doing to me?"

Without missing a beat, she responds, "Nothing . . . apparently."

"How are there not a hundred guys begging you to fall in love with them?"

Playing coy, she says, "Well, I don't get out much."

Groaning, I resume my spot, rolling over and planking my arms on either side of her head, hovering my torso above hers so I don't crush her and straddle her with my legs. I press my forehead to hers and watch her wet her lips with her tongue. *God, I want this girl so much.* My groin aches with the need to sink into her. But now that I know she's a virgin, I also know I've got no business going there—yet. Or possibly ever. There would be a special place in hell for me for thinking I even deserve her. I must've done something to make the gods believe I deserve another chance at something, someone so breathtaking.

Her fingernail is tracing the heart outline on my chest, and her touch alone is striking a match. Her words douse the flames. "Do you miss her? Taya? That's her name, right? Your girlfriend who died?"

I resume my earlier spot, rolling onto my side, her finger sliding down my torso and landing softly on the bed between us as I shift. "I don't let myself." She nods her head slightly, absorbing my answer. "We were young," I add. "And . . . I don't know . . . clumsy. Kids. I think it's easy to idealize and romanticize something like that once it's gone. It's hard to even remember what it was really like. It's all wrapped up in this unjust pain of a life gone too soon. All the what-ifs and the should've-could've-would've thoughts. I don't know if I miss her or miss not feeling this hollowness in my chest."

She nods again like she knows what I mean, and I'm reminded of Allie telling me Everly lost her dad.

I want to take that faraway look off her face. I want to not think about the past. I try to shift the conversation to something safer. "When I'm with you, it's easy to forget. When I'm with you, it's like nothing existed before you." I don't choose my response. The words just spill out, shocking me because every one of them is true.

This enigma in my arms impresses me yet again by accepting my answer and shifting gears. "So, you think you might kiss me again?" She's tracing my tattoo again.

Chuckling, I nuzzle her neck and breathe in her intoxicating scent. "Yeah," I whisper into her ear, "I think I might."

I trail light kisses along her cheek until I reach her lips, which are slightly parted. She tilts her head toward me for better access. I feel her breath on my lips, and I can't not kiss her, even if I tried. I plunge my tongue into her mouth. Hers is there to meet mine, stroke for stroke. Like she's kissed a dozen boys a hundred times, likes he knows exactly what she's doing. And it drives me mad. I'm rolling onto her in seconds. Fitting perfectly between her legs, I grind into her. She raises her hips to meet every thrust. Her hands are gripping the sides of my face. Her nails scrape my neck as she pulls me down harder on her lips.

I'm going to have this girl. I decide right then that hell will be a worthy trade-off. I glide my hand over her ribs to the hem of her top and under it. Her skin is silk. Her stomach flat. As my fingers graze the underside of her breast, goose bumps raise on her skin. Her breast fills my hand fully and I squeeze, gently at first, then harder.

Her gasp fills my mouth in a sweet moan. She releases my neck and grips my bicep, nails digging in and pulling me to her. "Mmm."

Her soft moan spurs me on. I lower my head, ready to take the peak of her breast into my mouth. My phone vibrates on the nightstand, followed by Allie's familiar ringtone, sufficiently dousing ice water on the moment.

We spring apart like we're caught. Ever pulls her shirt down and rests her arm over her eyes, her chest rising and falling as she attempts to slow her breathing.

"Fuck," I say under my breath. I sit up on the edge of the bed and slide the phone to answer, placing it on speaker while I, too, try to control my breathing. "Hey, Allie. Good morning. How's the retreat?"

"Julian! Hey. You working out already? You sound out of breath."

"No, just ran back up the stairs when I heard my phone," I lie.

"I tried to call Evvie first, but she didn't answer."

"Oh, uh, I think I just heard the shower. She must be in there. Want me to have her call you?"

"No. No. It's fine. I just wanted to check in. See how things are going. The retreat is awesome. Thank you so much for running things so I could do this. I knew you were the exact right person to succeed me someday—"

I snag the phone off the nightstand and take it off speaker as I stand up, intending to walk out of the room to continue the conversation in private under the guise of making coffee downstairs. Before I leave my room, I turn and see Ever sitting on the edge of the bed now, gripping the edge of the mattress with both hands. She looks up at me, all expression gone from her face, just big gray eyes waiting to see what I'll do next. I tilt my head as if to say, *I'm sorry we were interrupted*, my mouth lifting in a sad smile before I turn and head down the stairs. *Shit!*

Chapter 22
Everly

I guess this is what sexual frustration feels like. Weirdly it's much like regular frustration, except for the ache in my lower region that's got me keyed up. I set a record for brushing my teeth, getting dressed and flying out of the house. I can still hear Julian talking in the kitchen when I quietly dip out the front door. I decide to run to Fit and take my frustration out on the punching bag again.

Spotting Lilly's car in the lot from a distance picks up my pace. Although we text daily, I haven't seen her in almost a week. I've been blowing off turning in my schoolwork because I don't have a car to get there. Allie offered hers any time I need it, but I'm trying not to need anything from anyone. The instructor is chill, provided I'm completing my assignments, and tells me to turn them in whenever I can. So I haven't even seen Lilly at school yet. I'm already smiling at the thought of catching up with her.

Old-school rock hits me as loud as her greeting when I walk through the doors.

"Davis! Where you been? I miss your face." Lilly is grinding on the elliptical in the empty gym. "I see you already got in your cardio. Wanna lift together?"

"I'd planned on hitting the shit out of the bag for a bit."

"Oh, it's like that, huh? Okay, give me five more minutes and I'll join you in there. You can tell Auntie Lilly all about it." She winks exaggeratedly.

Rolling my eyes at her auntie comment because we're the same age, I laugh and give her a thumbs-up.

***

"I knew there was something between you two. Not to be dramatic, but you both were giving *just kiss already* energy from day one. And honestly, I'm glad to see someone catching his interest besides the Cougar Club." She makes a barfing face and gagging noises with the last comment.

"Eww. We ran into one of them yesterday on the way out after our early workout. Sylvie. It's like she finds reasons to touch him. So gross."

"After you had your meltdown?"

"Yeah. I didn't mean to confess that. You just have a knack for dragging it out of me. Maybe you should become a therapist."

"Yeah, then I could charge you." She screeches when my face drops, embarrassed. "Kidding! Ev! Stop!" She halts slugging her bag to look at me. I stop, too, but don't make eye contact.

She adds, "I'm not like those douchebags you called friends in Oak Valley. I don't fuck people over to make myself feel better." She tosses her hand at me like shooing away a fly. "Wipe that guilty look off your face and let's get back to you and Julian." She wiggles her eyebrows and turns back to her bag.

At the mention of his name, I take a hard swing at the bag, then another picturing the Cougar Club. I continue to take my irritation out on the equipment and say, "Yeah, let's shelve the cougar discussion for now. I don't get it, and I don't know if I want to."

After a hot minute of hooks and jabs, I stop, turn to Lilly, panting, and say, "One minute I'm this virgin fantasizing about fictional characters and the next I'm ready to jump the bones of the most beautiful guy I've ever seen in real life like I've done it a million times. And the things I want to do to him . . ." I groan. "And I don't even know how to do them. But with him, I just feel . . . I don't know. My body takes over. But we keep getting interrupted. Maybe it's a sign."

"Yeah, a sign that you need to plan better." She cackles at her logic. "And if you ask me, that's the best way to figure it out. When it's all hot animal magnetism and instinct. You've got . . . how long till Allie comes back?"

"I don't know. It was originally three weeks, but she texted me this morning she may stay longer 'if we can hold down the fort' for her." I use finger quotes to mimic her words. "And of course, I agreed. She's kinda saving my ass right now with the place to live, the job, all of it."

"Plus, you get to continue being roommates with the hot cougar magnet."

Groaning, I ask, "Can we not call him that?"

"Speaking of . . ."

My heart lodges in my throat thinking—hoping—I'd turn and see Julian. It's Sylvie Dixon instead. She takes one look at us through the glass wall of the kickboxing room, tosses her flawlessly styled hair and hops onto the treadmill.

"That's my cue to get the hell out of here. Gotta get to the marina anyway." I move toward the door and toss over my shoulder, "Talk later?"

"You know it. I'm gonna want all the dirty details. Make me proud," she calls as I roll my eyes on my way out. I shoot my arm in the air in a backward wave as I move through the main workout area.

In the locker room, I douse my face and pits with water to cool down and attempt to freshen up before heading to work. If I wasn't in such a hurry, I would've planned better. Swiping the towel down my face, I startle when I see Sylvie standing a few feet behind me, watching me in the mirror.

"You know he's out of your league, right, Evvie?"

She says my nickname like it's making her point for her and inspects her polished, probably fake, nails as she speaks. "Something tells me you think he's your knight in shining armor," she says as she meets my eyes in the mirror. "Well, I assure you, he's not. He prefers . . . uncomplicated." She fans her hands out, palms up, in a gesture that implies she means like her. "Maybe he feels sorry for you and wants to help Allie's latest project, but he's incapable of the storybook ending every girl your age is so obviously looking for. Trust me." With a pitying smile, she turns and leaves me standing there, face dripping.

And I thought only male dogs marked their territory. Because that woman gives some serious female dog energy. My body involuntarily shivers—to shake the *ick* off.

***

Avoiding Lilly on my way out, I walk back to Allie's to change before heading to Brew for the day. Julian is already gone as I expected, but our shared bathroom still smells like him—which only reminds me of Cougar Bitch Sylvie and pisses me off more. I mean, I know these women all throw themselves at him. I've seen it. I just can't quite wrap my brain around him hooking up with them. It doesn't track with the guy I know and see when we're together. Then I remember his cryptic behavior with Allie on the phone this morning that sent me running, literally, out of the house.

She isn't one of them, is she?

Aware that my trust in people is reasonably skewed at the moment, I want to give Julian the benefit of the doubt, but between Sylvie coming at me in the Fit locker room and my recent past, and why I'm even in Blue Lake to begin with, I leap to distrust and anger first. Not letting people in seems like a reasonable plan to avoid a repeat of Oak Valley. Although Lilly feels safe. Not only safe but like water in a desert. She just makes me feel calm and seen. Her snark and candidness hit like a favorite song on repeat. I want to be more like her. Owning my inner snark. It's my brain's default setting. It just rarely slips out of my mouth. Except with Julian. He puts me at ease much like Lilly does. I'm not just freer in my actions, I speak my mind with him, and I'm feeling a little too exposed on both fronts right now. I need to reel it in. Or better yet avoid him as much as possible, which is my new plan—at least until I can cool down from my cougar encounter. I can't stand the thought of him with *that* cougar especially. Not that I could with any of them, but the rest seem kind of sweet in an attention-seeking kind of way. Sylvie is straight-up mean. And looking at him now would just make me picture them together. Like I am right now.

Ugh! Upchuck reflex activated.

***

"Hey, Pete." I step inside Brew and spot him behind the counter. I exhale. *No Julian.* "What can I help with?"

"Wanna inventory the new shipment of supplies? In the kitchen . . ." He points through the swinging doors. *Perfect!* A solo job away from everyone else and hopefully enough stock to keep me busy all day. I dip into the modest café kitchen and prepare to go through the boxes stacked next to the back door.

I missed Allie's call this morning because I left my phone in my room when I jumped up to rush to Julian in the middle of the night. Instead of calling her back, because I knew she was on the phone with him, I texted her to confirm—okay, lie—that I was in the shower as Julian suggested. She texted back that she was thinking about staying another couple weeks but wanted to ensure me she'd rush home if we wanted or needed her to. I know from hearing the stories over the years that Allie has essentially been married to this place since she took it over from her grandmother. She'd never miss camping season unless necessary. I've never heard of her missing one, so I'm curious what would prompt her to do so now. Maybe it's classic burnout. Maybe it's that she has Julian now to help her run things. Isn't that what she said before he went all cryptic on their call this morning? Yesterday, I would've relished her extended absence. Now I wonder how I'll avoid my houseguest for two more weeks. Maybe I can suggest

I don't need him there now that I've settled in. Surely I can handle the house maintenance on my own. If I can't, maybe I can ask Lilly and Noah to help me.

As if my thought spiral summoned him, Julian pokes his head in through the swinging doors. I see him in my peripheral vision but use my earbuds as an excuse not to acknowledge him. A tad bitchy maybe, but I'm not sure how to face him after his secret conversation with Allie and Sylvie marking her territory this morning. If I'd have thought it through, I would've looked up and acted natural. Fake ignoring him got him to come into the kitchen and place his hand on my lower back where he rubbed lightly to get my attention. I want to act aloof, but my body betrays me. Goose bumps cover my skin at his touch. It ignites where his hand rests. I look up, trying not to get lost in the pools of deep blue. I lower my gaze and freeze on the sweetest smile from the most perfect lips. A genuine smile that crinkles the corners of his eyes and raises his cheeks. My heart flips like the traitor it is.

He acts completely normal, if not a little extra familiar in front of Pete.

Granted, he doesn't know about Sylvie, but I left this morning without saying a word and it's now noon. We haven't seen or spoken to each other since he was on top of me, and we got interrupted by Allie's call. Pulling out an earbud, I look up from my task, take a step back and smile. I try to sound unfazed when I greet him. "Hey you, what's up?" I sound squeaky, even to my own ears, and my smile feels plastic.

"How's it going in here? Wanna break for lunch? Pete said he's making sandwiches." His smile looks genuine and hopeful.

I look over as Pete comes through the swinging doors. "Hey, Ev. You're killing it in here. Want a sandwich?"

"Uh, sure, Pete. Thanks. If I'm not in the way, I'll just keep working until they're ready."

"Just like Allie. No off switch." He flashes his teeth with a grin. "Suit yourself. But it's okay to take breaks." He reaches into the fridge, grabbing lettuce, tomatoes and sliced turkey, and dumps them onto the counter across from me.

I can feel Julian watching me and I know I should acknowledge him asking too. But Pete's presence is throwing me a lifeline. I smile and turn my face to meet his gaze. "Thanks for asking." I turn my lips up in a closed-mouth smile and add, "I'll just finish up here while he makes lunch."

He watches me intently as I place my earbud back in my ear and turn around. I don't see him leave, but I feel it. I know he can't question me in front of Pete, so I'm spared for now. When I see the swinging doors flapping in my peripheral, signaling his exit, I exhale and continue counting.

By the time I finish, I look up at the clock and see it's almost five p.m. I've successfully avoided him all day. When it's time to call it quits, I head to the bathroom to wash my hands and try to come up with the best way to leave undetected. Turns out there was no need. Julian's Jeep is gone when I walk outside. I don't know whether to be relieved or disappointed. Kicking a pebble, I begin my short walk home. As much as I don't want to be a burden to Allie or need anything from her, I admit I need to ask if I can use her car. I know she'll gladly let me; I just prefer not to need it. I pull my phone out of my hip pocket on the way home and find our text conversation.

Me: Hey Allie. Would you mind if I use your car when necessary? Like for turning in schoolwork or driving to the store?

She answers immediately.

Allie: Of course, Evvie. I'd assumed you'd been using it all along. Whatever you need. What's mine is yours. You know that. Are you sure you're okay if I extend my trip?

Me: Totally. I don't even think we have that many campers booked. And the remote access to Fit is working well. Haven't heard any complaints about the lack of classes either.

Allie: About that, I have a couple regulars that might be interested in hosting the basic classes. I may take them up on it. Julian said he'd arrange it.

Me: Great. Enjoy, Allie. Don't worry about a thing. We're solid. Thanks for letting me use your car. Totally appreciate it.

Yes! A car. I feel freer already.

Allie: Of course. And thank you for holding down the fort.

I reply with a smiley face and slide my phone back into my pocket.

Chapter 23

JULIAN

Sweat drips into my eyes. I pull my shirt up, swipe it down my face, grip the barbell and grind out another set. On the last rep, Sylvie steps up as if to spot me. I place the barbell back on the rack and sit up. Watching each other in the mirror, I greet her casually, belying my apprehension. "Hey, Sylvie. How's it going?"

"Hey, Julian. I've been talking with some of the other ladies, and we want to bring back some of the classes while Allie's gone."

"Allie and I just discussed that this morning."

Irritation flickers across her face before she plasters her lipstick-caked smile back in place. I'm not sure if it's someone beating her to the punch or the mention of Allie that causes it, but I ignore it all the same.

"Great. I can totally run the yoga classes. No more than two to three times a week though." She amends her offer to appear in charge.

"I'll talk to her about it and get back to you. Thanks for offering." I give a head nod and smile before adding, "I better get back to it before I cool down too much."

"Of course, sweetie. Don't go too hard."

Winking at me in the mirror, she drags her polished nails lightly along my shoulders as she saunters off, trying way too hard to make people look at her—which they do, because Sylvie is a beautiful woman. She takes immaculate care of herself and always has. Much more now that her husband divorced her and moved to the city he commuted to for years. She told me she never had kids. Maybe that's why Sylvie pretty much lives at the gym, and it shows. She looks half her age, unlike her friends. But the hard-won beauty only goes skin deep. Underneath, she's bitter about the cards she's been dealt. She considers herself the spokesperson for her group of ladies that frequent the gym—the ones that Lilly, Noah and probably everyone else around town refer to as the Cougar Club. They're mostly harmless busybodies, but Sylvie is a know-it-all and can be especially mean if she feels crossed or otherwise threatened. And she acts like she has a claim on my attention. If any other ladies sign up for personal training with me, Sylvie makes it her business to be around, interjecting her two cents. I humor her and her input because, again, she is mostly harmless. I've even let myself be drawn to her a few times. It happened that first year I landed in Blue Lake and started working at Fit for Allie.

Six months of shadowing Allie and finally completing my personal training certification caught me celebrating at the local bar where I got a little too drunk. While I was feeling proud of myself and like someone for the first time ever, it also sent me down a gloom spiral of the past. I ended up wandering into the tattoo shop next door to the bar and getting the heart outline on my chest.

Walking out, Sylvie met me on the sidewalk. She was in the bar that night, watching me, talking to me off and on, and offered to drive me home. That's how it began—a mutual scratching of an itch. It happened a few more times after that, strictly physical. She even offered to film and post a few training videos to the Fit website to attract memberships. Of course, the videos are just me training a client, which happened to be her. I didn't mind if it helped bring in business. And since Allie and I both shy away from the social aspects of business, it was a win-win. But it only encouraged her possessiveness and enhanced her claim on me. When her behavior began to cross the line of our unspoken no-strings agreement, I ended it.

Since well before Ever showed up, the thought of Sylvie held no lure—if it ever did. Again, to me it was scratching an itch, nothing more. And she claimed it was the same for her at first. She didn't want anyone to know her business, and I certainly didn't want anyone to know mine. So we'd been discreet first and foremost. It only happened a few times, in my weaker moments of loneliness, if I'm being honest, but once I could tell the dynamic was changing for her, I put a stop to it. I didn't want her to expect more from me. She was nice enough to me, if not to anyone else, and I didn't want to hurt her. I felt like a dick anyway. Like I was using her. I know she was using me too, but I started to feel like an asshole.

Maybe it's like Allie told me over the years: time and this place is healing me. What I was once able to do with no emotion I couldn't do anymore. Sylvie mostly took it like a champ, acting as though she wasn't invested either. She plays chill, the epitome of unbothered. But I know her better than most and I can tell I pissed her off by ending it. She likes to have the upper hand and feel like things are her idea. Maybe giving her a win and asking her to run the yoga classes is the peace treaty in our unspoken civil unrest.

I text Allie as soon as I leave the club to tell her Sylvie is down to host yoga. She sends a thumbs-up and a confetti emoji. I text Sylvie right after to let her know it's a go if she's willing. And to let me know her schedule so I can post it to the website and bulletin board. Her reply stops me cold.

Sylvie: Always happy to help. I can update the website. No worries. And Jules, that girl is . . . just a girl. You need a woman.

Fuck!

My chest tightens. So much for a truce. I mostly don't pay attention to the cougar drama. It's always something with that group. One thing I know is that none of them dare cross Sylvie. And I don't want Ever on her radar. I guess I wasn't as discreet as I thought or hoped. And fuck Sylvie. She doesn't know a damn thing about Ever, except maybe her age—which means nothing. Her inexperience is all but forgotten when we're together. Sylvie even saying her name has me seeing red and wanting to protect her from bullshit like this.

Approaching Allie's house, I slow the Jeep but don't stop. I admit I don't want to face Ever just yet after Sylvie's text. Besides, something is off with her today. She disappeared without a word this morning while I was talking to Allie. I didn't bother to text her because I knew I'd see her later at Brew, yet she purposely chose to work in the kitchen and avoid me all day. She even found a way not to eat lunch with the rest of us, saying she had some homework to finish. I wanted to confront her, make sure she's okay, but part of me is afraid she's changed her mind about me. Everything about her screams too good to be true. Ever changing her mind about me tracks more. I'm convinced I don't deserve her. But she's awoken something inside me that I'm not ready to analyze. And now I've put her on Sylvie's radar. She deserves better than me. Someone innocent, like her. Someone to learn all the firsts with together—like I had once. I'm convinced she'll realize it sooner or later. I choose cowardice and drive past Allie's to my place instead. Just to shower, I tell myself.

Thoughts of her in my arms flood my mind as I pull up to my place. Her body responding to me like it was made for me alone carries me up the stairs and through the door as I strip off my sweat-drenched clothes, leaving them where they fall, and head into my shower. Maybe she does deserve someone better than me, but I'm not ready to let her go. The cold spray stings at first but does nothing to stop my thoughts. Then it heats up, which aligns with the images tracking through my mind. Ever looking at me with those hungry gray eyes. Her nails digging into my arm, wanting more. The low moans that tell me she likes what I'm doing. So wet. So tight. So beautiful. I imagine her lips around me like my hand is now, moving up and down, taking all of me until I'm ready to erupt. My release is quick and consuming, taking the tension and buildup of wanting her and getting a taste but never the relief.

Looking at my dripping face in the mirror, gripping the sides of the sink, I take some slow, deep breaths. My body might feel the relief of my orgasm, but my thoughts are escalating.

What if she changed her mind? What if she realized I'm not good enough?

I could leave. I could go away and start over again. I dismiss the idea as fast as it slams into my mind. Allie and I just discussed this morning how my roles here in Blue Lake would be changing, how I'd eventually take over as her partner. Making something of myself after feeling like nothing most of my life is all due to Allie. I can't throw that away. I don't want to. When we first met, sometimes her belief in me was all that kept me going in some of the darkest moments of my life.

Tapping my fists on the sides of the sink, I step back and mentally prepare myself to head back to Allie's for the night. But did Ever really need me there? Hell, she comforted *me* last night when I apparently called out in my sleep. I was thinking about Taya more and more lately. The first year was hard. The next two years, I threw myself into becoming something—something Allie needed for the business-es. Someone Taya would've been proud of. People needing me is my weak spot. Allie calls it my love language. In this case though, Allie needing my help with her businesses created a life for me, one I enjoy and am good at. I'm not going to throw it all away now. Even if she changed her mind, I would eventually get over it.

Just like you got over losing Taya?

I absently rub the tattoo as I turn away from the liar in the mirror.

***

The house is quiet when I walk in. No lights on, no noise whatsoever. I drop my keys into the bowl on the entryway table and peek into the kitchen as I head for the stairs. Empty. Upstairs, her door stands open with a clear view of her neatly made bed and deserted room. She's been here because she left her bed unmade this morning when she ran out.

Standing in her doorway, I hear the front door open, keys jangle.

My heart pounds as if I've been caught doing something wrong and I dash into my room and silently push the door almost closed. Then immediately curse myself for acting like a pubescent kid.

What is this girl doing to me?

I reach for a book on the shelf and settle on my bed to distract myself from the sounds the girl I can't stop thinking about is making downstairs. She knows I'm here. My Jeep is in the driveway. Where has she been? I hear rustling in the kitchen, cabinets opening and closing, the sounds of pots and pans. Is she cooking? I shake my head to stop my swirling thoughts and try to read the book in my hands, *Wuthering Heights*. Something tells me the book is more for décor than reading. I'm not what you'd call bookish. I'm merely trying to distract myself. One paragraph in, I decide to google the gist of the book and read that instead.

The smell of food wafting up the stairs causes my stomach to growl. That answers the question of what she's doing down there. I wrestle with whether to go down and offer to help or wait for her to finish what she's doing and then go down and feed myself.

As if she can read my thoughts, she lightly taps on the door I didn't completely close just before she peeks her head in. "I cooked. You hungry? I made plenty, but I can't guarantee it's on the approved healthy list."

"I'm starved. Thanks, Ev. I'll be right down."

She nods and disappears as quickly as she popped in.

I'm almost giddy as I descend the stairs. Relieved she's not acting mad at me anymore. She's got what looks like a pasta dish ready on the bar and two place settings, along with salad and garlic bread. Walking into the kitchen, the scene gives fifties sitcom energy. I subconsciously rub the tattoo on my chest as I lean on the doorframe and take it in.

"Smells amazing in here. Thanks for including me. Need any help with anything?"

"Nope, it's ready. I'm sure the bread isn't on your approved food list, but it's delicious and worth the cheat."

"It looks delicious. Thank you, Ever." I take a seat at the bar.

At the mention of her name, she looks up from filling two glasses with water, smiles and nods as she brings the glasses over and sits across from me on the kitchen side of the bar. She's already moved one of the three stools over to the opposite side.

Was that so she didn't have to sit next to me? I like this better anyway. I can see her face.

As she sets a glass down in front of me, she announces, "This is my go-to comfort meal, and I've been craving it. Hope you like it."

The pasta with cream sauce is not a "health food" but it melted in my mouth. The meal itself wasn't as unhealthy as she claimed, like most comfort meals. She combined the pasta with grilled chicken and broccoli. The green salad she dressed with olive oil, vinegar and spices. I was impressed. My resolve to stay away from her disintegrated with every bite. Not because of the food, although I love it. As we eat, she tells me how she's been making this dish since her dad died. The only real meal she knows how to cook, she says. After all the relatives left and the delivered casseroles went away, it was the first meal they shared as a family of three. They—her mom, sister and her—made it together. It was the first time she felt happy after his passing. She said it became her favorite meal after that.

The fact that she made it to share with me has my mind spinning hopeful thoughts and my heart thumping in a way that makes me want to take her upstairs and thank her with more than words. To distract myself from . . . myself, I change the subject. "We're a week or so away from spring break and our first campers. You ready?" I wink and stuff another bite into my mouth.

"For campers? Yeah. Jumping into Blue Lake at the cliffs? Not so much." Her expression is playful, but I see the dread behind her eyes.

"You don't have to jump if you don't want to," I assure her.

"A deal's a deal. Besides, I'm eager to shed my hoolie status." She winks at me.

My heart flips—like in the movies or the books. I think she's flirting. *Please, let her be flirting.* My fingers itch with the need to touch her. Rubbing my hands along my thighs, I clear my throat and lower my gaze to my now empty plate.

"You cooked. I'm on dish duty." I stand up and begin stacking our dishes.

"Oh, you don't have to. I cleaned up most of it as I cooked. It's just a few dishes to throw into the dishwasher. I can manage." She stands and reaches for the plates in my hand.

"Ever, let me do the damn dishes. As a thank-you for dinner. Okay?" I carry the plates to the sink.

She drops her hands and quietly says, "Sure, okay. I'll just go take a shower if you don't need the bathroom."

"All yours." A moment later, I hear her on the stairs and let out a breath I didn't realize I was holding.

Chapter 24

Everly

Driving myself to the grocery store, buying supplies for dinner and making it myself felt freeing. I feel like my old self for the first time since coming to Blue Lake. And just like how I made it countless times in my kitchen at home, I whipped it up effortlessly. As I cooked and listened to my favorite playlist, I found I wasn't mad anymore. I wasn't even sure what I was mad about. Maybe it was that we were so intimate one minute and the next he was hurrying to take the call off speaker for privacy. There's still so much I don't know about him. I let my guard down so easily with him, yet I don't know him at all. Maybe I was mad we got interrupted again. If Allie hadn't called, would we have stopped? Would I no longer be a virgin at this very moment? I feel my face flush despite the steamy shower already heating my skin. The tightening between my legs causes me to lean back against the tiled wall and place both hands flat against my stomach to stop the flutters.

Mentally shaking myself to stop the Julian spiral of my thoughts, I quickly finish my shower and move into my room to throw on some sweats. I intend to go outside and watch the sun set. Blue Lake boasts the most spectacular sunsets. Since the recent time change, we get daylight longer. Watching it sink settles me in a way nothing else does. Down in OV, the city hides the sunset behind, well, the city. I remember loving the sunsets up here even as a kid.

Stepping through the sliding doors of my bedroom, I intend to sit in one of the loungers on the deck. I stop short when I see Julian in the opposite chair near the sliding door off his room. "Oh, sorry, I didn't know you were out here."

"No, Ever, it's fine. Come watch. It's a good one."

I hesitate.

He turns, holding his hand out to me. "C'mon. Join me. Please?" He presses when I still don't move.

I'm unable to resist him, nor do I want to. I just don't want to intrude. I take his hand and walk over to take the lounger next to his. I drop his hand as soon as it feels natural to do so. I'm not mad anymore, but I'm also resolved to not being so available to him. I would gladly give myself to him and not think twice about it. He's the only guy I've ever wanted to do . . . anything with. I just know though that the aftermath would be unbearable. Not knowing him as well as I'd like to, trying to decipher his closed-off nature, or if he shut down emotionally as I've seen him do on occasion, would haunt me and fill me with stage five clinger level insecurity. I want to avoid that more than I want his hands on me. Okay, that's a lie. But at least just as much. I push my hands under my legs to still the tug of war and silently watch the sun set the lake on fire and turn the sky five different colors, aware of every rise and fall of his chest with each breath he takes.

So much for settling sunsets. Afterwards, when the darkness takes over, I find myself more keyed up than ever. I'm wondering the best way to escape back into my room.

"Julie."

"Ever."

We call each other in unison.

I laugh softly. "You first."

Which he quickly tosses back at me. "No, you go. Please," he adds when he sees the protest loading.

"I was just going to say, I'm going to head to my room now, maybe read a little before bed. What were you going to say?"

"I just . . . wanted to thank you again for dinner."

I don't trust my voice to keep my disappointment hidden. I nod and turn to go inside.

"Goodnight, Ever," he says in an almost whisper.

Closing my eyes, I pause my steps and murmur, "Night."

As I step through the sliding doors into my room, my phone vibrates in my hand. It's a text from Via.

Via: I miss you, sister. Can you talk?

Me: YES! Call me.

An hour ticks by in a blink catching up with her on the phone—about everything. I don't mention Julian except in a vague work capacity. And she doesn't bring up Chase and Kendall except in group reference—"the crew." I want to be pissed she's still friends with them, but I don't have the energy for that conversation. Her next statement wipes all thoughts of them from my mind.

"I think Ryan's going to propose," Via gushes breathlessly on her end.

"Way to bury the lead, Via," I exclaim.

She giggles. "We'd talked about living together after graduation, so Mom suggested we live here. That it would be doing her a favor since she's gone so much. Her latest client will be a semi-permanent one—a music superstar with a world tour coming up. They want her to be their personal flight attendant. She sounded so excited about it, Ev. She'd be gone for a year or more though."

We talk details for a few more minutes. I tell her Allie is gone, too, at the training retreat, but she already knows that. I guess Allie and my mom talk regularly, and Mom told Via.

"I work with the coolest girl, Lilly, and her boyfriend, Noah. She feels like the first legit friend I've ever had."

"I think I was just insulted." But she laughs as she says it, so I know she's not really offended. I walk her through a day in my new life. She sounds relieved that I have a friend to laugh with and confide in, but she's most surprised and impressed to hear how much I like working out, kickboxing especially and working at Fit.

"I thought you were allergic to organized fitness. 'Running is nature's gym.' Isn't that the Evvie workout slogan?"

"But Fit isn't a regular gym. It feels more like a retreat and smells like one too." Selling it to Via drives home how much I like it here. In fact, I love it here. I can see myself being happy right here in Blue Lake every day, but the picture in my head includes the mystery man across the bathroom from me that I'm not ready to tell her about.

After we hang up, I sit for a moment, listening for any sound coming from Julian's room. I pad softly into the bathroom to brush my teeth. Before I tap the light switch, I can see a soft glow coming from under the adjoining door. I don't bother to lock his side and quickly brush my teeth and retreat to my room. I pace for a moment, unable to settle. I don't want to read. I don't want to watch TV. The tingle in my lower region tells me exactly what I want, and he's ten steps away.

Music might be a remedy. Placing my earbuds in and queuing my favorite old-school playlist, I settle into my sheets and stare at the ceiling. The second song on the shuffle: "Feel Like Makin' Love" by Bad Company. Of course! And yes, I think I do.

I tug the earbuds out of my ears and toss them on the bed. Reaching into the nightstand, I take out my journal. I haven't written in it for a hot minute. Maybe getting my raging thoughts down on paper will give me some relief.

I decide to do the thing the therapist made us do when my dad died—write the letter we'd never send.

Dear Julian,

You're never going to read this so here it goes.

I want you! I've never wanted anyone the way I want you. I've never wanted anyone—period! That's not to say I haven't had attention from boys before, but they were clumsy and dumb and painfully transparent. They didn't want me. They wanted someone or the experience. I could've been any girl. That didn't exactly make me want to rip my clothes off and have all the sex. Or even kiss. I began to wonder if there was something wrong with me that I didn't want to be with a guy. Now I know it was the guy. Because with you, I want . . . everything. I want you to touch me. I want to touch you. When I'm with you, it's like they describe it in the books. Everything else fades away and all I see is you. All I think about is you. All I feel is you. The loneliness, anger, pain . . . . It all goes away when I'm with you.

Sometimes, I wish we could stay in this Blue Lake bubble forever and not have to face the world and all the stupid, senseless bullshit that comes with it. Sometimes, I wonder if I've built all of this up in my mind and it's not as earth-shattering as it seems. You make me feel seen for the first time in my life. You make me feel beautiful and sexy and like I could deserve a man as beautiful as you. I know fairy tales don't exist. My sister has always said I set myself up for disappointment because I expect guys to act like the ones in my books. Maybe that's true. I don't know. I just know that I've never wanted to experience all the things I want to experience with you. No one has ever made me crave being kissed or touched the way you do.

Maybe the gods are rewarding me for enduring all the bullying and lies in my hometown, for being ostracized and forced to leave the only life I've ever known. Maybe I'm being given a gift for being the perfect daughter all these years that never made waves and always did what was expected of her. I don't know! Maybe it's that I never took any of those fumbling guys up on their offers and waited patiently for you. All I know is I'm yours, all of me. If you want me, and I think you do. I don't even care if it's not forever. Although I'm sure it would break me if it wasn't, because I'm convinced no one will ever make me feel the way you make me feel. No one will ever smell the way you smell. Kiss me the way you kiss me. Touch me the way you touch me. Make my body come alive the way it does for you.

It's physically painful that you're only a few steps away, across a cold tile floor, probably naked except for the soft cotton pajama bottoms I love that hang low on your hips. My mouth goes dry at the memory of how soft and smooth the skin of your chest is. The way it heats my fingertips when I touch you. The way your biceps ripple when I grip them tight, wanting more of whatever you're giving me. Is this what falling feels like? If it is, then here's the spoiler. It's better than the books, Julie. You're better than all my imaginings of what the guy I'd fall for would be. You're perfect and beautiful. And I don't mind saying it because you'll never read this anyway.

Good night, sweet Julian. I hope you dream of me as I'll surely dream of you.

Love, Ever

Closing my journal, placing it back in the nightstand, I find I'm more relaxed now. I retrieve my earbuds and phone from across the bed where I flung them earlier and place them on my charger. I'm sleepy now, my mind clearer. Therapy tools really do work. *Inhale. Exhale. Inhale. Exhale. Inhale. Exhale.* After three deep breaths, I settle into my bed and drift off to the lingering but faint scent of Julian on my pillow.

Dreams are bizarre. Especially when you know you're dreaming while you're dreaming. Julian comes to my room just as I wished for right before falling asleep. I can tell he's there before I open my eyes because his scent is stronger now. He smells like a shower and laundry and warm skin. I reach out hoping to find him there as I open my eyes, but it's not Julian. It's Chase. What's Chase doing in Blue Lake? He's reaching out to me, touching me. I want to scream, but my voice is frozen like my body. If I just call out, Julian will hear me and come running. And he'll throw Chase out effortlessly. Chase used to look so big to me, like the big man on campus everyone saw him as. But compared to Julian, he looks like a boy. A sad boy who tries too hard to look important. Clearly so after the way he let me take the blame for everything he did that night. I see it all now. He woke me up by touching me. He shushed me just like he's shushing me now in my dream. I try to push his hand off me and sit up. That's when I see the hall light and hear Kendall. He must've blamed it all on me. Just like before, I feel the light behind my eyelids. It's dim but it's the wrong direction. It's not coming from the hallway. It's coming from the bathroom. My bathroom. My bathroom at Allie's. How did Chase find Allie's? I open my eyes and see the shadow approaching me just like that night but from the bathroom.

"No, Kendall, it's not what you think!"

"Ever, stop, it's okay."

Kendall doesn't call me Ever. It's Julian. His voice is dragging me up from the depths of the dream. I'm awake now and there's only me and Julian.

The bed dips where he sits down. His hand rests on my sweaty cheek, his palm cool and dry. He's shushing me, like in the dream. But this sound calms me. He drops his hand and blows softly on my sweat-slicked neck, pushing the hair sticking to my skin behind my ear.

I look up into his shadowed face, the glow from the bathroom doorway backlighting him. I make out his half smile and it trips my heartbeat before he says, "Hi."

He lifts his other hand that was leaning across me on the bed and pushes a lock of hair behind my other ear. He cradles my face with both hands, his thumbs tracing soft circles on either side of my lips.

Still disoriented from sleep, I reply hoarsely, "Hi."

"You were dreaming. Wanna talk about it? A drink of water maybe?"

"Uh, no. I'm okay, thanks. I, uh, guess it's my turn. Tag you're it." I try to laugh but it comes out in a half sob. I fight the tears that want to fall.

He tilts my face toward him and pierces me with his stare. "Ever . . ." he sighs. "Let me help you. Let me be here for you."

One traitorous tear slides down my face, then another. "I can't, okay?"

"Why?" He drops his hands from my face and holds them out to his sides in question.

"Because if I let you 'help' me, I let you touch me. And when you touch me, I want to touch you. And when we touch each other, I don't want to stop." I exhale a shaky breath.

"Okay?" He says it like a question and exhales loudly.

I continue before he can interject. "No. It's not okay. I ran away from the only home I've ever known because I was labeled a slut and a home-wrecker. And maybe I am. Because I can't remember what happened that night. And even though I'm still the dictionary definition of a virgin, I don't feel like one when I'm with you . . . and I can't be . . . I don't want to be logical and responsible when you 'help' me." I use quotes when I say it, staring blindly at my hands while he leans over me.

Another exhale escapes his lips before he responds. "Then let me be logical and responsible enough for both of us." He stands up and moves in behind me on my bed, then brings my back up against his chest as he settles his against the tufted linen headboard. He places his hands over mine, interlocking our fingers, and wraps our arms around my waist with his on top of mine. He tucks my head under his chin. "I care about you, Ever. When I'm with you, I feel things I thought I'd never feel again. I want to stay away from you because you deserve better than me. And I don't know what happened in Oak Valley, but you're not a slut. Or a home-wrecker. I'd bet money on it. You're perfect. Probably the most perfect girl I've ever met. Undeniably the most beautiful."

"*You're* beautiful," I barely whisper.

I know he hears me. The lazy circles his fingers were drawing on my hands stop with my words, then he squeezes them in his hands, slowly inching up to rub my arms. "We don't have to rush this. We can go slow."

"Between the bad dreams, the interruptions and bully cougars, I think we've covered slow. If we want to actually do anything, we may need to go off grid."

Chuckling, he wraps his arms tighter around me. "Oh, sassy girl. What am I going to do with you?"

"Are you asking for suggestions?"

I'm rewarded with another low laugh and his arms squeezing me, but then my words sink in, and he leans his face down and tilts my chin so we can see each other squarely. "Wait. What bully cougars?"

Chapter 25

JULIAN

My dick wakes up before I do. More accurately, Ever wakes my dick up when she rolls over on top of me. She fell asleep with her head tucked under my chin last night, and once her breathing slowed to a rhythmic pace, it lulled me to sleep too. Not the most comfortable position I've slept in, but Ever between my legs, pressed to my chest, more than makes up for it.

I glance at her phone on the charger to check the time. It's early. I'm careful not to move because I don't want to wake her. The raging hard-on isn't helping though. And I could really use the bathroom. I'm wondering how long I can hold it with her leaning on my bladder when I feel her head tilt up under my chin. Since she's awake, I do what my fingers are aching to do. I run them through her hair, which always smells like sunshine and feels like silk. Swiping it off her neck to flow down her back, I look down into her sleepy gray eyes.

She smiles shyly at me. She's always shy in the mornings.

That I know this little quirk about her makes my crotch tighten. I touch my lips to her forehead and rub my thumb up and down the spot behind her ear. "Hi, pretty girl."

"Hi, Julie." She dips her head back down to nuzzle under my chin as she answers.

"Sleep okay?" I ignore the ache in my crotch and aim for politeness.

"Mm, yeah. Thanks for . . . This couldn't have been very comfortable for you. So thanks."

"It was fine. Good. I slept well." I'm awkward, tripping over my words.

"Liar." She calls me out, her raspy voice making the ache in my crotch worse.

I chuckle at her sass. "No, it was fine. I swear. But I could use the, uh, restroom."

"Oh, of course." She rolls off me and the bed so quickly that she stumbles until she finds her footing. Realizing she doesn't have anywhere to escape to, being we're in her room, she looks at me and shrugs while her face blooms crimson.

Ugh, this sweet girl is breaking me. And I don't care if I'm undeserving or if it makes me a selfish asshole. I want her. And I know it's a matter of time before we cross that line. She wants me just as much, which makes the ache in my chest match the ache in my crotch.

I tap her on the chin as I head to the bathroom. I keep my other hand in front of my lower half to hopefully hide my morning wood, or at least not draw attention to it. After I take a piss and brush my teeth, I pace back and forth a few steps. Should I go back to her room and . . . check on her? I decide to go outside and absorb the crisp morning air instead.

After a few stretches and deep breaths, I lean on the railing, wondering how to make this girl mine. The tug of war inside my soul is slowly dying. My desire is no match for my conscience.

I hear Ever's door and turn as she steps outside. Her hair is knotted on top of her head in a strategic messy bun, her face looks freshly washed and she's dressed in leggings and a cropped hoodie. One of my favorite outfits of hers.

My hand immediately flies to my chest, making small circles over the tattoo. "I was just about to head down and make some coffee. Want some?" I ask to distract myself from the skin peeking out from the bottom band of her hoodie.

"Let's go grab some in town before we head to Fit. Wanna?" She dangles what I assume are Allie's keys.

"Sure. Let me throw on some clothes. Two minutes." I'd go anywhere with her right now if she asked. Her capacity to compartmentalize and get on with her day amazes me. I know some of the shit that could easily jade her, the small amount she's shared with me, but here she is, sunny and bright, asking me to coffee. She'd make a great first responder—the way she can tuck it all away. Maybe that's why she gives old soul energy. Clearly this young beauty in front of me has lived before. I shake my head at my romantic musings.

Sweet Everly is turning me into a . . . poet? Dreamer?

Speaking of dreams, I want to propose something. I'm not sure she'll go for it. I'm not sure I'm capable of living up to my end of it. But I find I can't help suggesting it. Once the idea struck me, I wanted her to agree to it more than I've wanted anything, save one, but we don't get do-overs. I shake the thought away as quickly as it comes. But, yeah, the only thing I might want more would involve turning back time, and I'm not even sure if *more* is accurate. But since that's not an option, I mentally shake off that train of thought as we head into town.

Town is only a few blocks away by city standards. In Blue Lake, those blocks are stretches of country highway, fields and fence lines with houses spaced acres apart. I switch my focus to how to pose the question I want to ask Ever. I start with small talk—which I'm admittedly bad at.

"So, how'd you sleep?"

"Still good. Just like the first time you asked me." She softens her response with a wink.

"Oh, yeah, I did ask already. Didn't I?"

"Yeah," she says with a giggle. "Spit it out, Julie. What's up?"

"That," he exclaimed, like it explained everything.

"That, what? Gonna need a little more here."

"I know." I blow out a breath. "Okay, here's the thing. We seem to be in tune to each other. Get each other. And we even . . . we sleep better together, right?" I rush on before she can answer. "I mean, we both seem to . . . I don't know . . . torment ourselves in sleep with . . . bad dreams of the past. But you said you slept well last night. And you did. I was there. And the other night, when I . . . when you came in . . . . it . . . helped. Maybe we could just sleep together. To . . . you know . . ." *Fuck, why did I always feel like a stupid kid around her?* I backpedal. "It's probably a terrible idea. Would probably just torture ourselves in a new way. Forget I brought it up."

Chapter 26

Everly

"No. I think you have a point. But first . . . coffee," I wink, turning my head quickly from the driver's seat to face him and smile. Hair whips across my face with the breeze from the open windows. I'm thrilled that Blue Lake boasts a Starbucks. I'm too excited to go there. Like a slice of my old life, but a part that doesn't haunt me. One that feels like a favorite book. Before we leave the driveway, I use my app to place our drink order so it'll be ready when we get there. Julian requests black coffee. *Boring.* I ask him to trust me and add vanilla cold foam to the top. And in the spirit of being healthier, I plug in my order the same way. The approval on his face is as clear as if he'd spoken it out loud. I couldn't contain the eye roll as I pull out onto the highway. Granted, Starbucks coffees could contain more sugar than coffee depending on the order, but they're damn delicious. And all this health stuff really does make me feel better physically than I ever have. I'm just not ready to admit that to Julian.

I catch his dimple from the corner of my eye before I return my gaze to the road. When his hand reaches out and tucks my hair behind my ear, I want to freeze the moment. Julian riding in the passenger seat, that lazy half smile, me driving to my favorite coffee shop on this hypnotic tree-lined highway, green velvet stretching over rolling hills. Maybe it's the fresh air up here or all the working out or finally finding someone who makes me want all the things every other girl my age seems to find so easily, but my thoughts rush like a river. My feelings settle like a bubbling brook. I can't keep up with the contrast—a raging flood and a peaceful flow.

For the first time that I can recall, my external life matches my internal one. I feel seen. Wanted. Beautiful. I love who I am with him. I want to raise my hands to the sky like some born-again holy roller and thank God or the universe for everything that has led me to this moment, to this person next to me. Instead, I reach across the center console of Allie's 4Runner and place my hand on top of his much larger one, clasp my fingers around it and squeeze.

He turns his over and laces our fingers together. Then he brings our hands to his lips and kisses the back of mine.

My tummy flips at the touch of his lips on my skin.

Yep, book boyfriends have nothing on this guy.

Pulling into the Starbucks parking lot, the app notifies me that our order is ready for pickup. I feel him tense before he lets go of my hand. I track his line of vision to the red convertible with the custom plate, SYLVIED. Before I put the car in park, he removes his seat belt and offers to go inside and pick up our drinks from the mobile counter. I envisioned us sitting at a table, sharing a coffee over conversation. I stamp down my disappointment.

As he steps out of the car, he reaches for my hand and squeezes. "Let's take ours to the lake. It's a perfect day out."

I smile and nod, grateful for the shades I'm wearing, knowing my eyes would belie my cheerful compliance. If I wasn't totally sure Julian and Sylvie had hooked up, I'd bet money on it now. I try not to let this realization dampen my spirits. The guy is twenty-one years old. To think he wouldn't have a past is ridiculous. I just wish it didn't have to be with a hot cougar reliving her glory days. I hate myself a little for the bitchy description. In my defense, Sylvie was bitchy to me first.

It takes Julian no time to return with our coffees. I take some small satisfaction in watching him tip his cup to the cougar table on his way out the door, knowing he didn't stop to talk to any of them, especially Sylvie. But I still want to know what that situation was . . . or is. I'm just not sure it's my place to ask.

Since he requested drinking our coffee at the lake, I head to Brew. Julian said he wanted to check in on his apartment and pick up his mail. I hang back, not wanting to intrude on his space.

"C'mon, it'll just take a second." He tosses his head toward his place as he says it.

I don't analyze my delight at being invited to join him.

The apartment above a garage implies simple, possibly rundown. It isn't. The inside is breathtaking. Elegant, even. I mean, it screams *single guy* but in a cool, rustic way. Open beams on vaulted ceilings, remodeled kitchen with granite counters and an island bar. The furniture is muted in color and shouts cozy. The whole place begs you to snuggle in and stay awhile. And I want to. This urge to hide away right here from the rest of the world and keep this place and the man in it all to myself is powerful. My old therapist would have a field day unpacking that trauma response to abandonment.

I turn a complete circle before I catch Julian staring at me. I grin at him, unable to contain my delight. He smiles back almost shyly but doesn't speak. Like he's waiting for me to say something. I don't hold back. "I love your place. It feels . . . safe." My confession has his smile claiming his whole face, forcing his dimples and creasing the corners of his eyes.

"I'll just be a second. Gonna grab a couple things from the bedroom." As he moves down the short hall and disappears through one of two doors, I ignore the urge to follow him. What does his bedroom, his bed, look like? Feel like? Smell like? My foot takes an involuntary step in that direction. I pivot and turn toward the wall of windows that look out across the lake. Wrapping my arms around my stomach, I take in the view. I understand the sway of so many windows with a view like this and the one at Allie's. It's so beautiful, it stings my eyes. It swirls around you, envelops you and promises to make everything alright. *I wanna stay.* I jerk at that thought like it was audible. I look over both shoulders to ensure someone hasn't spoken it out loud.

Julian appears from the hallway with a lightweight drawstring backpack over his shoulder. He stops short when he sees my face. "You okay?"

"Yeah, totally. I just really like it here."

"Thanks. It didn't always look like this. And we can have our coffee date here if you want. On the deck?"

My heart trips on the word date. I swallow and clear my throat. "I do."

On the deck, kicked back on two chaise lounges, our coffees resting on the short table between us, he starts telling me how he remodeled the place. On and off throughout the story, he would pause and get a faraway look on his face. When he did, I wouldn't ask, but I wanted to. He caught himself quickly each time and continued. Turns out Julian is quite the handyman. He worked some construction during summer breaks throughout high school and has a passion for carpentry. He also has a stylistic eye for detail. His tastes run to classic and clean with a hint of rustic. Kinda like him.

That faraway look is back.

"What's going on in there, Julie?" I don't want to ask because I can tell he doesn't want to explain, or he would've. I can't help myself though. I want to know this man and what makes him disappear like that. And where he goes when he does.

Chapter 27

Julian

Three-ish Years Ago

The dangling raw hamburger that used to be my forearm is making me kinda nauseous. Maybe it's the head gash causing the nausea. I don't know how bad it is, just that I have blood trailing into my eye. I try to sit up, but the wave of dizziness has me sliding back onto the gravel. It's so dark outside I can barely see my hand in front of my face, so I can't tell what shape my bike is in. If my body is any indication, the bike is toast.

I hear the rustling footsteps before I see the bobbing orb of the flashlight coming at me. I struggle again into a semi-sitting position. Taking a breath is like inhaling broken glass. I clutch my chest with the effort.

"Are you okay? Should I call 911?" Her voice is soft, sweet, like a melody.

I can't see her in the pitch black, but I can tell her hair is light colored, illuminated by the flashlight.

"I heard the crash from my house. It's just up this embankment." The crunching footsteps get closer. "Lucky you. I'm the only house for miles." Her voice is next to me. "How bad are you hurt? Do you know what happened?" She's kneeling beside me in the dirt and gravel and reaches out to touch my face.

I jerk back, causing her to do the same.

"I'm not going to . . . I just want to . . . Let me help you. You're hurt."

"No shit. And I don't want any help. No one can help me."

"Honey, let me just get you inside. Wait here. I'm going to get my car. You're not gonna make it up my driveway and I can't carry you."

She doesn't wait for my response. She hasn't asked me a question anyway. Her crunching footsteps fade as she leaves, presumably to get her car and give me a ride to her . . . driveway?

Maybe I'll die before she gets back. Then all the pain will stop. The nightmare will be over. No such luck. I hear the motor of a vehicle just before the headlights spotlight me, blinding me until I put my hand up to shield my face.

She leaves them trained on me as she parks halfway in the ditch and gets out. "Oh my God, you're pretty torn up. I think I should take you to a hospital."

"No. I'm fine." I try to stand up, but my body won't cooperate. I turn sideways and get on all fours, wait for the wave of dizziness and nausea to pass and try again.

She's instantly beside me, helping me stand.

My vision starts closing in on me. I know I'm going down if I don't let her help me. She walks me to the passenger side of her car, a Toyota 4Runner, and eases me into the seat. My body slumps against the door as she closes it. My head feels sticky. I know I'm leaving blood on her window. I'm trashing her nice car with blood, dirt and gravel. *Her choice to put me in it*, I think, like an asshole. Before I can straighten myself in the seat or pass out, the door is opening again, and she's walking me up a front path onto a lighted porch and through her front door.

I have no reference of time, but it feels like I sit at her kitchen table for hours while she meticulously pulls gravel out of my arms, head, face and torso.

"I'm Allie." She looks older than me but not by much. She has a pretty face that matches her calm voice. She looks physically fit but petite. And obviously strong enough to half carry me to her car.

I'm not exactly a small person. Maybe a little thinner than I usually am, but not small by any means. She doesn't ask me any questions. I know she can smell the alcohol on me. I can smell it. I guess life has other plans for me than my death wish. I didn't exactly try to kill myself driving my motorcycle intoxicated. Not consciously anyway. Although death would be preferable to this searing pain in my chest.

Remembering why I was drunk and riding too fast in the first place causes a fresh wave of nausea. I can't swallow the urge this time. I stand and fight the dizziness and bolt for the kitchen sink and throw up everything in my stomach—which is alcohol and bile. I can't remember the last time I ate. With my hands gripping the edge of the counter, my head dangling over the copper farmhouse sink, I try to apologize for fucking up her pretty sink. "I'm sorry. I didn't mean to

. . ." Another wave of dizziness cuts me off. I dry heave into the sink. There's nothing left to throw up.

"Let's just sit you back down. How about the couch? I'll bring you some water." She helps me walk into the open floor living room and over to an L-shaped, linen-colored couch.

I protest sitting on it and sink to the floor in front of it. I already fucked up her car and her sink. "Pretty sure blood won't come out of this white sofa."

That got a smirk and a nod from her. "Well, when you're steady enough, we'll get you in the shower."

"Why are you being so nice to me? What if I'm a serial killer?"

"Well, no offense, but if you are, I might be able to take you in your current state. And if you're faking to get the upper hand, your makeup people are phenomenal, because that blood looks real. And that fake vomiting scene in the kitchen? Oscar worthy."

I chuckle, then immediately grab my ribs. Yep, pretty sure a few of those are cracked.

"Look, if I'd caught serial killer vibes from you, I would've left you on the street and called 911."

"Fair," I concede. I extend my arm and take the glass of water she's offering, still gripping my ribs with the other. The water soothes my throat, raw from vomiting. I take small sips to test if it will stay down.

"I've got some sweats and a hoodie you can change into. Wanna try a shower? Just go slow and hold on to something in there. I don't wanna have to come in there and rescue Naked Crash Stranger."

I vaguely wonder who the clothes belong to. Not that I care. I just wonder if some husband is going to come home and find me in the shower and kick my ass. Maybe he would put me out of my misery.

A hot shower does sound amazing. Every part of me throbs in pain. I hunch onto my knees and slowly get to my feet, balancing my hands on the coffee table. No nausea, just mild dizziness. I think I can make it through a shower. I follow her down the short hall into what I assume is a guest bathroom.

She places a fresh towel on the counter and disappears upstairs. She's back in a blink with some folded clothes and sets them near the towel. She moves past me, turns on the shower and leaves me standing in the blue, ocean-inspired bathroom. "I'll be in the kitchen when you're done. Take your time and holler if you need me."

"Thanks, uh . . ."

"Allie," we say in unison.

"Yeah, memory works." She softly giggles and closes the door.

I wish it didn't.

I don't know if it's her kindness, the alcohol or the concussion I've likely given myself, but I'm suddenly overcome with emotion. I peel off my torn, bloody clothes, step into the steamy spray, sink to the floor and hug my knees and let the water pound my skin like a thousand tiny hot needles. I don't know how long I sit on the tiled floor under the stream, shaking, crying into my folded arms with my forehead on my knees.

She can't be gone.

I don't want to live in a world without her in it. Her father killed her. He said she did it. He said she took pills. He blames me, but he did this to her. And he wouldn't let me see her. But I loved her. She loved me. He did it. By not letting us be together. By threatening to send her away. If he'd just let her stay, let us be together, she'd still be here. God, I wanted to kill him. He said if I ever showed my face around there again, he'd have me arrested. For rape. How could he say that, think that? I would never. We loved each other. He said other stuff too. About how he could convince a judge it was felony statutory rape because I'm an adult now. So I left. It doesn't matter now because I won't be back. There was nothing to go back to.

Everything I've ever loved about that town died with her. I wish I had too. I wasn't consciously trying to kill myself when I tore out of there on my bike. I just wanted distance between me and the searing, soul-crushing pain of losing Taya. Taking corners sideways and well over the speed limit, all it took was a little loose gravel to send me sliding off the road down the embankment in front of Allie's house. That and slow enough reflexes from the alcohol to render me incapable of recovering the turn. I didn't know what small town I was even in. They all went by in a blur from the moment I downed the fifth I picked up at the liquor store, where I hit the road in a fury—no destination in mind.

I purposely drove in the opposite direction of South Point. No good could come of me confronting Bennick. He owns that town and they'd be rallying around him in his grief. No one knew about me and Taya except him. I could disappear and no one would miss me. Not even my parents. She was the only good thing I had going for me in my shit life. She made me feel like someone, like I was worth something.

The water turning colder drags me out of thoughts and into the now. I force myself upright, feeling the soreness more now. My entire body screams, my ribs ache, my head pounds like it's caught in a vise. The cuts on my arms, head and face sting in the ever-cooling spray. I quickly lather my body, ignoring the sting from the soap on the open wounds. Once I dress in the sweats Allie offered—commando because my boxer briefs were full of dirt, gravel and blood—I make my way back to the kitchen, my clothes and towel piled in my arms.

Allie is placing two mugs of steamy liquid down on the kitchen table when I walk in. She sets one in front of a plate bearing a grilled cheese sandwich and a pickle wedge.

"Sit. Eat. I'll toss your clothes in the wash." She takes the pile from my arms and disappears through a door off the back wall of the kitchen—laundry room I surmise.

I'm not sure I can eat, but I sit anyway and vow to try because this guardian angel cared enough to make it for me. And she must be a guardian angel. Either that or a figment of my concussed imagination.

I take a tentative bite of the sandwich to test my stomach. It happens to be the best grilled cheese I've ever tasted. My stomach growls in approval. I take another bite. Bigger this time. I must've made a sound of approval because Allie speaks up behind me.

"I know, right? I make it with garlic buttered bread. Takes a plain grilled cheese to another level."

"M-hm," I agree with my mouth full.

"The tea is a favorite of mine. My go-to calming, stress-reducing blend. I promise it doesn't suck."

"Why?"

"Why doesn't it suck?"

"Why are you doing this?" I ask around a mouthful of sandwich.

"Oh. Well, the obvious answer is because you needed help. And you sort of waved that 'help wanted' flag right in front of me by crashing your bike outside my door."

"That's fair. So . . . thanks for all this, but I'll just get out of your way and . . ."

"And? Go where? With what? And how?" She folds her arms across her chest like a mom scolding a child. Not my mom, but regular moms I assume. Like TV moms do.

"Look . . . Allie, you seem really nice and uh, kind, but I could be a serial killer."

"Are you?" She raises one eyebrow and waits.

"No, but I'm an ugly drunk. And not very good company."

"What's your name?"

"Doesn't matter. I'm nobody. Nothing." I unclench my hands I unknowingly fisted and look at the scrapes, rubbing my sweaty palms down my thighs.

"Well, Nobody Nothing, as unfortunate as that name is, I have a place that's empty. It could use some work. I'd planned to hire someone to help me fix it up. I mean, you're not in any shape to . . . do much of anything right now, except heal. But would you . . . want a job? A place to stay?" She places dishes in the dishwasher as she talks.

"What makes you think I want a job? Or a place to stay?"

"Let's call it a hunch." She folds her arms across her chest again, tilts her head and studies me.

"You're too trusting." I shake my head slowly and put the last bite of sandwich in my mouth, staring down at my plate as I chew.

"I'd like to think of it as being a good human and hopefully solid at reading people. Sleep here on the couch tonight. We'll assess your injuries in the morning and see if you need a doctor."

"What about your husband?" I pick up the pickle wedge as she takes the plate from in front of me.

"No husband. The sweats were my dad's. And in case I'm bad at reading people, I have a black belt in karate and I'm pretty sure I could kick your ass—even without your injuries."

That earned another bark of laughter that has me gripping my ribs again and hissing through clenched teeth at the stabbing pain. I drop the pickle on my napkin. "I'll be fine. But, uh, thanks. Allie. For . . ." I stop to breathe through a wave of nausea.

She doesn't wait for me to finish my sentence. "You're welcome, Nobody. Glad you're not a serial killer."

"It's Jay—Julian."

"Jay Julian? That's different."

"Just Julian."

"Okay, night, Just Julian. Get some rest."

Before I drift off into a fitful sleep on the pretty white couch, I decide that if God won't put me out of my misery and let me die, maybe I'll stay and help this woman who was nice enough to help me. Even if I believe she's dangerously too trusting.

What else do I have going for me anyway?

Chapter 28

Julian

Present Day

"Where'd you go?" Ever's question pulls me out of my flashback.

"I . . . I guess seeing my place through someone else's eyes for the first time took me back to when I first moved in. Allie gave me room and board to fix the place up. It took about a year to get it just the way I wanted it. The project and this place kinda saved me, I guess. Gave me a new lease on life, a new path. But . . ." I give an involuntary shiver. "Enough of my memory lane. Tell me something I don't know about you, your life."

She considers me for a few seconds.

I hold my breath hoping she'll play along and we can stop talking about my past.

"Sylvie cornered me in the gym and told me to stay away from you. And I know that's why you wanted to come here instead of staying at the coffee shop. I saw her car."

I bark a short laugh. "You aren't afraid to just say the truth, are you?"

"I mean, it seems to me it's the shortest route to getting to the point of a thing."

"Tell the truth. You're a reincarnated thirty-year-old, aren't you?"

"If I were concerned about aging, I think I'd be insulted right now. But in case you're serious, I'm really eighteen. I probably sound older because I read a lot."

I feel my grin in my cheeks. Shaking my head and chuckling, I subconsciously rub the tattoo on my chest. This enchanting being is seeping into my skin, my bones. Easing the ache. And for the first time in three years, I welcome it. "And what are you currently reading?"

I watch her forehead crease. Maybe because I don't address the Sylvie topic, although it wasn't unintentional. I'm just insatiably curious about her. I want to know everything.

"I'm in between books right now."

"Why is that troubling?" If her frown isn't about books, as I suspect it's not, now is her chance to say it.

"Troubling?"

"Yeah, you're frowning like it bothers you not having an answer to that question." I leave the door wide open for her to bring up Sylvie again. She doesn't.

"Oh, it's just weird not to have a book to read. For me, anyway. I DNF'd the last book I started. It wasn't doing it for me. I've been writing more instead of reading. But I may reread an old favorite until I find a new one that gets me out of my slump."

"Hmm, okay." A slump? As in a reading slump? "So, what's DNF?"

I'll never tire of watching the flush bloom on her cheeks. "Oh, Did Not Finish. It's a bookish term for—"

"Not finishing a book?" I say, cutting her off, winking.

"Yeah." She smiles shyly.

"And you write, too?" She intrigues me so much. "What do you write? Stories, or . . . ?"

"Someday, hopefully. But I mostly journal, maybe some poetry, but honestly, I haven't written poems in a long time. Kinda lost my passion for it."

"I think I'd love to read some of those."

"You read? Sorry. That sounded rude. I meant, do you like to read? I've just never seen you with a book, so I didn't think . . . I just . . . wow. Sorry, Julian. I sounded like a snob just now."

"Ever, you're good. I'm not offended." I want to laugh because she looks like someone just kicked her puppy. I don't think I even know another guy who would be offended by this. But I want to let her off the hook, so I say, "I really didn't love reading most of my life. I started really enjoying it about three years ago. I, uh, I got into a bad accident and spent some down time recovering. Reading was a great way to kill time while lying around, and it distracted me from the pain." I don't elaborate that the pain I'm referring to had nothing to do with my injuries.

"What was the first book you read three years ago?"

"Ah, promise not to laugh?"

"I don't lie so I can't make that promise. What was it?"

She had a perfect, enchanting response for everything. I rub my chest again as I answer.

"*Catcher in the Rye.*"

She looks surprised. Probably because most people read that in high school.

I quickly follow it up to fill the silence and try not to be offended. "What is your go-to favorite book?"

She pulls her chin back up, closing her slightly agape mouth at my answer, her forehead creasing again as she considers the question. "*Pride and Prejudice?*"

"Why did that sound like a question? Because that's the book a respectable book girl like you should call her favorite?" I raise one eyebrow in challenge. Before she can answer, I add, "What's your real favorite?"

"So . . . Sylvie—"

"Nooo, first tell me your book. Then we can talk about Sylvie."

"It's called *Paradise*. It's by a popular romance author of the eighties, weirdly enough. I found it at a secondhand bookstore and bought it for the title alone. But I love it."

"It's a good title." I pause and raise my hands out at my side, purse my lips together and tilt my head to the side as if to say, *I guess it's time to do this*. I bring my hands back together lacing my fingers and rest my elbows on my parted legs. "Sylvie and I . . . had a thing." I feel the embarrassment like a weight around my neck. I want to be better for this girl. I want her to think I'm better than I am. The weight settles in that empty spot in my chest. "Just physical and only a few times. I thought it was mutual. And I think it was at first. When it got weird, I ended it." I pause in case she wants to say something. She doesn't, so I add, "I'm sorry she came at you. I wish you'd told me when it happened. I promise I'll be talking to her about that. It won't happen again." I say all this looking Ever squarely in the eyes, so she knows I mean every word.

"I just don't want to cause any problems. For you. Or Allie. And I really don't want to cause any problems for me. I don't have any other towns to run away to." She adds the last part with a half smile and a shrug.

"You're not causing anyone problems. This isn't on you. This is the fallout of my poor decisions. This is what happens when guys think with their . . . when they don't think."

She purses her lips together in a straight-lined smile but says nothing. Her eyes say it all.

"Don't give up on me, Ever. I'm going to fix this." I reach across the little table and clasp my hand around hers, never breaking eye contact. "If I'd known . . . if I'd had any idea I'd meet someone like you, I'd have never given Sylvie the time of day. And I'm not hating on her. I'm just saying, I never thought I'd ever want to feel anything below the surface. Sylvie was surface. I thought it was for her too."

She crinkled her nose. "I get it. I do. It's just . . . icky."

"Hmph," I snorted. "Fair. And I admit, through this new lens . . ." I wag my finger between us to imply her and me. "I might have to agree." I turn her hand over and draw lazy circles on her palm. "Truth?"

"Always."

"Does that mean that you think I'm . . . icky?"

"It would simplify things if I did. Wouldn't it? But no. Believe me when I say I get being closed off. It's just way less acceptable if, say, I, a young girl, chose to go . . . scratch an itch with a man twenty years older than me."

Leaning my head back on the lounger, I wrinkle my nose at the thought of Everly with some old guy. Or any guy. Except me. I want her all to myself. I love that I'm the only one who's ever seen her in the height of pleasure. I want to be the only one to ever see it. I look up at the sky as I bring our joined hands to my chest, stretching her arm out straight across the table and our forgotten coffees that are surely cold now. Fingers intertwined, I press the back of her hand over my hollow heart tattoo. My boxers pull tight over my junk at the image of her in my arms coming apart for me alone, my thin joggers doing nothing to conceal it. I prop up my knee that's closest to her to camouflage it.

Her train of thought must mirror mine because she brings up the sleeping arrangement I proposed on the way to get coffee.

Chapter 29

EVERLY

I t's finally the night before camping season begins. Lilly insists on celebrating tonight, before we get so busy "we won't even be able to even go pee." That's a direct quote. She invited herself to stay the night at Allie's with me, after our pre-season bonfire at Brew. Pete's bonfire is flaming in the rock-lined fire pit. His wife, Shelley, and their kids are roasting marshmallows. Lilly and Noah's little sisters hunch over their phones, heads huddled together, sitting two to a chair around the fire. The glow dances off their faces as they trade tea back and forth.

I didn't tell Lilly about my sleeping arrangement with Julian, but she knows we're . . . something. I don't hide that we're interested in each other and neither does he. We just don't make a habit of flaunting it with PDAs—especially at Fit.

That day over coffee, Julian and I agreed to sleep together—just sleep—and to take everything else slow—his suggestion. And I must admit, I've never slept so soundly. The waiting I solve by journaling. Abstinence seems to be the key to unlocking a creative streak. Although I don't get why we're waiting, other than his desire to take it slow. I can only imagine how Julian is dealing with waiting, but he seems perfectly fine with it and curiously relaxed after longer than normal showers right before bed. Although I can't confirm this and he wasn't offering, I find it . . . weirdly respectful, if not frustrating. And it obviously does its intended job, because he gets into bed and spoons me, and besides nuzzling my neck and a soft kiss on my cheek, he doesn't touch me.

On that first night of our arrangement, I waited for him to join me after his shower breathless with anticipation. Then . . . nothing. I wanted to be disappointed—I was, if I'm being honest—but his restraint gave perfect book boyfriend energy, and frustration aside, I'm here for it. Plus, I don't really know what I'm missing . . . yet. And I took my own edge off after I knew what to expect with his long showers. Still, I wished it were his hands instead of mine.

With Lilly sleeping over, Julian offered to stay at his own place tonight. He said he needs to be at Brew early tomorrow anyway, so it's more convenient. I suspect he's just giving us space and friend time, because everything is more than ready for the first wave of the season. Forget book boyfriend energy, it's just perfect boyfriend energy. And I know he's not my boyfriend, but our little arrangement is sure channeling relationship vibes.

Lilly returns from the deck and hands me a Solo cup as she takes the seat next to me. I take a tentative sip, knowing the last cup of liquid burned my throat from start to finish, but it gives me a warm, slightly numb feeling. I haven't felt anything like it since coming here and honestly wasn't sure I ever would again, but Blue Lake and the people here feel safe.

So did the Oak Valley crew once.

I push that thought away and take a sip of the new cup. It's delicious and doesn't burn like the first one. Lilly's "famous jungle juice" she calls it. I can tell by how easy it goes down it'll sneak up on me and put me on my ass. I vow to pace myself. But letting things fall out of focus feels so good, like I've been juggling nonstop since I got here, and tonight I get permission to let the balls drop.

Julian watches me sip the new drink from across the bonfire. The orange glow on his face makes him even more gorgeous, if that's possible. I ignore the concern in his eyes. I know he won't bring it up in front of Pete and Shelley. Hell, he even edits himself around Noah and Lilly. But I know I won't be able to ignore him for long.

"I've gotta pee," I announce to Lilly as I stand up and set my drink on the wide arm of my Adirondack chair.

"Want me to go with?"

"No, no. You just got back. I'll be quick." I turn and head for the stairs and bathroom inside Brew.

Coming out of the Brew bathroom, I collide with Julian's chest. Clasping my arms, he steadies me. I snake my arms around his neck intending to kiss him. My inhibitions disappear with the alcohol buzz along with my discretion, apparently. It doesn't occur to me to check if anyone else is around.

It must occur to Julian though, because he reaches up and takes my hands off his neck and holds them in his. Never taking his eyes off me, he drops my hands to my sides, places his on either side of my face and brings my lips to his.

Maybe he's not.

His kiss is soft, lingering. And when he pulls back, I lean into him, not wanting it to stop. Instead of kissing me again though, he places his lips on my forehead and wraps his arms around me. Tucking my head under his chin, he swings slowly side to side, once, twice. Then he moves his hands to my shoulders and pulls back to look at me again. "Be careful, Ever, okay? I like seeing you relax and have fun. Just be safe tonight. When I'm not there. Please?"

"Yeah, totally. Don't worry." I clench his soft heather-gray tee lightly in both my fists and rock them back and forth against his chest like pulling on suspenders. "Just letting off a little steam. But I'll miss my spooning buddy tonight."

His chuckle is more groan. "Careful what you wish for. Lilly may offer herself as tribute. Especially if she drinks enough jungle juice."

"Ha, ha. Yeah, I think I'll draw the line at letting her share half my bed."

"Fair enough. I guess we better get back to the fire before they miss us."

"Don't you have to use the bathroom?"

"No, I came in here for you."

"Okay."

"Okay." He turns to head toward the door, taking my hand to lace our fingers. As soon as we walk through the door to the deck, he squeezes my hand and releases it.

"Julie?" I stop just outside the Brew doors, so he does too.

"Ever?" He looks sideways at me and waits.

"Can I ask you something?"

"Of course. Anything."

"I'm just wondering what your definition of slow is. Because to me it's landing like a hard stop instead of slow progression. And really my question is, what are you waiting for?"

Groaning, he faces me and places his hands on my shoulders and squeezes lightly. "Smart, sassy girl, you don't fight fair."

"Are we fighting?" I arch my eyebrow in challenge.

With a chuckle and another little squeeze of my shoulders, he drops his hands, letting the one closest to me slide down my back to my ass.

The rub pat thing he does heats me more thoroughly than any fire could. It makes saliva gather in my mouth. His touch sparks a flame in my lower region that has me fighting the urge to squirm as we walk. When he doesn't speak but keeps moving toward the others, I stop. He takes a couple more steps before he realizes I'm not keeping pace.

Sighing audibly, he faces me and says, "I guess I just want to make sure I'm being respectful of our situation. We were kinda thrown together to help Allie and . . . I don't want to . . . I don't know . . . take advantage. And maybe we should have this conversation when you're not drinking."

I place my hands on my hips and face him squarely as I consider his words. "First, I'm not drunk. I'm happily buzzed and very much in control of my faculties."

"Hmf." The corner of his mouth tilts up as he sighs and nods at me, but he stays silent, waiting for me to continue.

"Second, and I want you to hear me on this. You are probably the best thing that's ever happened to me. I've never felt more myself than when I'm with you. If you're worried about my innocence, don't." I spread my hands wide, palms up. "I'm a big girl. And honestly, I've been patient. I wasn't one of those girls that hooked up with randos for the sake of the experience. I've finally met someone who makes me want to . . . I don't know . . . be less innocent." I look down at my feet after that confession, feeling a little exposed and surprised by my own frankness. Maybe the buzz is making me bolder because I add, "And I just don't understand why we stopped."

Julian's footsteps thud before his shoes come into my line of vision. His fingertips under my chin draw my gaze up to his. "Is there a third?" His face is so close I feel his breath on my lips, making mine part in anticipation, invitation.

I barely swivel my head side to side to say *no*.

"You done?"

I nod, his fingers still under my chin.

He's nodding too, mirroring me. "Good." His lips touch mine, softly at first as his hands rush along my cheeks and into my hair, curling around the back of my neck. Pulling me to him, he deepens the kiss, lifting me onto my toes.

I twine my arms around his neck as his slide down to grasp my thighs under my ass and pick me up. I wrap my legs around him, molding my torso to his.

He rains kisses along my jaw, neck and behind my ear. His breath rushes against my ear, sending flutters to my belly and lower. His arms snug around my back, hugging me tightly. His voice is a heated whisper. "I want you, Everly. So much. More than I've ever wanted anything." He kisses the spot in front of my ear before he continues. "How could I not? Don't ever think I don't. I just want it to be . . . special. For you." With a squeezing hug, he sets me on my feet, plants small kisses on my lips, slips my hair behind my ears and draws lazy circles around the shells.

I nod, breathless, resting my forehead on his.

"C'mon, before they miss us." He clasps my hand and tugs me toward the group.

I follow, feeling warm and fuzzy. Whether from the jungle juice or the guy, I'm not sure, but he holds my hand all the way back to the bonfire. I'm leaning toward it being the guy.

As we approach the fire, no one turns or even seems to notice us. Pete and Shelley are dancing to the song Noah plays on his guitar and Lilly sings softly beside him. These two are true couples goals. The young boys are making gagging noises as their parents dance. The high school girls are taking selfies. As I take my seat next to Lilly, she puts her arm around me and bumps my arm in invitation to sing along. The song is a country song I've heard plenty of times, but not well enough to offer more than chorus support. And I do so, shamelessly. Liquid courage, compliments of the jungle juice. I'm shocked when Julian joins in. And his voice isn't half bad.

This night is perfect. Another one I want to stay frozen in.

After the song ends, I take another gulp of my drink. I don't look up to see if Julian is watching me. I know he is. I ignore the nagging guilt to be the good girl I always am. I deserve to act my age. Noah is driving us home, so I don't have to worry about that. And by most eighteen-year-old standards, I'm boring as hell. *Fuck it!* I down the rest of contents of my cup.

Speaking of Noah, he starts playing "Hey Ho" by The Lumineers, and Lilly taps her Solo cup to mine and begins belting out the lyrics. It's not long before we all join in—even the *cooler than us* Little Sister Gang. We all continue to sing while Noah plays until the fire starts to fade. Pete and Shelley carry the boys, who've finally passed out, to their car, the Little Sister Gang pile into Noah's SUV, filling up all the seatbelts, and that's when Julian offers to drive us over to Allie's.

Lilly proposes we walk and that the fresh air would be good for us.

"I agree with the fresh air. But let's not risk it. The path is dark and . . . you know . . . snake season," Julian warns.

"Fine. You win! All you had to say was snake." Lilly marches to Julian's Jeep in a fake tantrum and hops into the backseat.

Laughing, I follow her, secretly glad he offered. The critters of Blue Lake take some getting used to.

***

"Y ou've never done it before?" Lilly is not one to mince words.

My face is on fire. My brain is spinning with ways to get out of answering this. While I seem to lose my shyness with Julian, I don't know how to have these kinds of blunt girlfriend conversations. My sister and I never did. My mom was never around long enough to delve into anything beyond basic survival needs. And in their defense, I never had anything or anyone to ask or answer questions about. Until now.

She started peppering me with questions about Julian as soon as we walked into Allie's. I didn't hide the goodnight kiss Julian and I shared through the window of his Jeep when he dropped us off. When she came around to how he was, as in *in bed*, my face gave it all away, prompting her shocked accusation. A pillow puffs against my face at my silence.

"Spill it," Lilly squeals, rearing back with her pillow in a threat to repeat the offense if I don't answer.

"Have you?" I buy myself time by throwing it back at her.

"Nope. Nope." She's shaking her head adamantly. "I asked you first."

I want to talk to her about Julian, but I also don't know how much to say or how to say it. She's the least judgy person I've ever met, unless she's joking about hoolies and cougars. But that's in the name of sarcasm and comedy. I respect this. I'm just not sure I can handle my sex life or lack thereof being her comic relief.

"Promise not to laugh?" When she opens her mouth with a smirk on her face—a knowing tell when something inappropriate is about to fly out—I add, "Or make jokes."

She clamps her mouth shut and raises her hand in a mock scout promise. With her other hand she mimics zipping her lips closed.

I snatch the pillow off her lap and press it to my chest, wrap both arms around it and settle back against my headboard. She's facing me, sitting with her legs crossed at the end of my bed. She flops onto her side and stretches out across the foot of the bed, propping her hand on the side of her head and resting on her elbow like she's settling in for story time. She keeps her mouth shut, but her eyes are aglow with anticipation.

"I almost did."

"With Julian?"

"Yeah."

"Oh my God, I knew it." She sits back up, wrapping her arms around her knees and rests her chin on them. "What stopped you?"

"Ugh, that's a longer story."

"I'm not going anywhere. Spill."

So I do. All of it. Chase. Kendall. The crew. How it got even stickier because my sister and her boyfriend are their best friends. I feel the weight of it all falling away with the telling. Lilly's animated and supportive indignation prove to be the comfort I didn't know I was missing. Hearing it from her point of view makes me realize how much more fucked up it all was than I even let myself believe.

After I pour it all out, including all the Julian stuff, she hops onto her knees and clasps my legs with both hands. She pounces on them, playfully exclaiming, "You are so doing it. Like probably tomorrow. Shit, I cock-blocked you. God, if anyone deserves an epic first time, it's you. And I fucking cock-blocked you." She plops backward onto the bed and smashes the pillow over her face.

"You're not the only one. Julian's been doing that all week. Says he wants it to be special. And don't start planning or romanticizing this," I say when she drags the pillow off her face and studies me like the wheels are turning. "If it happens, I want it to be organic. Not orchestrated. I'm so awkward. If I tried to plan anything, I'd just fuck it up. When I don't have time to think, I'm way better."

She sits up on her heels and ponders me silently. This is why Lilly is probably my favorite person—and I just met her. She can be so passionate and fired up about something but can stop the momentum and really listen when someone throws the brakes on her steamroll.

"Okay, but you promise to tell me everything?"

"I'm not promising that. I don't know what to expect or if I'll be able to talk about it without dying of embarrassment. But I promise to confirm the event. Okay?"

"Ugh, okay."

"Now it's your turn. Noah?"

Her smile takes over her face and I know I'm in for a riveting Lilly B. tale.

Chapter 30

Everly

Opening day at Brew is a success, but I hide out at Fit all day with Lilly. Although no one knew I was hiding out except me. Over breakfast I mention to Lilly that I wish I'd gotten the Fit shift instead of the Brew shift, that crowds sometimes make me anxious. Ever the accommodating friend, she calls Noah and asks him to take opening day with Julian so I can help her with some aesthetic stuff at Fit. I know she doesn't entirely buy the crowd anxiety thing but mistakenly thinks I might have nerves about my first time with Julian.

During our morning workout, after about the fifteenth time Lilly brings it up, I tell her about the camping reservation from Oak Valley under the last name Young. I'd mostly put it out of my mind since that day I discovered it. But now that opening day is here, it's living rent free in my head. In Lilly's, too, apparently.

"Okay, but why is your sister still friends with them? Especially Kendall?"

"Maybe because she tried to leave the planet over it. I mean, the thought that I may have contributed to that . . . to her trying to . . ." I shudder.

"But did she?" Lilly holds up her hands in surrender before she adds, "No, hear me out. I'm just saying the suicide thing doesn't track for me. The aftermath . . ." She shakes her head.

I pause mid-squat. "What? You think she lied?"

"Or faked it." Lilly finishes her leg press sets so we switch places. She begins dumbbell squats, and I start my sets on the leg press machine.

"How do you fake it?" I find her eyes in the mirror.

She shrugs her shoulders, arching one brow in question.

We finish the rest of our sets in silence, both lost in our own thoughts. I can't quite wrap my head around someone faking a suicide attempt—even Kendall, who arguably got a whole town to bully and cancel me on her behalf.

But did she?

The few times Via and I talked about it, she said Kendall vehemently maintained she had no part in it. That she never asked anyone to treat me badly. Maybe that's true. Maybe she didn't have to. As the golden girl of OV, maybe they did it out of some twisted loyalty and alliance to her and her family. I guess I'll never know the truth. Doesn't matter anyway. Wouldn't change my circumstances now. Which leads me down another rabbit hole as we switch to abs to finish our workout. What happened in Oak Valley sucked. It beyond sucked. But if it hadn't happened and sucked so completely, I would've never moved to Blue Lake. And never met Julian.

Julian's face slams into my mind, and my heart drops into my kicks at the thought of never knowing him. I don't know how or when this person became such a huge part of my life, but I can't imagine my life without him in it. Which feels premature at best and delusional at worst. I know we've got something. I know that much. But this is my first time ever being interested in anyone. Julian has had plenty of experience and may not find all of this as earth-shattering as I do. I stamp the doubt down and focus on my work.

The day at Fit flies by. After we work out, help regulars, sign up new members and sell juice shots for Letty, we close just before sunset, program the doors for app entry and make our way to Brew to catch the sunset with Noah and Julian. I'm twitchy to hear how the first day went and to scope out the campers.

My heart thuds harder the closer we get, so I take some measured deep breaths. I'm sure the last name is a coincidence. Even if it is him, Chase doesn't know I'm here. I'm aware this thought loop is playing like a track on repeat.

Now that Lilly knows about Chase, I can just tell her my fear. I know she'd appoint herself my personal guard. That's how she rolls. And Brew would no doubt be buzzing with campers. All the cabins boast kitchenettes, and most campers relish the idea of making their own meals. But a young group of tent campers like the crew would most likely rely on Brew for their meals. I almost suggest we watch the sunset on Julian's deck, separate from the camping world, but I don't want to explain why. I decide to put it out of my mind and not to worry until there is something to worry about.

Compartmentalizing isn't new to me. It's a family trait.

We get to Brew with minutes to spare before the sun completely sinks into Blue Lake. The place is buzzing with activity. The parking lot is full. The outdoor string lights twinkle everywhere, creating a festive mood, as colorful umbrellas, chairs and ice chests litter the camping areas. Adults and kids scatter around the beach, on the patio, the walking trail—their energy infectious. Still in our gym clothes, we carry a change with us but hold off changing so we don't miss the sunset. That we're all equally obsessed with Blue Lake sunsets feels like I've clicked into my piece of the puzzle. My spot in the world. I can breathe here—in this place with these people. I hug my clothes tighter to my chest as I take it all in.

Julian's placing chairs around an outdoor propane heater when we walk up. He stops and smiles when we make eye contact. As he drapes a blanket across the back of the chair he moved, he offers it to me, sweeping his hand out invitingly.

"Thanks. The place looks amazing." You can feel the joy in the air, the anticipation of the season. Warmth and sunshine just make everything better, everyone happier. Even the little sisters are more social, stashing their phones for a millisecond and joining the conversation.

Lilly sits in the chair on my right; Julian takes the one on my left. Pete and Shelley join us while their two boys throw a Nerf football nearby.

"Hey, Littles," Noah aims at the sisters, "you're about to miss your photo op," and points to the glowing orb about to dip into the lake.

"Save our seats," Sydney, Noah's sister and the oldest of the group, calls as they dash down to the beach, phones in hand.

"Such a sweet big bro." Lilly sweeps the back of her index finger along Noah's cheek.

He captures her hand and kisses it, still watching the sisters pose.

The automatic gesture has me glancing sideways at the quiet figure to my left. When I do, hungry blue eyes lock on mine. I might not have as much experience, but I can read that look like it's spoken out loud. And the pull is like gravity. My head leans into that look. His hand reaches for mine.

"You guys want a photo of the four of you, commemorating opening day?" Shelley asks, pulling me out of the trance.

I surprise myself by speaking up first and passing my phone to her before anyone else. "Allie will love it." *I'll love it.* Why can I not admit that to myself? Admitting you need someone or love someone means it can wreck you if you lose them. It's why I don't begrudge my mom's absence from my life. Losing my dad didn't change the day to day for me and Via, except for seeing our mom broken down. But my mom lost her person. Tears sprang to my eyes at the thought of ever losing Julian permanently—and he wasn't even mine to lose. I shake my head to clear the trajectory of my thoughts.

"How's her trip going anyway?" Pete asks as Shelley gestures to us to scrunch closer together for the picture.

"Good," Julian and I answer at the same time.

Shit! We even sound like a couple.

Julian chuckles before he elaborates. "She says she's learning a lot and is excited to offer more features at Fit."

"Yeah, when she checked in with me a couple days ago, she sounded like she was loving it—especially the weather," I add. "Who knew the small-town girl was going to love Southern California?"

"You couldn't pay me enough to live in Southern California. Too many people," Lilly spouts loudly to the group.

One by one everyone chimes in agreeing with her—except the little sisters, who all declare they plan to go to college down there. An enthusiastic debate ensues, prompting varying opinions from their older siblings and even Pete and Shelley, who got to close Brew early and join us because, surprisingly, no campers need food tonight.

I don't weigh in and instead stare into the growing darkness, watching the color die on the water, turning it to black. I feel Julian's touch, small and unnoticed by everyone else.

He locks pinkies with me and leans his head over until I can feel his breath on my ear. "What's going on in there, Ever?" He speaks so low, no one would hear over the *best colleges* discussion.

"Hmm?" I play dumb. "Just enjoying the view."

"Mmm." He mimics my response. With a little squeeze of my pinkie, he drops his hand back into his lap but doesn't push me on it.

I force thoughts of college and the future from my mind, to be present in my new life, with these incredible people I consider my friends. It's been amazingly easy to immerse myself in life at Blue Lake. The place, the work, the beauty of it all and the relationships I'm making. For the first time, I feel like I truly belong. Like people see me and get me. And like me—for me. But if I pull back the lens a bit, what am I doing? Am I just going to hide out here in Blue Lake forever? Work at the gym and the café, tend to campers every season? Be a small-town girl, content with small-town life? I mean I could become a writer anywhere, any time. I don't even need a degree to do it. But learning, being in a classroom, it gives me all the feels. There was a time not so long ago I couldn't wait to get to a big campus and disappear among the throngs of students. Now all I want to do is work out and *play house* with this magnetic man next to me. Am I selling out for the first guy to ever pay attention to me? I don't want to believe that. I love my life here. Maybe dreams have a way of changing over time. We grow up and life changes us—our desires, goals, dreams.

Could I be content to learn online?

Online high school was one thing. It stopped being challenging anyway. The assignments were beyond easy and, because of that, the instructor let me grind out the rest of my assignments and turn them all in at once. I'm now technically and quietly a high school graduate. I didn't tell anyone—not even Via. I just did it. I appreciate the efficiency of getting my diploma through remote learning. But college? Part of the allure is going away and having the college experience. I'm not one for rushing sororities or anything, but there was a time in the recent past where I couldn't wait to study in those gorgeous libraries, sit in lecture halls, listen to thought-provoking discussions, expand my knowledge of and gain insight on the world around me. Maybe I'm more like my mom than I like to think and have a little wanderlust of my own.

"Well, if you're sure you can handle locking up, we'll get out of here." So much for dialing down my thoughts of the future. I zero back in on Pete and Shelley saying their goodbyes and Julian standing, shaking hands with Pete and assuring him he'd take care of everything.

"Come on, boys, time to go." Shelley gathers items strewn about by her "gremlins," as she calls them, while saying goodbye to all of us and inviting us to have café breakfast with them before work tomorrow. They kind of declare themselves our unofficial parents, although I guess they're only ten or fifteen years older than us.

As they herd their boys toward the parking lot and their vehicle, Julian asks Noah to help him lock up. When they walk away, Lilly pounces. "Girl, what's going on with you? You're so quiet. Tell Auntie Lilly what's going on."

"Eww, it creeps me out when you call yourself that. I'm technically older than you are anyway. And I'm good. Just got in my head about the future. All the college talk. I had it all planned out until I came here. I guess I'm feeling a little lost. But on the other hand, nothing in my life has ever felt more like home than this place feels right now. I'm just in my feels right now. Ignore me."

"Well, this place has a way of doing that to people. My advice—I know you didn't ask, but when has that ever stopped me?"

I arch an eyebrow and wait for her to continue.

"Don't overthink it. Things have a way of working out the way they're supposed to. And maybe for the first time in your life, you're not supposed to have it all figured out, planned, scheduled." She shrugs her shoulders with her hands out on either side. "Except for breakfast. Don't be late or there won't be any left." With that, she hugs me and kisses me on my cheek. "Love you, Davis. I'm glad you're here. See you tomorrow."

"Night, Lilly. Thanks."

"You can repay me with tea. I'm gonna want details." She smirks and blows me a kiss as she spins toward the parking lot where Noah waits by his truck.

After she turns to go, I stand, hugging myself, staring at the blackness of the lake, the chirp of crickets competing with the muted voices of settling campers. I remain contemplative after the debate over best college towns. I've mostly put all thoughts of my future out of my mind when I moved here. I only applied to a few schools—all in California and mostly down south. I didn't even know if I got into any.

The letters would've come to Oak Valley. And since arriving, I've been too preoccupied with my new life (and roommate) to worry about any of it. Part of me wants to freeze time and let it always stay this simple and peaceful. Logical me knew it couldn't.

Warm arms snake around me from behind. I can smell his now familiar scent before he speaks a word and lean back into his chest. Everything about him makes my nervous system exhale. My back melts into his chest as I lock my arms over his. His lips graze my ear and my head tilts to them instinctively.

"I kinda need to stay here tonight as the camp host. Wanna join me? Or should I drive you back to Allie's?" When I don't answer right away, he continues. "I mean, I want you to stay. If you want to. I want—"

"Tell me," I cut him off, turning in his arms. "What do you want?" I ask, surprising myself but needing to hear the words.

"I want you with me, next to me."

I smile in response, even though he can't see my face in the dark. His heartbeat thuds steadily in the ear pressed to his chest. "Okay." I feel his exhale like he held his breath waiting for my reply.

"Do you need to get anything from Allie's?"

"No, Lilly and I brought a change of clothes because we weren't sure what was on the agenda for tonight." I add with a low laugh, "We all technically still owe each other a cliff jump, but I'm not reminding them."

"Me neither." His deep chuckle rumbles against my cheek.

As I raise my face to his, he moves a lock of my hair behind my ear, letting his fingers skim my cheek. He dips his head and touches his lips to mine, so softly I almost wonder if I imagined it, but my lips tingle in the cooling air where his leave a touch of moisture. His fingers trail down my cheek to my neck, across my shoulder and down my arm as lightly as his lips touched mine. Goose bumps follow his trail.

Once his hand reaches mine, he laces our fingers, turns and pulls me toward him. In a pseudo dance move, he swings our joined hands across my body and over my head, releases my hand and drapes his arm around my shoulders as we walk toward his apartment.

I wrap my arm low around his waist as we walk and want to overanalyze how normal it all feels. Because I've never done anything like this in my life. But I've read about it plenty. It's not lost on me that Julian is as epic as any book boyfriend I've ever fantasized about. I catch myself holding my breath waiting for it all to vaporize before my eyes. Him. Blue Lake. All of it.

Has my life taught me not to trust the good times? Nothing lasts forever and people don't stay. That's what life has taught me so far. I want to hold on to him and this moment so tightly, but I'm equally scared to want or need it too much in case it goes away. I make my fingers unclench the side of his shirt and slide my hand down and hook two fingers on the side pocket of his joggers. While his thumb and index finger draw lazy circles on the ball of my shoulder, we walk in silence. Not awkward silence, peaceful silence. And I am at peace, aside from my constant internal dialogue that I've learned to function around and mostly ignore.

***

Stepping into his apartment, I take in the low lights—a lamp on the end table, a muted can light over the kitchen sink, the moonlight pouring in from the open slider. It's giving romantic vibes without the thirst, and it's working. Every cell in my body exhales as I step over the threshold.

"Hungry?" He drops his arm from my shoulders and ushers me inside. He stands just behind me when he asks.

I feel like I know him so well now. At least his energy, if not a lot of life details. We're both good at glazing over the specifics while sharing big moments of our pasts. Honesty without the vulnerability, I guess. "Maybe a little. Are you?"

His baritone chuckle is his only reply. He clears his throat. "I, uh, raided Brew for some snacks—cheese, olives, bread. Shelley made a little snack board for me to take home because we were all so busy, no one stopped to eat."

My stomach growls as he talks. With a small laugh he tugs me by the hand into the kitchen.

Whether it's the low lights, the familiar smell of his place—which smells like him—or the man himself, I tell myself to calm the hell down. My anticipation is palpable. To feign calmness, I hoist myself up onto the island bar, dangling my legs as he rummages through the fridge. He sets the snack board on the counter next to me and pulls the wrapping off the top. I reach down for an olive and pop one into my mouth. When I look up, he's watching my mouth and visibly swallows as I do. I lick my bottom lip as he turns back to the fridge and produces a bottle of champagne.

"Are we celebrating something?" I search his face, curious.

He nods, never taking his eyes off mine. I know him well enough to know he's not trying to get me drunk. He's trying to be romantic

. . . or thoughtful? And I want to let him. My heart flips at the sweet charm of this walking daydream of a man in front of me.

"Yeah. Graduation?" he asks, hopeful, and turns to get glasses.

He doesn't wait for an answer and pops the cork gently, instead of with party-like fanfare. I like that he doesn't disturb the quiet. He pours the gold bubbly into two stemless narrow glasses—real champagne flutes. I'm impressed and further captivated by the subtle class. He brings them to where I sit perched on the counter. As he hands me one, he clinks his to mine.

"Congratulations, Everly Davis."

My eyes widen.

"Were you not going to celebrate?" He raises his glass to his lips, so I do the same.

We both take a sip. It tickles my nose. He sets his down on the other side of the snack board, so I do the same. Then he takes a half step toward me, which puts his body between my legs. He places his hands on my legs just above my knees and softly moves them up and down my thighs.

"How'd you know?"

"Don't get mad. I swear it was accidental. But I saw the text from Mr. Rossi on your screen the other morning in my Jeep when you ran back inside for your water bottle. It dinged; I looked down. There it was." He leans his forehead into mine. "Why didn't you tell me? Or anyone?"

Wrapping my legs around his body, I hook them on his hips and lock my ankles.

He curls his hands around the underside of my legs and squeezes, his face inches from mine.

I shrug in his embrace. "Dubious honor?" I say it like a question, but I'm not looking for an answer. Graduation ceremonies are unnecessarily long and tedious, and finishing high school remotely seemed a great excuse to avoid it all.

"Well, my little genius, I think it's a big deal—especially since you finished early."

His breath heats my parted lips. They catch his exhale as my hands rise from the edge of the counter where my fingers curl around the granite. They land delicately on his biceps. His muscles contract at my touch. I glide my hands up his arms to his shoulders, then the sides of his neck. His pulse thuds under my palms.

"Say it again." My nails curl into his skin at the nape of his neck, urging him closer.

"Say what?" His lids flutter closed, and a low, almost undetectable growl sounds from his throat just before his lips meet mine. A light kiss at first.

I tilt my head and lean in, pressing our lips together harder, pulling him closer, my nails digging in just a little more.

His lips close over my bottom lip, sucking softly. The wayward curl that always falls on his forehead tickles my temple before his tongue meets mine, soft and cool and tasting like champagne. My legs tighten around his waist and my body inches closer. His hands curl around my lower back and down, cupping my ass. He scoots me all the way off the counter, carrying me now, never breaking the kiss. With my eyes closed, still kissing him, I can tell we're moving out of the kitchen and down the hall. To his bedroom. He wraps both arms around my back tightly, pressing every part of my torso against him. The heat rushing to my lower region has me grinding against him.

Julian's strength turns me on. He effortlessly carries me into his room. Him calling me his? Swoon-worthy. More low light flickers from a small candle on his dresser, another reflecting off the mirror in the attached bathroom. The slider is open in here too and the breeze coming in cools my fevered skin. Still holding me, still kissing me, he leans one knee on his bed. With my eyes still closed, lost in the kiss, I feel the dip. Smoother than a Hollywood sex scene, he lays me down on the bed. As soon as my back meets the cushion of the mattress, I unwrap my legs from his hips and he settles his body between them, his excitement hard against my inner thigh. He doesn't press into me, so I fight the urge to press into him. My body knows what it wants, but I have no idea what I'm doing. I tell myself not to think, just feel. I want him to set the pace, show me how. And I want him to call me his again. His lips pull back from mine and my eyes flutter open to drown in the deep blue of his.

"Hi, pretty girl." He traces a finger down my cheek as he says it.

"Hi, Julie." My lashes lower and my cheeks heat.

"Congratulations."

"You already said that."

He made that low chuckling sound I love and pecks my lips with his, resting his forehead on mine. "You told me to say it again." Then his lips lightly kiss the tip of my nose.

"Not that part. You said 'my little genius before.'" I lower my eyes to hide my neediness.

"Ohhh. You like being called genius. Well, you are. I'm proud of you, Ever."

"Not that part. You said 'my.'" My voice is barely above a whisper.

He lifts his head in acknowledgment, then rests his forehead on mine for a second. Bringing his lips to my ear, he whispers, "You want to be mine, Ever?"

"M-hm." I nod and trace a fingernail around the shell of his ear.

His low deep laugh tickles my ear before he says, "What am I gonna do with you?"

"Are you asking for suggestions? Because I was hoping you'd lead."

He barks a loud short laugh, pecking me soundly on the lips. "My sassy girl." With another quick kiss, he rolls off the bed and stands as he says, "I'll be right back."

Without his body covering mine, the cool breeze wafting in from the open slider chills my skin. An involuntary shiver sends me to the slider, closing it. I stand with my arms wrapped around me, gazing out into the darkness of the lake. I can see the surface reflected in the moonlight. Beautiful and dark, promising and haunting.

Julian comes back with our glasses of champagne. He hands me one and takes a small sip of his.

"I don't think I've ever seen you drink. I thought maybe you didn't," I say as I take a sip.

"I really don't. An occasional beer, but I just don't care for it, I guess."

"Bad experience?"

"You could say that."

"But you don't want to talk about it." And really, neither do I, but this is a rare time I felt the need to fill the silence.

Julian sees through it. He tucks a lock of hair behind my ear and says, "I just wanted to celebrate you and your milestone. That calls for a toast. And . . . I thought it would be . . . relaxing."

He's nervous.

I was counting on him to show me the way, but somehow recognizing his nerves gives me confidence, like I couldn't fuck this up if I tried. I take another a sip of my champagne and set it down on the desk next to the slider. I keep my eyes on his as he stretches to set his glass beside mine.

I curl my fingers into the soft cotton covering his chest and pull the wad of gray fabric toward me. When his lips meet mine, I open mine and deepen the kiss. I let go of the clenched-up fabric and slide my hands down to the hem of his shirt and push it up his torso, feeling every defined ab muscle as I go.

His body is a specimen.

Once I push it up to his chest, he reaches above and behind him, pulls it over his head with one hand and drops it to the floor. He reaches down and does the same thing to my top. I lift my arms over my head as he pulls it up and off, dropping it next to his on the floor. Even with my sports bra tight across my breasts, I can feel my nipples straining against the material. His free hand grazes across one nipple, sliding down my body, and hooks inside my leggings. The other hand joins it, and they slide the leggings over my hips and down my legs. Once they're halfway down, I use my feet to push them the rest of the way and step out of them.

I mirror him and push my hands into the waistband of his joggers and begin sliding them down. He steps out of them easily when they puddle at his feet.

Standing in front of each other, me in a sports bra and thong, him in boxer briefs, I back up toward the bed. He follows me, clasping our hands together down at our sides, locking our fingers. When the backs of my knees meet the edge of the mattress, I sit and edge backward until I can lie back.

Julian doesn't release my hands. Instead, he pins my forearms down above my head with his, our hands still locked and settles himself on top of me. He partially supports his weight with his legs, so he doesn't crush me.

I think I want him to crush me. I know I want more. I want his full weight on me. To feel his hard body pressing into my softness. When I squirm a little to try to free my hands, which I plan to use to pull him to me, he gives me what I want.

He doesn't let my arms go, but he presses into me, sending a rush of moisture between my legs.

"Mmm, Julie." I lift my hips, begging for what I want with my body.

"I know, Ever. Me too." This he whispers in my ear, his breath heavy and hot. He kisses the tender spot behind my ear and places tiny kisses down my neck, sucking slightly on my pulse. He pulls the strap of my bra off my shoulder and kisses the skin it reveals. He keeps pulling it down until the fabric gives and uncloaks one breast. His hand goes to the side of my breast, softly clenching as his lips settle around the jut of my nipple while his tongue draws lazy circles, teasing the peak.

My back arches off the bed, seeking more.

His other hand follows suit, dragging the constricting fabric off my other breast and lightly squeezing as his mouth finds and gives equal time to that nipple.

My hands that were clenching the pillowy comforter fly to curl around his neck and pull his head down harder. The fade of hair on his nape, the texture, has me scraping my nails back and forth, almost scratching his skin there. He moans a little and rolls his neck like he likes it. I rub my hand up the back of his head, loving the soft spikiness of it, and press him tight to my chest.

His teeth nip at the sensitive bud, and I gasp. While one hand holds him down tight to my chest, the other flies back to the comforter, clenching it in my fist. With a low chuckle, he releases it with a pop and trails kisses down my stomach, dragging the bra with him as he goes.

I lift my hips as he shimmies it over them and down my legs, where I pull each leg free one by one. I didn't know my bra would come off over my hips and ass. Where there is a will, I guess. The thought extracts a giggle that quickly turns to a moan when his lips find my center through my thong.

His lips tighten around my hardened bud as his fingers pull my thong to the side. He slides into the slick wetness effortlessly.

My hips rise to meet the welcome invasion.

"So wet, so soft."

I barely hear him as his mouth continues to put pressure on my most sensitive spot. My hand moves from the back of his neck to his wrist, urging his hand to give me more. A second finger joins the first one, and I cry out.

His hand freezes, his fingers still inside me. His mouth stops. He eases his fingers out of me and reaches his other hand up to stretch himself out beside me. He nuzzles my neck and places soft kisses near my ear.

My chest heaves with intensity. I roll somewhat to face him, resting my hand on his chest. I feel his heart racing in time with mine and peer up into his eyes under my lashes. "Why'd you stop?"

"I just . . . want to be careful with you." He heaves in a breath, telling me the restraint costs him. "I don't want to hurt you."

"Mmm," I moan. "I could argue that you . . . stopping . . . hurts."

His half smile shows in the moonlight and comes with that deep chuckle I love so much. It sends another flood of moisture rushing between my legs, and I squirm slightly. He brings his hand up to my face and traces one finger down my cheek. The finger he just used on me. The finger that was just inside me?

I take his hand and lead it down my body to the vee of my legs and push his palm into my heat. "Don't make me beg, Julie."

"I think I'd probably like that."

"Yeah? Like this? Please, Julie." I lower my lashes, wanting to turn him on the way he turns me on, but I'm not sure I can pull it off without melting into a puddle of embarrassment. His hard-on twitches against my leg, and it empowers me. I say more as he draws circles around my sensitive bud through the satin lace of my thong. "I want you. So much. Please."

"Please what, Ever? Tell me. What do you want?"

I'm new to all of this, especially the sexy talk. Not even in my fantasies do I do that. But I like it, and I want to play along, because it's turning me on. I shut off the part of my brain that wants to overthink this and try to feel my way. "I want to feel you, your hands on me. In me again. Please." I beg as my pelvis squirms, unintentionally emphasizing my words.

"I got you, Ever. Easy, babe." With that, he pulls my thong to the side and slides his finger into me again.

I moan deep in my throat. "Yesssss," I hiss this through clenched teeth. My body feels like coiled wire ready to snap. God, I want this man. There's no room in my brain for anything but him and what he's doing to me and what I want him to do to me. I can't think, only feel.

He's pulling out and pushing into me harder and faster. I feel the pressure when he adds another finger and can't help raising my hips to meet each thrust. His thumb hits my clit with each thrust and sends my back bowing off the bed each time.

I'm panting with the pressure building inside me.

His labored breath brushes my neck, my ear, my cheek as he places fevered kisses along my jaw. "Are you gonna come for me, sweet girl? Come for me, Ever."

I cry out as my body clenches around his fingers and begins throbbing with my orgasm. He slows his thrust and keeps moving in small circles inside me. Every nerve ending down there is twitching, and I almost can't take the sensation of his movements. I reach down to clasp his wrist, to still his hand.

He pushes against my resistance and continues to make me come.

I feel the wetness seeping out of me. My breathing is so labored it's more panting.

As he keeps moving his fingers lightly now and the waves subside, his lips touch my ear and he whispers, "Easy, babe. I got you. So beautiful, Ever."

A tear slips down my cheek and stops when it meets his lips.

He kisses the trail of it all the way to the corner of my eye and rests his forehead on my temple. He slowly removes his fingers from me, and I immediately mourn the loss. I feel swollen and sore, but in a good way. And now empty and wanting more.

Julian rolls away from me, leaving his hand on my stomach as if to say he's not going anywhere.

In the moonlight, I see him reach into the nightstand drawer and hear him grasp what sounds like a plastic wrapper. A condom. My heart leaps in my chest as heat and moisture rush to my center again. "I'm . . . on the pill . . . for my periods. If you . . . if we don't . . . you know . . ."

He looks over his shoulder at me, and even in the darkness his eyes look dark, pupils huge. "I've been tested, and I've always used protection. I just want to be safe, responsible."

I nod my head. "Yeah, okay." I reach up to clasp his arm.

He rubs his hand in short strokes on my tummy before reaching into the drawer.

I let my arm fall and drape across my body, waiting. I want to touch myself, I'm so keyed up. I hear a top flip open on what sounds like a tube.

Julian stands, strips off his boxer briefs and returns to the edge of the bed. He rolls on the condom and strokes himself in the flickering candlelight. "This will help. I don't want to hurt you," he says, his hand moving up and down on himself.

I swallow. My throat is desert dry as I watch.

He turns his body toward me, one leg curled beside mine, the other bent over the edge of the bed. The hand he just had on himself reaches for me, touching me again. As soon as his fingers make contact, it sends a jolt straight to my sweet spot. He slips a finger inside me again and moves his thumb in circles on my clit while his finger crooks in a come here motion, eliciting a deep moan from me. He leans over to capture my moan with his lips, his tongue.

I can't even kiss him back and instead pant as another orgasm starts to take over my body. I'm not even sure it took more than two minutes to send me writhing again. I can't control my body or the sounds I'm making. I vaguely wonder if anyone has ever hyperventilated from an orgasm.

Then he's whispering in my ear, "Sweet, Ever. So beautiful. I got you."

As I come back to earth and my breathing slows, he gently positions himself between my legs. He lifts one of my legs, pushing it up and bending it at the knee. I instinctively hook it onto his hip, wrapping it around him. I feel his smooth tip at my opening. He uses his hand to slowly ease himself in. The tip slips in effortlessly. Pressing, he inches into me until he meets resistance and stops.

Don't think. Just feel.

I grasp his hips and pull him down toward me, wanting all of him, my heart thudding so hard and so loud in my ears it's like white noise.

In a blink he grabs my arms and pins them to the bed with his own, interlocking our fingers so we're touching elbow to palm. Our hands on either side of my head. He dips his head to mine and whispers urgently into my ear, "Let me go slow, Ever. I don't want to hurt you." With our bodies touching from groin to forehead, he grinds his hips a little and rocks into me.

I feel the slipperiness, despite the tightness. With each rocking motion, I feel him push into me a little more. His chest grazes my nipples as he moves up and down, sending shock waves with each pass. I'm experiencing so many sensations at once, I feel like I'll break apart. A slight burn down below, the electric shock in each nipple and now he's kissing the side of my neck, which is curling my toes. Then I feel it. The searing burn as the pressure intensifies. Then a rip. I cry out, and Julian freezes. I know he's all the way in now because I can feel his rough manscaped stubble tickling the bundle of swollen and hypersensitive nerves.

After a few frozen moments, Julian kisses the corner of my lips, my temple. He rocks back and forth little by little, stretching me to accommodate him, placing tiny kisses along my neck. Sucking my pulse there as the pain eases, the burn subsides, and the sensitivity increases.

I'm digging my nails into the backs of his hands and arching my back. The sting of penetration is still there, but the urgency and craving is rivaling my discomfort.

He releases one of my hands to cradle my breast, lowers his head and takes my nipple into his mouth, sucking hard. With my now freed hand, I cling to the back of his neck and pull him to my breast tighter. The rocking motion turns to grinding, then he slowly eases out of me an inch, maybe two and back in repeatedly until he slips in easily. He repeats it, pulling out a little more, pushing back in a little harder each time. The tension building in both of us.

I feel him shaking with restraint, and I'm undone for the heart of this man. So gentle. So careful. I moan his name. "Julie."

He answers right back. "Yeah? You okay, Ever?"

"M-hm. So good. Please don't stop." I breath the words more than say them.

That little chuckle again. "No chance. Ugh. You feel so good. So perfect." He pulls out almost all the way and slams into me kind of hard. "You okay?" His words are breathless. "Feel good? Ugh, so wet. Tell me it feels good, Ever."

"So good, Julie. I ... ung, I'm gonna ..." A half cry, half scream rips from my throat.

I wrap my legs tight around him and raise my hips to meet his thrust. I start shaking with the release of my orgasm and feel the convulsions in Julian inside me. I cling to him as we both fall off the edge. I feel the tears track into my ears from the corners of my eyes. Just a couple. I've never read about that in any books. I don't know what to make of them, but so far, it's my norm. Maybe my body can't take all the emotions and needs another avenue of release. I squeeze my eyes shut, provoking another trail of tears.

Julian's head was tucked into my neck as he came, his lips parted on my skin. Now he rains little kisses on my neck, cheek, lips. Light, feathery kisses as he rolls to the side and pulls my body with him, keeping our bodies as close together as he can. "Hi," he says when I roll toward him and look up at him under my lashes.

"Hi." My brain wants to be shy, but my body is singing, so I say what my body wants to say. "Best graduation gift ever."

It's met with his alluring chuckle and a sweet kiss on the lips.

Chapter 31

Julian

"Why do I feel like the one who got a gift?" I wrap my arms around her and squeeze.

"Mmmm." She sighs next to me.

"You tired? Sleepy?"

"Not really. Just relaxed. You?"

"Same. But thirsty. Want some water?"

"Sure, thanks."

I get up, snag my boxers from the floor, slip them on and head to the kitchen. When I return with two glasses of water, Ever is coming out of the bathroom with my T-shirt on. It barely covers her ass. It's now officially my favorite shirt, as long as she's wearing it just like that. My phone vibrates on the nightstand. It's my alarm tone. "You're officially out of high school. Congratulations, Ever."

"Thanks, Julie. Um, you set an alarm?"

"I did." Why do I feel embarrassed by this? "I wanted to make sure we commemorated the occasion," I add shyly.

"Did I tell you how much I liked my gift?" She, on the other hand, is less shy around me, and I love that she seems more her authentic self.

"I think you did. And even if you didn't, I got the impression you enjoyed it."

"I did. I didn't think I was supposed to."

My eyebrow arches at her comment.

"You know, you hear the horror stories." She sits down on my bed and crosses her legs, looking very much at home, to my delight.

I sit down facing her, one leg half curled in front of me, the other hanging off the side with my foot resting on the floor. I reach for her and place my hand flat on her thigh. The index finger of my other hand draws lazy circles around her ankle on the opposite leg. I lean in and kiss her lightly on the lips. I couldn't stop touching her right now with a gun to my head.

As if she can read my mind, she asks, "So, can we do it again?"

With a half laugh, half groan, I reach my hands under her ass and hoist her up onto my lap.

She instinctively straddles me, wrapping her legs around me. Her hands toy with the buzzed hair above the back of my neck, sending goose bumps down my arms and heat to my groin. She presses into me lightly, causing my dick to twitch.

"Uhhh, I don't want to hurt you."

Her eyelids drop with the faint nod of her head.

I lift her chin with my finger and thumb. "Ever, believe me when I say I want you every second of every day. We just need to . . . go slow at first. Okay?"

Her nod this time is less subtle. She adds a half-crooked smile to go with it.

I pull her lips to mine with the slight grip I have on her chin. Her tongue finds mine eagerly as her hands clench my neck. She grinds on me roughly and I feel her whole body tense. Her tongue freezes. She scoots herself back from my quickly hardening crotch.

I know it must've hurt her, which causes a pit in my stomach.

She tries to start kissing me again, but I stop her. "Hey. Let's go sit in the hot tub."

"Okay."

She's shy and unsure of herself again.

I hate it, because she's perfect. I want her to never feel less than perfect. I stand and bring her with me, setting her on the ground facing me. "The hot tub will make . . . ease any soreness you may have." I feel my face flushing, but I continue because I hate that she might be in any pain at all because of me. "And it won't always feel that way after. Just the first time, as far as I know."

"Okay."

"Ever."

"Julie."

"Look at me."

She looks up under her lashes.

My gut clenches at how young and fragile she looks, half shadowed in the moonlight. I want to protect her from every shitty thing this world might throw at her. Except me. I selfishly won't save her from me. But I can try to make her happy. And I will try. I promise myself that. "You're the most beautiful and perfect girl I've ever seen in my life. I can't even describe how beautiful—inside and out. Don't think for one second that I don't want you—"

"Every second of every day?" She interrupts me with her signature sass.

I love this girl.

That thought slams into my brain without warning. I quickly turn from her in case my face gives away the shock it prompted. Clutching her hand, I snag two robes from the closet, head through the slider, and out to the hot tub.

I leave the outdoor lights off. The moon illuminates our way as steam billows toward the sky when I lift the lid. Still holding her hand, I guide her shirt up over her head and drop it on a nearby chair, leading her up the steps and down into the tub. Once I sink in next to her, I ask "Jets?"

She opts for the silence.

I like that. Although the crickets are loud and conversations from campers waft up to us every so often, it's still quiet. Her sigh flutters my heart. She leans her head back and gazes up at the sky looking utterly content. I reach for her and run my finger down the side of her neck from behind her ear. She turns her angelic face to me and flashes the sweetest smile. The flutter becomes a hammer. She ducks under the surface and pops up in front of me. Slithering onto my lap, she straddles me on her knees. Ever is gorgeous any day. Ever gleaming wet in the moonlight? Drop-dead. I swallow as she inches her face toward mine. My shy girl is nowhere to be found. The warm, wet heat must agree with her body.

She tilts her head and locks her parted lips on mine, delving in with her tongue. She strokes mine, in and out. Much like the way I plunged in and out of her earlier. It sends a message straight to my cock.

My hands travel down her naked body, curving around both cheeks of her ass. I pull her toward me, my erection flat against her navel. Before she can grind herself on me, I reach between us and draw light circles until she's panting in my ear and biting my neck. I know she's never done any of this before, so her response to me is even more of a turn-on.

"Please," she breathes into my ear, pressing into my hand.

I keep teasing her sensitive bud and slip a finger inside her.

Her teeth scrape the sensitive skin on my neck on her sharp inhale. "Too much?"

"No. Don't. Ung. Stop."

I oblige gently until it's not enough.

She grips my bicep in a now familiar unspoken "more."

I lift her out of the water, drape a robe carelessly over her shoulders and cradle her as I walk us back inside. Laying her down on the robe on the bed, I waste no time kissing down her body until I get to the center of her heat. There I kiss her softly at first, then increase the intensity. Slipping a finger inside her, I curl the tip up toward me over and over.

Combined with the circles my tongue draws on her clit, she bows off the bed and clasps her hands around my head. The sound she makes as she comes is part moan, part cry and utterly primal.

I could almost explode watching her come undone. I want inside her so badly, but I want to give her body some time. When she settles down, still panting a little, I stretch out next to her and blow softly on the side of her neck where her wet hair clings to her skin.

She rolls to face me and reaches down to touch me, shyly at first. Then she wraps her hand around my head and squeezes a little, like she's unsure of herself.

I take her hand in mine and interlock our fingers. "It's okay, Ever. You don't have to."

"Julie, stop being so careful with me." When I don't immediately respond, she adds, "Okay?" She traces a fingernail around the hollow heart tattoo. "So what if I'm sore? Maybe it hurts in a good way." Her fingernail lightly follows the trail of hair down until it's grazing the head of my dick. Her voice is barely a whisper. "I want to be good for you too. Show me?" She looks up from under her lashes. "Please."

I bring her hand to my lips and kiss her palm. "Ever? The way you feel? That's how I feel. You feel so good to me. Whatever we do . . . or don't do." But I want to give her what she wants, because I want it too. I stand from the bed and lean my knees on the edge of the mattress and hold my hand out to her.

She takes it and kneels on the bed in front of me.

I place her hand lightly around me and guide it along my hard length. She touches her lips to the head of my dick, then peeks her tongue out between her lips and grazes the opening and the sensitive underside. I arch at the intensity. I want her to know how good this feels. Running my fingers through her hair, my thumb draws circles around her ear.

She opens her mouth and sinks her lips down my shaft, ripping a groan from my throat. I feel the tip touch the back of her throat and hiss through my teeth. I tug a handful of her hair back, encouraging her to slide her lips back. She does and then plunges them around me again. Over and over, I watch her cheeks hollow with each effort until I can't take it anymore. With my palms under her jaw, I bring her lips to mine and kiss her until we're both panting.

I lay her back onto the bed and settle myself between her legs. I dip my finger into her and find her wet and ready. I stretch to reach a condom on the nightstand and tear it open with my teeth. She takes it from my hand, so I help her guide it on the tip of my dick and roll it down my shaft before I edge myself into her and sink.

She squeezes my ass with both hands, urging me deeper. I resist, bracing my arms on each side of her, supporting my weight. A frustrated groan escapes her lips. She wraps her legs tight around me and tries to roll us so that she's on top. With a quiet laugh, I let her. When she's sitting on top of me, still joined together, I lift her hips a little and slide out of her, then lower her slowly until she gasps. I know she doesn't get that it's more intense with her on top. But I want her to feel empowered, like she's in control. Once I'm completely sheathed, I hold her hips still. She tries to arch up again, but I hold her steady, then I rock her hips back and forth.

I feel her clit on my pelvic bone. Her guttural gasp tells me she likes this. I do it again. She takes over, rocking, gasping until she's on the edge. I use my thumb to coax her over as she cries out and collapses on me, convulsing around me, and I realize I'm shaking. I hold her until her breathing calms. Her orgasm slicks over me. I know any pain will be minimal now. I lift her head to look at me and kiss her softly.

"Hi, Ever."

"Hi, Julie." She smiles so sweetly.

I raise her hips and drop her down suddenly and completely on me. Her mouth makes a perfect, mind-numbing O as her cry rips through the silent room. She quickly lifts her hips and drops her ass down on me again, harder. I let her set the rhythm and she does. She drives me up into her over and over until I can't breathe. All I see is her body moving up and down on me and I can't control myself. I grab her hips and bury myself deep inside her with one final thrust as my orgasm pulses into her. And I feel her walls tighten around me and contract again as she collapses on me, kissing my chest, my nipples, my tattoo.

As our orgasms subside, she rests her face against my neck, her soft breaths creating moisture there. I nuzzle into her lips, and she rewards me with light kisses. How is she so perfect? She knows exactly what I want in this moment and she's brand new at this. It's like she was made just for me. Even though I know that can't be true because I don't deserve her or this. It won't stop me from having it though. I can't deny her, even if I wanted to. I'm putty in her hands, but she's too innocent to know that.

Her breathing evens out and I dip my chin to look at her face. She's asleep. And if tonight and everything we shared wasn't enough to do it, this exquisite creature sound asleep, spent from her first night of sex, splayed out on top of me surely did it. The heart I was convinced I no longer had fell out of my chest and lay bleeding on the floor at her feet. She could break me if she wanted. Destroy me. Even more than my past has already tried.

Slowly and silently, I shift with her in my arms onto our sides and pull the edge of the comforter around us. In seconds, I follow her into sleep.

Chapter 32
Everly

I smell the rain before my ears track the patter outside. The slider is still partly open, and I can see the day is giving coastal vibes without the coast. Warm, muggy, overcast. I've always loved it. Kinda mirrors my soul. Dark and broody. But today it looks fresh and cleansing. Just like it smells.

I'm not surprised to wake up alone. In all the weeks we've shared living space and then a bed, I've never woken before him. I've wondered more than once if the guy even sleeps. I figure he's up drinking coffee, maybe even outside on the deck. I wonder how he'll greet me. Will we kiss? Hug? More? My cheeks warm at the thought, and my center tingles. I clench my thighs and feel the soreness with the pressure. I press my hand to my crotch to both stave off my body's reaction and ease the discomfort. I'm smiling so wide my cheeks ache.

I swipe his discarded shirt from the end of the bed and pull it down over my head and stretch my arms. Swinging my legs over the side, resting my toes on the floor, I reach for my phone on the nightstand. I see his name on the screen, notifying me of a text—from him. My heart sinks. He's not here? This insecure morning-after mindset is something the books don't prepare you for. It's all snuggly and sweet between the pages. The real world launches a swarm of nervous butterflies and spiraling what-ifs.

Julian: Brew is slammed with campers dodging the rain. Helping Pete and Shelley man the crowd. I didn't want to wake you. Take your time but come join the party when you wake up. I made you coffee.

Phew. The helper in me wants to run right down and get to work, but I need a shower. I shift into work mode though and jet into the bathroom to crank the shower. While the water warms, I head to the kitchen to pour coffee. All thoughts of slow good morning kisses squelched, although it lands equal parts gloom and relief. The rush would surely stave off any awkwardness. Maybe by the time the crowd dissipates, we'll have moved past the awkward *morning-after* portion of the program.

***

I've never had so much fun in a frenzied swarm. Okay, I've never experienced or worked in a "frenzied swarm" before. But still. Brew has been at capacity since I walked through the doors. An "all hands on deck" scenario, and everyone showed up. Lilly and Noah, their sisters, Pete and Shelley, of course. The whole atmosphere is one of connected cheerfulness. The gloomy weather did nothing to dampen spirits of the campers or the employees. Even Letty came to seat people and bus tables. She also brought a cooler full of juice shots and offered them to the waiting patrons.

"Most of the tables are low on napkins. I can fill them, but where do you keep the stock?" She pokes her head into the kitchen from the swinging doors.

"I got you, Letty. They're on a shelf in the office. I'll run and grab them." I set down the unopened pack of tortillas I just took from the refrigerator to continue our breakfast burrito assembly line. "Be right back, guys," I call to the little sisters over my shoulder as I push past the swinging doors into the main dining room of the café. My cheeks hurt from smiling as I rush down the hall to the office. The crack of the cue ball on the pool table in the game room just adds to the vibe. Rushing past, I catch the group of young men playing pool. My mind has seconds to register the familiar faces just before I hear his voice.

"Evvie? Oh my God. It *is* you."

I freeze.

My heart slams against my rib cage like it wants to escape my chest. His hand on my shoulder turning my body is gentle but feels like a vise. My teeth clamp down on my lower lip after my tongue juts out to pull it inward. I look up into Chase's face, beaming like we're long-lost friends. Like he isn't the one who turned my life upside down.

"What are you doing here?" he asks conversationally. Looking down my body and back up to my face, taking in my appearance—leggings and a knotted oversized Brew shirt I snagged from Julian's closet this morning. "Do you . . . work here?"

Work. Brew. Julian.

I snap out of my freeze state. "Uh, yeah, and . . . you can see we're slammed so . . . I better get back to it." I turn and rush into the office, closing and locking the door behind me. Leaning against the door, I begin to shake. Tears roll down my cheeks one after the other silently as I sink to the floor.

Fuck! I knew it! I knew it would be him.

I let myself forget for a minute. *Goddammit.* I want to run. Disappear. But I can't go back out there. I don't want any of them to know I'm here. But now he knows. I don't want to leave Blue Lake. That thought makes my stomach twist sickeningly. I don't know what to do. I wish I could rewind the morning. I'd think more clearly. I'd pay more attention. I could've seen him before he saw me. I could've avoided him, all of them, until they left. No one would've known. Now it's ruined. This place. This life. I can't start over again. Where would I even go this time?

The doorknob jiggling above my head sends me scurrying back from the door. "Ev?" *Lilly.* "Hey, you in there?"

"Uh, yeah." I force my voice to project normalcy. "Just had to, uh, just needed a minute. I'll be right out." I hold my breath, waiting, listening. After a moment, I hear her footsteps retreat. I exhale. I pull my legs up to my chest and curl my arms around them and, with my chin on my knees, I stare at the door. I should be thinking of what to do next, but my mind is a blinding white room. They say the mind is powerful. Mine is blank. Beyond wishing this would all go away, I can't figure my way out of this. Did they all see me? Would he tell them if they didn't? I only noticed guys. Is Kendall here? Although I can't see her camping, cabin or not.

The sound of a key sliding into the lock pierces my thought spiral moments before Julian's frame fills the doorway. He's crouching in front of me as the door latches behind him.

I look into the blue pools staring back at me and take a shaky breath. "Hi, pretty girl."

"Hi, Julie."

"What's going on in there?" His finger swipes my hair back from my temple and tucks it behind my ear.

My head swivels slowly from side to side as I lower my gaze. "I knew it would be him."

His hand stills where it's tracing lazy circles around my ear. His fingers snake around the back of my neck while his thumb urges my chin up. "Him who, Ever?" His jaw clenches on the question.

Blowing a shaky breath through my pursed lips, I confess. "Chase. I saw his last name. On the reservations. I didn't think . . . I'd hoped it wasn't. I should've checked. Been more careful. He saw me." Another shaky breath. "He stopped me. He knows I'm here."

"Okay." Julian mirrors my exhale and sinks to the floor in front of me, crossing his legs. That someone as muscled as him is flexible enough to cross his legs travels through the head haze and makes my radar, raising the corner of my mouth in a half smile. His palms pace up and down along the sides of my thighs that are still tucked against my stomach. Dipping his head to get in my line of vision again, he asks, "Did he hurt you? Touch you?"

I quickly shake my head. "No. no. He just . . . he called out to me. He stopped me. He knows it's me. I can't go back out there."

"Ever." Squeezing my thighs as he says my name brings my eyes level with his. "You're one of the strongest people I've ever met."

I roll mine at that.

"You are," he repeats. "And brave." He nods as he adds that. "Give me a minute, okay? I'll be right back." When I don't readily agree, he leans his face toward mine and presses his lips to my forehead. "Okay?" he asks again and then pecks my lips.

I nod.

He fluidly rises and disappears, closing the door behind him.

I stay as I am, turning my cheek to rest it on one knee. I wipe the dampness on the fabric of my leggings. Heat rises from my stomach and burns my chest, then my face.

I'm pissed.

Fuck Chase! Fuck all of them! I left their stupid town they seem to think they run. They can have Oak Valley. Blue Lake is mine. I'm starting to make a life here. One I like. Maybe love. One I'm not letting go of. Or running from. Fuck him. And Kendall. And all of them. Except Via and maybe Ryan. *Shit!* Are they here too? Via would've told me. Right? The fact that I'm not a hundred-percent confident of the answer pisses me off more. I gather myself and stand with a half-cocked notion to call Via immediately and demand to know.

Then Julian is filling my vision again. His hands clasp my shoulders, drawing me into his arms. His wingspan impresses me despite my current meltdown. Each arm extends across my back, hands resting on opposite shoulders. "He's gone." He rests his chin on top of my head as he says it.

Stepping back, I drop my hands from his back to each hip and pin my stare on his. "For real?"

"For real." He adds, "Can I fill you in later, after the crowd? But I promise, Ever, he's gone. They all are." He releases me from his grasp but wraps his pinkie around my forefinger as he pivots and softly tugs me toward the door.

I tug back and release his pinkie, my bottom lip finding my teeth again. "Here." I spin and reach up for the box of napkins on the stock shelves to my right. "Can you give these to Letty on your way to the kitchen? I just need a minute."

"Yeah." He winks at me on his way out like he has every confidence I won't bail.

And maybe that's why I don't.

I dip into the bathroom right outside the office door and peek at my reflection. Splotchy skin, bloodshot eyes. *Great!* I wet my hands with the frigid tap water and place them on my cheeks. I expect them to sizzle. I do that a few more times and decide it's as good as it's gonna get. I swallow the urge to punch the image in the mirror. When did the self-loathing start? Maybe when I ran instead of told Chase to fuck off to his face. I hope Julian did. I stare back at the smug smile in the mirror.

You're so brave behind your ripped . . . Is he my boyfriend? I shake off the train of my thoughts. *One mental spiral at a time, Ev, okay?*

I take three deep breaths and turn to rejoin the others. I want to help with the crowd. Via would be my first order of business when I finish at Brew.

***

"Oh my God, Evvie. WTF?" Via says the letters instead of the words. She rarely says the word fuck. "If I'd had any idea, I would've said. I swear. Ryan too. He said he didn't know. And he's never mentioned you being at Allie's. To any of the crew. Not even Chase. He admits that Chase has brought you up a few times. And he did ask Ryan to go camping with them. Guy trip. But we already had plans."

I don't know what to say to Via. I just listen to her spiral, wondering what to tell her about my life here. So much has happened since I first arrived. I feel like a completely different person from the one who walked away from Oak Valley just weeks ago.

"So, what did he say to you anyway?" Her question stops my musing.

"Nothing. I didn't really give him the chance. We were slammed at Brew because of the rain so I made an excuse and bailed. When I came back from getting supplies, they were gone. But he texted me once, a while back. I didn't respond and blocked the number."

I purposely leave out that Julian took care of it. First because I don't know yet how he "took care of it." And second, because Via doesn't know about Julian yet. I don't even know how to explain Julian. Except to say that I'd finally done what everyone in Oak Valley already accused me of and that it was mind blowing and that I couldn't wait to do it again. But Via isn't going to hear any of that anyway. I'm not even sure I can tell Lilly without setting my face on fire. Just thinking about it sends heat to my cheeks and my center at once.

"Shit. He just texted Ryan, asking to swing by here. Shit, Evvie. Want me to ask him about texting you?"

"No!" I spit out instantly. "Let him wonder if he texted the wrong person."

"Okay, I won't say a word. Promise. Listen, Evvie, I wanted to tell you something. I was going to call you anyway. I wanted you to be the first to hear. Forget about Chase for a second. Fuck him. I have news."

My heart skips then triple thuds in my chest. I can feel my pulse in the fingertips gripping my phone. But I fake calm well, or I used to. "Did you just say the F word, Via? Wow. This must be big." I giggle. Not that Via doesn't swear. She's just selective about it so it tends to make the radar.

"Let's just say Ryan and Chase have had some growing pains lately. But that's a story for another day. So, listen, he didn't go camping with them because he took me to the coast instead, where he . . . proposed."

"Holy shit. You're getting married?"

Chapter 33

JULIAN

Ever squeals. I'm halfway through our joined bathroom before I hear her follow-up giggle and stop my charge. She's been on the phone with her sister for a while now. Relief to hear her excitement has me padding back into my room, folding laundry in my lame attempt at hovering. Like I hovered all afternoon. If she noticed, she didn't let on. This girl rallies better than people twice her age. She simply got back to work. She bantered, made jokes and hustled her ass off until the last of the campers cleared out and went back to their campsites. Some choosing to leave early, the diehards sticking it out, rain or shine.

She took off for Allie's as soon as she felt cleared to leave, saying she needed to call her sister. I told her I'd meet her there shortly. No one at Brew knew about her meltdown except me and Lilly. Lilly hugged her on her way out, but I never saw them discuss it. We were all too busy keeping the guests happy. As soon as I could leave, I dashed into my place, grabbed my laundry bag, threw it into the Jeep and rushed to Allie's. As I stepped through the door, the hum of her muted voice filtered down the stairs. She didn't sound distressed, but I used my laundry as a reason to be in my room. Not to eavesdrop I told myself, just to be close if she needed me.

Seeing her shut down on the office floor earlier gutted me. I stayed calm for her. But I wanted to smash that fucking dick's face. I knew I didn't have all the details. I wanted her to tell me on her own. I didn't want to pry. But based on the reaction I got from Chase, he felt plenty responsible and possibly even guilty. It wasn't hard to get him to leave.

"Young? Chase Young?" I stand at the arched entrance to the game room and call his name like a hostess calling for a reservation. When he answers, I ask to speak with him outside. We step away from the group and he follows me out the double doors of the café.

Once outdoors, I turn and face him squarely. "You and your group need to leave." The look on his face tells me he knows that I know exactly who he is. And I know he wonders who the hell I am and how much I know. I can tell when he makes the decision to gamble on me not knowing all the details. He squares his shoulders and tilts his chin up to make himself taller. I take pleasure in seeing that he still has to look up to look me in the eyes.

When he opens his mouth to argue, I stop him with one finger raised between us. I move my face to within an inch of his and say, "You can tell your friends whatever you want. I'd go with something believable and blame it on the marina. We overbooked the site and the people coming in are celebrating a special occasion. And you're just such a standup guy, you agreed to give up your space and go home early. The weather sucks anyway. And for your kindness, the marina agreed to waive your fees. Or you can tell them that you're not welcomed here, and we reserve the right to refuse service to anyone. Or you can tell them what a fucking douche you are, and you had the choice to leave or get your ass kicked. Either way, you're going to haul your ass back to your camp, pack your shit and leave. We clear?"

He opens his mouth again to speak, and I roll my weight onto the balls of my feet. My fingers twitch as I clench my fists at my side. I really don't like violence. I've seen enough of it within the walls of my own house growing up. But that doesn't mean I'm not human. Every cell in my body wants to beat the shit out of this asshole. Part of me wants him to give me a reason. It must show, because after a brief stare down, he nods and turns to go back to the game room, presumably to tell his friends. I stay busy in the dining area checking on guests, making small talk until I see him and his group leave the café. Once I tell Ever he's gone, I stay in the dining area until I watch his group's vehicles leave the marina.

Ever has already returned to the kitchen making burritos with the littles when I rejoin them. She laughs and banters with them like she didn't just have a meltdown in the office. My chest swells watching her. That she doesn't realize her own strength makes her stronger. She's not actively projecting strength. She's just strong.

Picturing her like that stamps down the surge of anger from reliving the morning. The click of the bathroom door reaches my ears just before her hands snake around my middle and her cheek presses into my shoulder blade.

"Hi." Her soft breath warms my skin through my shirt.

"Hi, sweet girl." I turn in her arms and clasp mine loosely around her lower back and look down into her flushed face. Her cheeks always go pink when I call her sweet girl. I kiss each one lightly. "Your talk with your sister sounded . . . exciting?"

"She's engaged." Her eyes go wide, brows arching up.

"Isn't she my age?" I share her surprise.

"M-hm."

"Wow." I snug my arms tighter around her.

"But they act like an old married couple already, so I guess it's good they're making it official. They're both like old souls."

"You sound thrilled for them." My words drip sarcasm. My chin is tilted up and resting on top of her head, my arms still wrapped securely around her.

"No, I am. I just . . . Chase is Ryan's best friend. I'm going to have to see him at the wedding. Fuck, am I going to have to walk down the aisle with him?" She pulls back and turns her frown on me, eyes wide.

"Well, it's not happening right now, so that's a worry for another day."

"No . . . you're right." Then with a heavy sigh, she adds, "Thanks for today, Julie. Sorry for the meltdown."

"Why do you do that?" I tighten my arms around her again. I want to shelter her from all the shit that makes her want to shrink, apologize for who she is.

She shrugs in my arms and squeezes me a little tighter. "What'd you say to him anyway?"

"Basically, for him to tell his friends there was a mix-up in the schedule and they needed to check out early. Or I would tell them my version. He agreed to go quietly." I feel her cheeks arch up against my chest.

"Thanks for that."

"You already said that." I toss her line at her. "And you're welcome, Ever. Always. Whatever you need." I want her to explain what happened back home. But I don't want to push her, take her back to that panic she felt. I exhale a deep sigh and wait. When she says nothing, I ask instead what she feels like doing with the rest of the day. It's late afternoon and I think we all were glad to leave Brew and hope that the campers didn't need us until tomorrow. "We could go grab a quick workout. Or figure out what to make for dinner. Or maybe you just want to be alone?"

"I'm kinda beat. Aren't you tired? You were awake before I was. Not that that's anything new."

"I'm not tired. But I'm more in the mood to relax than workout."

"Same. In fact, I could use a hot shower."

"Okay, maybe I'll go figure out dinner while you shower." The domestic vibe of our conversation puts a dull ache in my chest and a longing in my gut. I ignore the urge to rub the tattoo on my chest.

Ever leans up on her toes and presses a soft kiss just below my ear. Before she releases her arms from my waist, she speaks so close to my ear her breath raises the hair on my arms. "Maybe you could just help me . . . wash my back?"

Her words send blood rushing to my crotch.

She turns and steps toward the bathroom, and I follow in her trance. She turns on the spray and closes the door to wait for it to heat. I'm there in her space. I step to her and capture her lips in mine, pushing hers apart with my tongue and tangling it with hers. I clench the hem of her shirt and roll it up her body, only breaking the kiss to whip it over her head. She does the same to my shirt.

I roll her leggings off her hips and down her thighs. No thong! My pants strain with that knowledge. Her fingers fumble with the waistband of my joggers and push them down my hips, taking my boxer briefs with them. My hands cup her face as I kiss her deeply, and she's panting when I pull back.

The bathroom is steaming and fogging the air.

As I reach for the door handle on the shower, Ever pulls her sports bra over her head. I hold the door open, and she dips under my arm, steps into the spray, closes her eyes and leans her head back under the showerhead. Water sluices off her body. I step in and close the door. She opens her eyes as it clicks and pins me with her storm-cloud gaze, dropping her hands to her sides.

I step to her and join her under the spray, swiping my hand down my face to clear the water from my eyes. I seize her hips and brace her against the side wall, so the spray still reaches both of us. I lean my face into her and kiss her again while I pull her hips to mine. Her hands flying to my ass, fingers digging in, is all the encouragement I need. My hand drops to her vee. I touch her slowly, tentatively. I break the kiss to ask, "Are you sore?"

"Uh-uh. Maybe a little. I don't care." She grinds into my hand, reaching for my wrist to make me give her what she wants.

She's so wet, and not from the shower. I slip a finger inside her and swallow her moan with another deep kiss, my tongue mimicking my finger. She lifts her leg and hooks it on my hip, giving me more access. She's never done this. She's moving on instinct.

And that's my undoing. I slide my finger out and reach down to guide myself into her. *Ugh, no condom. Shit!* "Ever, no condom."

"I don't care."

I should care. I should stop and get one, but she's clenching my pecs, dragging her nails across my nipples, and I can't stop even if I want to. I grip my hands under her ass, lift her off the floor and drive into her. Slowly at first, swiveling my hips, eliciting more gasps and moans from her throat with each thrust.

Her hands clamp onto my shoulders, her fingernails leaving crescents on my skin. Her ankles lock against the base of my spine.

The sensation of no condom is taking all the restraint I've got. So tight and smooth, I glide in easily. I continue my slow grind until her breath quickens, her cry is deeper, longer, and I know she's almost there. I trail my kisses to her ear and whisper sweet things to her. With every plunge. Things I won't examine until later. "Sweet Ever. My Ever. Ugh. So good. All. Mine. Ever. Say you're all mine."

"Yes. Fuck, yes." Her words are breathy, lips parted and dripping wet. So fucking hot. "Ugh, Julie." My name is ripped from her throat.

"I got you, Ever."

Her body convulses with her orgasm, and it's all I need to follow her.

Afterward, my girl is playful, soaping loofahs and scrubbing my back, throwing one at me and giving me her back to return the favor. We make quick work of bathing and finish just as the water begins to turn cold.

On our way downstairs to figure out what to do for dinner, Ever brings it up on her own. "You know," she begins conversationally, "I was thinking, when I was sitting there on the floor in the office, in freeze mode, that I wished I never met Chase. Or Kendall." She says it so matter-of-factly and not at all as traumatized as she looked on that office floor. "But then I thought if I'd never met them, I wouldn't have gone to the party, got drunk, passed out, woken up to him trying to kiss me, Kendall walking in on us, accusing me of sleeping with him, her trying to kill herself, all her friends bullying me until I left town . .

." She pauses for a breath as she steps off the last stair, turns to look at me and continues with this proud "aha" look on her face. "I would've never moved in with Allie. I would've never worked at Fit. I would've never crashed into you that first day." She smiles at me with her whole face and touches my lips with her finger. "I would've never met you, Julie. And I wouldn't take that back. Not even to erase all that."

I kiss the tip of her finger and reach up to take her hand. I press my lips to her palm, clasp her hand and pull her with me into the kitchen. "Permission to revisit this story in more detail later, please." I ask boldly because she brought it up, and I want to know exactly what happened to bring her here. I choose comfort food for dinner. I introduce her to Allie's grilled cheese sandwiches, and she throws together a salad as our nod to healthy.

I try not to overanalyze why I choose to make them tonight. I haven't had one since that night I crashed here three years ago, but it left its mark. I know why I choose them, even if I don't want to acknowledge it.

Without realizing it, Ever asked me if I'd trade meeting her if it meant I could bring Taya back. Okay, she didn't ask. But it made me ask myself that after listening to her reason through seeing Chase today. I know I'm in my head and being too quiet. I rally and focus on her, our dinner, us.

She tells me all the bullshit she went through in OV—how people came out of the woodwork to make it their business to defend Kendall and vilify Everly. She tells me they even vandalized her car. I don't get how Via and Ryan are still friends with these assholes. But Everly gives me some flimsy excuse of not being able to really pin any of it on Kendall and Chase directly. And while half of me is fuming over the injustice she experienced, half of my head is recognizing that it brought her here and it's taking me back in time, to a blonde-haired, green-eyed girl who made me feel like someone for the first time in my life. But she didn't stay. Which just reinforces in my fucked-up logic that I'm not worth staying for. Which, in turn, brings me to how I don't deserve the chestnut-haired, gray-eyed girl that makes me feel like I'm not just someone, but everything. Yes, my brain is making unfair comparisons. I can't help it. But truly there are none. Taya and I were kids. Ever might be the same age I was when I lost her, but she is far from the typical eighteen-year-old. She's more mature and grounded than a lot of people twice her age. I know I don't deserve someone so perfect. But truly, the biggest fear—the one I don't want to admit—what if I can't keep her safe? What if I'm not enough to make her stay?

When we make our way upstairs to turn in for the night, I tell her I have some work to do and would just be across the bathroom if she needs me. It feels shitty to lie next to her, kiss her, touch her when my head is fucking with me that I don't deserve her—like I'm shitty for not saving her from me. I just need to take a beat and get my head straight.

If she notices my distant behavior, she doesn't bring it up. Which fucks with me more. That she doesn't call me on my shit because maybe she's used to people not measuring up. She brushes her teeth, touches my face with her delicate fingers and kisses me sweetly on the lips. I watch her retreat into her room and softly close the bathroom door.

Bracing my arms, hands fisted on either side of the sink, I stare at my reflection and want to punch the face in the mirror. *Why don't I deserve her?* I tap my fists on the countertop a couple times and watch my reflection take some deep breaths. Padding into my room, I sit down at the desk and open my laptop to make good on my excuse of work.

Several emails from Allie top my inbox. I tap the one displaying a business opportunity in the subject line. Apparently, a YouTube video, several actually, showcasing our kickboxing class, featuring me, has gone viral. *Sylvie.* As I read the words, my mind reels in too many directions. Somehow it, or I, as Allie made a point of saying, caught public attention. A famous trainer in Southern California Allie met during her training, the one running the event, wants to propose a lucrative opportunity to us both—a way to cash in on the virality.

I click on the link she attached. Luke Ashley Fitness has it all: training programs, his own supplements and health drinks, a merch line, a fitness app and a slogan that no doubt reels people in. *Real strength. Real life. No filters.* This guy is impressive. I just wonder how two small-town trainers fit into his world. I reply to Allie that I'll make time for a Zoom meeting tomorrow and to let me know when. I ignore the rest of the emails, unable to concentrate. Instead, I opt for the fresh air of the balcony, hoping it'll clear my head and snap me out of this doom spiral of what-ifs. Staring into the inky oblivion, I let the night air soothe me, the darkness lull me.

"Taya, don't go yet. We've got time." I forgot how much I love her laugh. I tighten my grip on the delicate fingers laced with mine. But hers are slippery. They're sliding through mine as I stretch to cling on, her laugh lilting through the air.

She floats farther away, looking over her shoulder at me. Her sage eyes smile, her lips parted with her melodic laugh. Her arm stretches out to mine.

Does she want me to follow her? I reach out, but she's too far away now.

I get up to join her but my feet tangle beneath me. I fall, but she doesn't stop. "Taya. Wait. I'll go with you." She's no longer looking back, and I can barely make out her figure in the waning light. "Taya!" I'm shouting now.

She keeps moving like she can't hear me.

Over and over, I scream her name until there are only shadows. I feel the cold now. She's gone. It's black out now and I'm all alone.

I jolt awake, the dream still fresh in my mind. I'm still on the deck, my skin slicked with sweat despite the chilled air. Shivering, I dash inside and crank the shower. After I let the water pelt the chill away, I slip into Ever's room. I hear her slow, rhythmic breathing in the silence and see her sleeping silhouette in the muted moonlight cast on her bed. I peel back the covers on the opposite side and slide in behind her.

Her body is so warm.

I fit mine to her back and curve around her as unobtrusively as possible. She sighs and presses into me but stays otherwise undisturbed. I'd never know what it's like to sleep next to or wake up with Taya. We were too young. We were Ever's age now, which seems impossible. She feels much older than Taya seemed back then. But lying with her in my arms, smelling her scent, feeling her body pressed against the length of mine, I have my answer. I wouldn't give back my time with Ever. I couldn't. She's part of me, like my skin.

I turn my face up to the ceiling and stare into the dark and feel the tear slip into my ear. I turn my face into the pillow to wipe the moisture away, then bury my nose in the hair just behind her ear and breathe in deep, slow, and beg for sleep. I hate myself because it feels like I'm saying I'm glad she's gone, and my heart breaks for the young green-eyed girl that never got to grow up to feel love like this.

Love. Like. This.

I love her. How can I hate myself and love her?

Chapter 34

Everly

I set my alarm for six a.m. hoping Julian and I could work out before the day gets busy. As usual, Julian is already awake. I think so anyway, because I fell asleep before he came to bed. I didn't hear him come in, but the other side of my bed shows evidence of him sleeping there. As soon as I open the door to the hallway though, I smell the coffee. It's not lost on me that we have a routine now. It makes me grin and puts flutters in my stomach. I've always teased Via that she and Ryan are like an old married couple, but Julian and I seem to be doing our best imitation of one. My cheeks ache with the effortless grin.

Before I step into the kitchen, I swipe the smile from my face. Just as I'm about to greet Julian with something familiar and likely inappropriate, he begins talking like he's in the middle of a conversation. He looks up from his laptop screen when he sees me, holds up his hand with one finger in the air as if to say, *just a sec.*

I pad over to the coffee pot and fill the mug he set out for me. My smile creeps back into place with the gesture. I wander to the windows and gaze out, conscious to stay out of the Zoom camera field of vision. He has earbuds in, so I can't hear the other half of the conversation, but from Julian's side I think it must be Allie. Whoever it is, they're talking fitness, content and social platforms. The thought of social media puts a pit in my stomach. I haven't even missed it since I came here. But it lost its allure way before that, when Kendall's posse decided to post slander and death threats about me. Of course, Kendall would "never condone that kind of hate." She never had to. She had loyal minions for that. I never put much effort into having a social presence in the first place, but I got popular quick when they decided to spotlight me with their venom and lies. It didn't take me long to shut down my accounts. Good riddance. Social media always came off a little fake and desperate to me. Like a drug for attention seekers.

Julian and I haven't discussed it in any depth, but he admitted he didn't do social media either except the few things he posted on the Fit website for members and potential members. It was such a relief to hear that I wouldn't have to explain why I didn't want my picture posted or why I didn't want to be tagged in places and activities. Not that I could be anymore without active accounts. And Lilly got it too. She has a loyalty streak a mile wide, so once she knew why, it was never an issue. I stumbled into this alternate universe where these few people I've come to adore don't give a shit about the social status of highlight reels and documenting every aspect of their lives. I thank the gods, the universe, the magic of Blue Lake and of course my unintentional fairy godmother, Allie, for the gift of this new life.

Like I told Julian last night, I could thank the shit show I went through in Oak Valley because it brought me here. I hug myself, the warmth of the mug heating my bicep. If I stay in the bubble of Blue

Lake, I can breathe. I can relax, be myself. Except that Chase found his way into my bubble. Would he tell Kendall? Any one of them could and likely would. And what about Via and Ryan's engagement? There'll be festivities. They're all still friends, though I wonder why. Maybe because we can't prove Kendall was behind the social take-down. And maybe she wasn't. She just had enough loyal sheep to do it for her whether she asked point-blank or not. Maniacal, mean sheep, but sheep nonetheless.

I need to call Via and find out what they're planning for the en-gagement.

Lost in my thoughts, I don't hear Julian end his Zoom call or walk up behind me. When his hands skim down my arms, I instinctively lean back into his chest and rest the back of my neck on his shoulder.

His lips find the side of my neck. His breath just behind my ear makes the hair on my arms prickle. This beautiful, beautiful man makes my whole body exhale and sing all at once.

"Hi, sweet girl. Sleep well?"

Setting my coffee on the window ledge, I turn in his arms. "Hi, Julie. Like a rock. You?" I wrap my arms around the middle of his back and press a kiss to his neck.

"M-hm." He mumbles his agreement and steps back before I con-tinue my intended attack on his neck.

I assume his distracted retreat is about the call he just had. "What was all that about?" I toss my head toward his laptop.

"Hmph," he chuckles, shaking his head a little. "Allie . . ."

"And . . ."

"C'mere." He pulls me toward the bar and sits, pulling me to half sit half lean on his thigh. He opens the laptop and starts showing me websites and videos. First ours at Fit, then someone's named Luke Ashley. Then he pulls up YouTube and shows me a video of him just like the one on the Fit website, but it has millions of views and comments. Surprising but not. He looks like a Greek god.

Pride swells in my chest. A twinge of jealousy does too. And it grows the more he talks. I've never had a boyfriend, and I'm not sure if I do now. I just know I like having Julian all to myself. Without the complications of life and people outside of Blue Lake. I also know that isn't sustainable or realistic. Any real relationship has to survive in the real world. And I'm not sure Blue Lake qualifies. Real world adjacent maybe, but a little more isolated, a little slower, a lot more peaceful. It's looking like I'm about to find out if our . . . whatever this is . . . would sink or swim.

Julian says he's flying to Southern California to meet up with Allie and Ashley. Ashley claims he can take Julian to the "next level." He'd become his own business. People would subscribe to his fitness videos. Ashley already established himself in that space and plans to get Julian and Allie there too. I had no idea that any of that was on Allie's or Julian's radar, especially Julian's. And maybe it wasn't initially. Maybe Ashley planted that seed. He's stunning to look at. So is Julian. What do I really know about Julian other than our simple little life and routine we created here?

Julian and Allie have apparently been in talks since just before I arrived to transition him into her partner at both Blue Fit and Brew. He obtained his degree in business online and secured his personal training credentials over the three years he's lived here. I can tell he's downplaying his excitement as he explains the concept Ashley's proposing.

I want to be proud of him. I *am* proud of him.

He grins like a kid as he rubs his hand up and down my thigh and leans in to kiss me on the lips. But his grin doesn't reach all the way to his eyes. His words don't match the deep blue pools. He looks sad or tired, despite his exciting news.

It reminds me of the look my mom gets sometimes. I want to ask him about it, but I'm not sure I want to hear his answers. Would he give me any if I did ask? I want him to ask me to fly down south with him. But Allie doesn't even know we are . . . whatever we are. The thought of explaining me and Julian to people makes my heart thud double time against my ribs.

My face must reveal my inner turmoil because he taps his index finger softly on my forehead and slides it down my nose before he asks, "What's going on in there?"

I go for directness and say, "I guess I'm feeling a little Cinderella-esque. Like the clock is about to strike midnight and everything is about to change."

"Hmmm," he murmurs, watching me. His chuckle is low and slow, but his eyes are sad. His finger trails the side of my face and tucks my hair behind my ear. "Ever, I know we haven't really 'gone there' about us. This." He wags his finger back and forth between us. "But nothing is going to change us, what we have. Not anyone from your hometown. Not any fitness guru from Southern California. Not Allie." He pauses, leaving his past hanging in the unspoken. "Unless . . . unless you want it to. If you don't want . . ." He trails off, dropping his hand into his lap and lowering his eyes to follow it.

My mouth drops open with my sharp intake of breath. Then snaps closed. I shake my head on his last words. "No," I bark, then stop myself, pursing my lips together, my gut clenching. I grab his forearms and turn my body on his thigh so I'm facing him squarely. I squeeze my fingers around the muscled skin until he raises his eyes to mine. "I don't want."

The storm in his eyes mirrors my thoughts.

"I wish we could stay right here forever and hide from every fucked-up thing this world has to offer. But we can't. I know that. And I'm happy for you, Julie. I'm proud of you. And I know Allie enough to know she just wants everything and everyone to be peaceful and happy."

He smiles sadly at that. Maybe he knows about all the pain and loss Allie has seen.

I don't know. I only know what my mom told us. But she's irony defined because her young life was anything but peaceful and happy. I guess for me that's the most beautiful display of humanity. That the world could throw utter shit at you and instead of letting it jade you, suck you into the bitterness, you come out on the other side wanting to save everyone around you from a similar fate.

My phone buzzes in my pocket, hitting the kill switch on our conversation, so I reach into my pocket to answer it. Via's face fills the screen. I hold my index finger up to my lips, set my phone on the counter in front of me and Julian, then slide the bar with the same finger to answer it and press the speaker button. "Hey, Via. You're up early." I smile at Julian apologetically.

He winks at me like it's all good.

"Yeah, well it's three hours later where Mom is, and she woke me up so . . . Did I wake you?"

"No, we start early at the fitness club and at the café when there are campers."

"Wow, that sounds . . . busy. How do you do it all?"

"I don't know. We all just pitch in wherever we're needed, and it somehow works out."

"You sound happy, Ev. And I'm happy for you. You deserve a happy life. We all do." Via's words mirror my thoughts exactly—maybe some sister telepathy.

"Yeah . . . we do. So . . . what's up? What's got you on my phone so early?"

Julian uses the conversation as his cue to retreat. He stops tracing circles around my ear with his index finger and stands, closing his laptop.

"I told Mom the news. I texted her yesterday after you and I talked. And well, I guess wherever she is, now is a good time for her to call me."

"What'd she say?"

"She's happy for us. Wants to do an engagement party when she can get home."

"Yeah? Did she say when that would be?"

Her giggle comes through the phone. "Yep, this weekend."

"Wait, like, in six days?"

"She said they have a break in the tour, and that's the only time she can get home for two days in a row."

"Wow. Okay. What can I do?"

"Just show up. I can do it all from here. Can you get the time off?"

I look at Julian, eyebrows raised in question.

He smirks a classic "of course" grin at me.

"Of course," I answer. "No problem. And Via, can I bring someone?"

He stops packing his laptop away, then resumes quickly.

My heart drops, then slams into my ribs. Would he not want to come with me? Meet my sister? My mom? Maybe we aren't a thing. I stamp down the rising panic, will the churning in my gut to chill.

Via coughs on the other end of the call like she choked on her drink. "Uh, sure," she responds, clearly shocked by my question. "Who?"

"His name is Julian and he's my . . . We're kind of . . . seeing each other?" I finish my sentence like a question, looking at Julian as I do. I drop my eyes quickly before he looks at me because I'm afraid of the answer I might see in his.

"Julian McKay? Allie's trainer at Fit?"

"Uh, yeah." I scoot my stool back from the bar and stand up, turning from him with my phone in my hand but still on speaker. "You know Julian?" I look at him now, askance.

He shakes his head, his lips arched up on one side in a wry face.

"Ev, that guy is famous. His training videos are viral on YouTube." Julian rolls his eyes at her declaration.

"Oh, yeah, well, you know I don't do social media anymore." I sound dejected, even to my own ears. I hope Via can't hear it. I turn my back on Julian again in case my face shows it.

"No, I know. But oh my God, Ev. Wow. So, are you guys dating? Is it serious? How long has this been going on? He's effing hot!"

At the last comment, Julian rolls his eyes again, smiling, stands up and mouths that he's going to take a shower and retreats up the stairs.

"We're . . . hanging out." I take the phone off speaker and hold it to my ear. Lowering my voice, I admit, "Oh my God, Via. I'm crazy about him," glancing over my shoulder to make sure he's gone. It feels good to admit that out loud.

"How old is he anyway?"

"Twenty-one."

"So, have you guys kissed? Is he a good kisser? I bet he's a good kisser."

"Okay, we're done with Q&A portion of the program. Can I bring him or not?"

"Yeah, of course. Totally. Oh my God, Mom's going to flip out. Little Evvie's got her first boyfriend."

"Shut up, Via. And don't tell Mom. One game of twenty questions is enough for today. And besides, he's not my boyfriend. He's . . . a situation. So . . . text me all the details. And seriously, let me know what I can do, bring, whatever. Seriously," I repeat when she doesn't respond.

"Yeah, okay. But, Evvie, you know some of the crew will be here for the party, right? I mean, we're not as close as we used to be. Mostly because I'm sure at least some of them are responsible for the hell you went through. Even if I can't prove it."

"I know. I'm going to be fine. I can do this. Fuck them. All of them. You're my sister. If they don't like that I'm there, they can leave. But also, Via, you don't always have to go along with the group. You don't always have to include them if they aren't your people anymore."

"Right." She drags the word out like it's not. "You've forgotten how things work in OV. But it's all good. If they don't behave, I'll fucking make them leave. And so will Ryan."

I drop it because I know it's useless. "Love you, Via. Miss you. And . . . congratulations. I'm so happy for you guys."

"Love you too. See you in six days. And, Ev, congrats on your . . . situationship."

"Don't tell Mom," I remind her and hang up.

***

Julian flew to Southern California to meet Allie and Luke Ashley early Wednesday morning. He promised he'd try to get back in time to go with me to my sister's engagement party Saturday afternoon, but something changed since the morning we discovered the viral videos. Since I walked in on that call with Allie and Ashley. I wouldn't peg Julian for someone who'd let fame go to his head. So I couldn't believe that knowledge of his viral status would be at the crux of the shift. We haven't had sex since then either. He wouldn't go to sleep with me, and I didn't wake up when he would come to bed. I'd see the evidence of his body next to mine in the morning, but he continued to wake before me. We all stayed so busy with camping season and the normal running of things that it didn't leave much time for anything else. Especially deep heart-to-heart conversations.

Sadness seemed to shadow his every word, smile and kiss. I couldn't find the confidence to bring it up. If my past taught me anything, it's that life rarely works out the way you hope. I weirdly prefer this state of limbo, the unknowing, to the surety that he'd changed his mind. Or that maybe he just doesn't feel the same about me that I feel about him. Maybe he thinks I'm too young. Maybe he's a typical guy who's gotten the goods and . . . I can't even finish that thought. That isn't Julian. He's the kind of green flag energy novels are written about. Despite the strange distance, he still shows me he cares. My coffee cup is out waiting for me every morning. Sweet kisses every night. But if I try to push the kisses further, he always has a ready excuse of work. So I don't push. Instead, I write him letters he'll never read. I wish for the happy ending my books always deliver. And I watch him grow more distant.

When Wednesday morning comes, I make sure to set my alarm to say goodbye to him before he leaves for the airport. I finally succeeded in waking up before he leaves the bed. But the unspoken strain between us makes my victory pointless. When I tap the alarm and roll over, he's awake and staring at the ceiling. I move into his side, rolling half on top of him, and my hand glosses down his smooth chest and chiseled abs until I reach the trail of dark hair and the waistband of his boxer briefs.

His hand shoots down and clasps mine, stopping my motion. Softening his abrupt response, he takes my hand and presses the palm to his lips. He's been doing this dance for days now.

I let him kiss my palm, but as soon as he stops, I pull my hand back, fling the covers off my body and stalk into the bathroom, snapping the door closed behind me. I don't know what to make of any of it. Does he not want me anymore? I want to ask. I just don't know that I want the answer. So I say nothing.

As I make my way downstairs after dawdling in the bathroom and getting dressed, I hear Julian's Jeep motor running outside. I know I'm cutting it close to the time he needs to leave for the airport, but I don't know what to do or say anymore. The awkward chasm between us is obvious and can't be ignored or excused. Something is up. Something changed. And my self-confidence is floundering. I stand on the bottom stair as he comes through the front door, presumably after loading his bag in the Jeep.

The shutters come down on his indigo eyes as he walks toward me. With me on the step, we stand almost eye to eye and he moves right into my space, breathing my air, causing my heart to pound in my throat.

I hold my breath.

He reaches out and swipes a lock of hair behind my ear with his index finger. "Hi, sweet girl."

"Hi, Julie," I reply out of habit, but I don't feel like his 'sweet girl' right now. I feel confused and squirrelly and . . . clingy. My eyes sting. I shut them and blow out the shaky breath I'd been holding.

"I'll be back as soon as I can, but I'll probably miss the engagement party."

My heart drops. "I know." But I don't know. I don't know what the fuck is going on or what changed. But I somehow expected him to say this. I want to ask him why. I want to ask a lot of things. Is meeting my family too much? Did I pressure him? Am I still his girl? Was I ever?

Say something, Everly.

"I'm sorry, Ever." He has the grace to look . . . embarrassed, ashamed? Both?

"For what exactly? Missingthe party? Ignoring me all week? Changing your mind? What?"

He sighs audibly, resting his forehead against mine and digging his fingers into my waist. "All of it. Everything. I don't want to hurt you, Ever. I just don't . . . You deserve better than this. Better than me." He brings his hands to either side of my face like he wants to kiss me, but he doesn't.

"What are you saying?" I hold my breath.

"I can't get into this. I—we don't have time to discuss this right now."

"But there's something to discuss. Just say it, Julian. If you changed your mind, just say it." I hurl the last part, wanting to hurl my fists at his chest. I push against it instead.

He drops his hands. "It's not that simple."

"It really is." I hold my breath again, waiting for him to deny it. He doesn't. "Just go before you miss your plane."

"I hate leaving like this.We'll talk when I get back. Ever, it's going to be alright. I promise." His eyes try to meet mine.

I don't look at him. I focus instead on my clasped hands, my thumbnails flicking against each other. "You can't promise that. You don't know. No one knows. It just is what it is."

"Hey. I'll see you when I get back. I'll hurry as much as I can. Okay?" He dips his head to try to catch my eye.

Always the accommodating one, I force a smile and nod.

He kisses me quickly on the lips as his his finger traces around my ear to a lock of my hair. He twirls it once, lets it slip free, and turns to go.

I stand on the bottom stair until the sound of his Jeep disappears, then I trudge back upstairs and straight into his room, where I find the hoodie he was wearing the night before on the foot of his bed. I drag it on over my head, stuff my arms into the sleeves and sink onto the mattress. As the first tear falls, I pull my knees up to my chest and yank the hem of the oversized hoodie over them.

Five minutes! I allow myself five minutes to feel sad and wallow in the unknown and what-ifs. Then I stand up, swipe my face with the dangling cuffs of the sleeves and leave for work. I stay so busy filling in the gaps of his absence between Fit and Brew that time flies. And I mostly sleep soundly with him gone, but it may have more to do with the hoodie I wear that smells like him. I've been wearing it since he left.

***

When I arrive home from Brew Friday night, I hope he's already there. He texts instead to say he can't get home until late the next day. We haven't texted much since he left. And I didn't initiate any. He texted the first night to say goodnight and that he's been busy all day with meetings. Somehow, I knew he wouldn't make it home for the party. I selfishly wanted him beside me to face the Oak Valley crew tomorrow. I know I'll have my sister and mom there, but Julian sparks a peace or confidence in me I can't readily explain. He grounds me. Or he did. I'm not sure I can even admit that to him now in this limbo state of *WTF* we're in. I'm caught somewhere between wanting him by my side and avoiding him entirely. Especially if he plans to end things. And this turmoil does nothing to put me in a celebratory mood. Skipping out on the festivities isn't an option though. Especially with my mom in town. They wanted me to come down last night, but I told them work was too busy. I knew that would shut my mom up, the dictionary definition of a workaholic. There's nothing to do now except show up and get through it. Maybe none of the crew will be there.

Yeah, right.

I know I won't get that lucky.

***

I arrive before anyone else. For almost two hours, it's just the three of us. I can't remember the last time we were all together, just us. My mom looks good. Happy. Via looks euphoric. Exactly how a newly engaged person should. We laugh, joke and prep for the party as if no time has passed between us. The Davis girls are superior at compartmentalizing. It's not like life gave us any other choice.

Via has no idea things changed since I brought up Julian on our call, so it's only a matter of time before she spills the tea to my mom. And I know she's dying for me to mention it, but considering our current dynamic, I can't bring myself to do it. Leave it to Via though.

"So, Mom. There's a guy. In Blue Lake. His name is Julian. And Everly likes him."

"Oh, honey, a real boyfriend. Wait, he's real, right? Or is this your latest book?"

Via snickers behind her.

"Really, guys?" They don't know anything, so I roll with it. Besides, if it is over, maybe I can just pretend for today. "He's real. He's a trainer at Fit. And he's nice and good looking. And nice."

"You already said that." That from Via.

"Shut up, Via."

"So where is Mr. Wonderful? You should've brought him." My mom keeps arranging the snack board like me having a boyfriend (if he is my boyfriend) is the most natural thing in the world.

"Working. He had to fly to L.A. to meet Allie for some work stuff."

"Mom, Julian is internet famous. Some workout videos of him went viral on YouTube."

"Okay, someone better pull those up."

"I got rid of my social media a long time ago, so I've never even seen them. And we don't have time for that right now. Later, okay? And where are the cupcakes?"

"Garage fridge," they say in unison.

I just ducked my head into the fridge when I hear her voice. "Everly. I figured we'd see you here. How are you?"

Kendall.

Her saccharine voice drips fake kindness. We left the rolling garage door open because our garage has always doubled as a game room with a pool table and dart board. First with my dad and his military buddies, then with Via and her friends through high school and college. Most people use the garage like a front door.

I straighten up and turn around, my back to the wide opening, and face Kendall. She stands between me and the door that leads through the laundry room into the kitchen and my family—the only people who have my back in this town.

Chase stands next to her looking like he wished the floor would open and swallow him. As he should. He could've cleared all this up a long time ago. When it first happened. He and I both know I didn't come on to him and that we didn't sleep together. His guilt casts his eyes to the floor he'd seemingly like to fall through while he shuffles from foot to foot beside her. What did I ever see in these two? They look fake and plastic and . . . small to me now.

"Look, Kendall. Today isn't about any of us. It's for Ryan and Via. Can you just not? We can ignore each other."

"Can I not? I just asked how you're doing. And I haven't done anything but be the victim here. We both are." She gestures to Chase. "You took advantage of our kindness and Chase's drunken state to sleep with him."

"I didn't sleep with Chase, and he knows it."

"So do I." Julian's voice hits me like a cleansing wave just before his arms snake around my middle, pull me back into his chest and squeeze just a little. Every cell of my body exhales as he dips his head, his nose nuzzling just behind my ear, and places a soft kiss on my neck. "Hi," he whispers in my ear.

"Hi." I close my eyes at his embrace. When I open them, Kendall and Chase are both staring, mouths agape.

"Chase, we've already met. Kendall, is it? I'm Julian, Everly's boyfriend. I'd say it's nice to meet you, but we both know that's not true. Shall we go inside and celebrate the happy couple? Or should we discuss how you and your boyfriend lied about my girlfriend and how I know it's true?"

"C'mon, Chase. We don't have to listen to this." Kendall grabs his hand to pull him inside.

"You're right," I find my voice. "You don't. But if you think you're going to continue your drama and bullshit inside, you can leave now. Today is for Via and you're not going to fuck with it like you fucked with me. Your choice."

"I think she means it, guys." I hear the smirk in Julian's words.

Then I see Via poke her head through the door, probably to see what's taking me so long. She takes in the scene, and we make eye contact just before she realizes Julian is behind me. Ignoring Kendall and Chase, she squeals, "Oh my God, Julian? You made it. Ev said you were out of town."

"Flew in just now. Didn't want to miss it. Congratulations."

That Via acted like she and Julian were old friends made me giggly. This is why Via fits in so well with the fake, plastic crowd. Not that she's fake herself, but that she knows how to play their game. Maybe better than they did.

"Get in here and meet our mom."

"We'll be right there. I'm going to help Ever—ly carry the . . ."

"Cupcakes," I fill in the rest of the sentence for him.

"Okay cool. Oh hey, Ken. Chase. C'mon in. Thanks for coming." Via ushers them inside and closes the door behind her, but not before giving me the eyebrows.

I roll my eyes and turn to face Julian.

"Hi, pretty girl." His finger traces circles around my ear—a habit that soothes me.

"Hi, Julie." I kiss him, fully. I kiss him so long and deep that we're both breathless when I pull away. "Perfect timing. How'd you even find me?"

"I've got your location." He winks at me. "And it turns out Ashley has a private plane." Raising his eyebrows, he adds, "He and Allie flew me into the little Oak Valley airport, and I took an Uber to your location. They're headed up to Blue Lake. We'll meet them there later. They'll be here for a couple days and then Allie will . . . wait for it . . . fly back with him." He wiggles his eyebrows on the last sentence.

"Allie and Ashley?"

"Yep." He nods swiftly, holding his hands out to his sides, palms up. "Like two school kids. I think that's why she's not coming here today.

The Ashley thing might overshadow the happy couple." He tosses his head toward the door Via disappeared into.

I nod, agreeing with that logic. "No wonder she extended her trip."

"Right? Worked out well for us too." He wiggles his eyebrows, his blue eyes sparkling. *The Julian I know.*

"So, those two?" He tosses his head toward the door they all just went through. "They gonna play nice in the sandbox today?"

"I think you intimidate them, so yeah. I think they'll behave."

"Maybe *you* intimidate them." He pins me pointedly with his dreamy eyes but quickly continues. "Olivia seems cool. Like her sister." He winks at me again and pecks a kiss on the tip of my nose.

"Oh, Via is way cooler than me." I don't bring up any of the stuff I'm thinking and feeling. Like how I could cry that he rushed here to be with me today. That he called himself my boyfriend. To Kendall and Chase! That he alluded to him knowing I was a virgin until him. My eyes well at the thoughts flooding my brain and that he's tracing circles around my ear with his finger. I still wanna know what the hell happened before he left. And more importantly what changed to bring back the Julian that I know and . . . yeah, love.

"What's going on in there?" He uses his finger to lift my chin.

"Julie, I . . . thank you."

"Shh." He shakes his head. "It's what boyfriends do, right?"

"Well, mine does." I shrug my shoulders as I say it.

That got the low chuckle from him that makes my tummy flutter and my body tingle. He wraps both arms around me and pulls me tight to him, tucking my head under his chin. "I missed you, Ever."

"I didn't miss you at all." I feel his low half laugh on my cheek that rests on his chest. "But I slept in your hoodie for three days." I look up into his face and lift the corner of my mouth.

His smile is sweet if not a tad regretful. "C'mon, let's go celebrate the happy couple so we can go home." He turns me toward the door and lets his hand drift down my back to rest between my hip and ass like it belongs there. And it does.

Epilogue
EVERLY

Julian and I are living together. I'll be starting online college classes in the fall. This isn't the life I dreamed for myself, but somehow, it's better. Except I know how. Julian. He confessed to me that my perspective on being grateful for the shitty parts of life because they lead to the good parts made him question his own shitty life. He carried some guilt over realizing he wouldn't trade me and us if it meant Taya never died. It made him question his moral compass and feel unworthy of our relationship. He confided all that to Allie when he arrived in Southern California. She told him that missing someone didn't have to rob today of its joy. That loving me didn't mean he didn't love Taya. Allie really does give fairy godmother vibes. Or at the least, she was a therapist in another life. Everyone needs an Allie in their lives. And apparently Luke Ashley agrees.

Ashley asked Allie to oversee the string of fitness centers he planned to open in L.A., so she planned to relocate there, temporarily. She asked Julian if he'd be willing to move into her place long term. When I first came to Blue Lake, it was to finish high school. I planned to go away to college and get as far away from Oak Valley as possible, but now, the thought of not being with Julian dimmed my world. He asked Allie how she felt about me staying there with him, and she surprised us both when she said it sounded perfect.

"If ever two people completed each other more, I've never seen it." *I couldn't agree more.*

Julian would fly to L.A. periodically to film content but would continue to run Fit and oversee Brew. As part owner, he'd be able to make decisions and run things while Allie opened the Ashley clubs down south. And it looked like Noah and Lilly wanted to rent the apartment at Brew and become the camp hosts for the summer. That meant I could join Julian on his trips to L.A. I've never looked forward to a summer more.

Today, we're meeting Lilly and Noah at the cliffs to finally carry out our jump. The air already feels thick with the promise of a three-digit scorcher. True to form, the spring season in Blue Lake lasted two minutes and now summer is upon us in full force. It means the lake water is warm though, which makes the idea of plunging more palatable—to me anyway. Never a fan of the cold plunge trend no matter how healthy Julian repeatedly tells me it is.

"Okay, hoolie, today you graduate to local. You ready?" Lilly, already perched on the edge of the shale rock, calls out as we emerge from the trail.

Julian and I step up to the edge alongside Noah and Lilly. Julian takes my hand as Noah takes Lilly's. Noah and Julian share a look over our heads.

"One, two . . .," they count together. After 'two,' they hurl us off the ledge together.

The rush of the water encasing me takes my breath away. Our hands release as soon as we crash under the surface. The whoosh sound is replaced by bubbles as I propel myself toward the light above me and tilt my head back as I break through the surface, smoothing my hair back away from my face.

Julian materializes in front of me, swiping his hair back from his face and sluicing the water out of his eyes. He reaches out and pulls me to him, a wide grin spread across his face.

My legs wrap around him instinctively. Lilly and Noah are splashing and trying to dunk each other next to us. Julian kisses me, lightly at first, then deeper, like the kiss has a mind of its own, prompting our friends to turn their splash attack on us. Julian pulls us under to avoid the onslaught, and we swim for the shore.

We all plop onto the rocky bank, backs splayed on the warm flat shale to dry off. The sun bakes the droplets on our skin dry within moments.

"Guys, it's going to be an epic summer." And for the first time in my life, I don't mean because of all the books I'll get to read.

"Epic, indeed," Julian says under his breath as he rolls himself half on top of me and plants a kiss on my sun-heated lips.

I reach up to pull on his neck, binding his lips harder to mine, tilting my head to deepen the kiss.

His tongue meets mine stroke for stroke.

"Get a room," Lilly groans, arm flung over her eyes to shield them from the sun as much as our PDA.

"We did," Julian retorts in an undertone between kisses.

***

I finish making the bed in the master suite and check the display on my phone. Julian would be back any time now from his latest trip down south. Allie insisted we make the place our home, starting with taking the master. She said either of the guest rooms would be perfect for her when she flies home between stints in L.A. Part of me wonders if she'll soon be moving there to live with Ashley full time. In my whole life, I've never seen Allie in a relationship or even date a man. It's special to see how well they complement each other. I guess it's true what they say: When you're in love, you want the whole world to be too.

Julian leans on the doorway watching as I straighten and fluff pillows. "The bed looks so neat. I almost hate to mess it up."

I jump at the sound of his voice. Then my stomach flips and my heart races. He's home. "You wouldn't," I challenge.

He moves toward me, his gait unhurried. "Of course not. If you don't want me to." He closes in without touching me. "Don't want me to?"

I feel his breath on my lips, my cheek, my ear, trailing down my neck. His lips inches from skin but never making contact. He sinks to his knees before me, and I collapse back onto the edge of the bed. My legs refuse to support me when his breath hits my navel. "I, uh, yeah." I run my fingers through the buzzed hair at his nape and pull him to me.

His lips rest on my lower stomach just above the waistline of my cotton shorts.

At the contact, my head falls back, and my lids flutter closed.

"Yeah, don't?" He teases, placing small kisses around my navel. His finger traces inside the waistband of my shorts.

"Ung, nooo. I . . . mmmean . . . mmm." The throbbing in my groin clenches my thigh muscles. I want to pinch my knees together, but he's filling the space between my legs. I squeeze his frame instead, clamping him to me.

His hands clasp under my knees and scoot my ass to the edge of the bed. His finger trails from the waistband to the leg hem of my shorts, pulling them to the side, then he places a soft kiss over my panties at my center and rises from his knees, leaning over me and pressing me back onto the mattress. As he hovers on top of me, somewhat on his side, he draws my panties aside and glides his finger softly along my opening and deep into me.

I clench my knees together then, unable to bear the intensity.

"You're so wet," he murmurs and plants tiny kisses on my lips between each word.

"I told you I missed you." My response is breathy and rewarded with another finger.

The kiss that follows is deeper and leaves me panting. His fingers build tension until I'm lifting myself off the bed, inviting more. I reach for his wrist, trying to control the intensity, but his thumb and fingers know my body too well now.

"Easy, Ever. I got you. I missed you so much. Too much. Come for me?" He says it like a question. But he knows the answer. Between his words and his hands, he knows how to make my body do exactly what he wants. His finger crooks and hits the spot that rips a cry from my throat and contracts my muscles around his fingers.

The force of my orgasm squeezes my lids shut. I feel the tear run sideways down my cheek into my hairline. His hand freezes until the waves subside. With my lips still parted on heaving breaths, I open my eyes and find his pools of blue, dark with desire, watching me.

"Hi, sweet girl."

"Hi, boyfriend."

He leans his face toward my ear. "I love you, Everly Davis. I missed you so much."

Another tear runs down my face sideways. Then another. "You already said that." I try for levity as another tear tracks into my hair.

"Baby, don't cry." He kisses each tear.

"It's okay. They're happy tears." I smile to make my point. "I love you too, Julian McKay."

The doorbell disrupts our moment. We freeze, our faces mirroring each other's thoughts. *Can we just ignore it?*

Rolling his eyes, Julian gets up, adjusts himself and heads downstairs to answer the door.

I stand up and pad over to the window that overlooks the driveway. My heart stumbles when I see the red convertible with the personal plates, SYLVIED. I want to hide upstairs and let Julian deal with her, but I also don't want to start my new life with him a coward. I fix my clothes, smooth down my hair and trek down the stairs.

Julian is facing the door with Sylvie just inside on the entryway tile, holding a basket of baked goods in his arms.

Sylvie sees me on the stairs and her words falter mid-sentence. "Oh, I didn't realize you had company." She sends me her saccharine smile and just as quickly dismisses me.

Julian clears his throat and says, "Actually, Sylvie, Everly lives here with me."

"Like roommates?" She doesn't hide the hopefulness in her question.

"As my girlfriend."

I gain the confidence to step off the last stair at the pointed certainty of his response. "Oh my gosh, homemade muffins?" I approach them and take the basket from Julian's arms. "Sylvie, that's beyond kind. Thank you. Allie will be back in a couple days, so this will make the perfect breakfast over coffee. I'll make sure to tell her they came from you." I turn and aim toward the kitchen.

"Of course. Just a little housewarming for . . . you."

As I disappear into the kitchen, I hear Julian thank her and impart some vague claims about settling in and making it ours.

I cringe on the word "ours" thinking it will just antagonize her. And maybe that's his goal, but I'd rather stay off any bully radar permanently. Considering Julian does not have an intentional mean streak, I deduce he said it out of loyalty to me and our relationship. That makes my heart trip in my chest. My pulse quickens, anticipating finishing what we started. I come around the corner and collide with the wall of his chest—like the first day we met.

Catching my weight and steadying me with his arms, flexed and taut, he lifts me effortlessly off the ground.

My legs twine around his back as he tucks his forearms under my hips.

"Hi, pretty girl."

"Hi, pretty boy."

He quirks his eyebrow at the new nickname, one dimple winking at me.

"Care to finish what you started?" I push my bottom lip out in a fake pout.

"Yeah, I do." He captures that lip in his and carries me up the stairs, his body not taxed even a little with the effort.

Thanks and Blame

ACKNOWLEDGEMENTS

I spend a crazy amount of time living in my head—plotting stories, arguing with imaginary people, and trying to convince myself caffeine counts as a food group. And I love it. I'm here for it. But it can also get a little isolating. So, to everyone who's supported me and this ridiculous dream of writing books—thank you. Whether you're bookish people or not, you've cheered me on, and I'm endlessly grateful.

To my beta readers, brainstormers, and the ones who let their ears bleed while I ramble endlessly about plot holes—"thank you" doesn't really cover it, but it's all I've got. Unless I name a character after you. Stay tuned...

To the bookstagrammers and booktokkers—every like, comment, and share has meant more than you know. You're a big reason we can do what we do without someone giving us permission first.

And to my friends and family—I love you, I really do. Thanks for pretending you're not tired of me answering "What are you working on?" with a 47-minute monologue. For that alone you deserve medals.

Last but not least, thank you to the cover designers and the editors. We all judge books by their covers. Thanks for making mine so pretty. And my editors...you make me sound smarter if not feel smarter when you point out how many times I used filler words and my beloved ellipses. You really are the unsung heroes of the circus.

This is just the beginning—so buckle up. Now go get book two already.

About the Author

C.M. Wyllie is a retired stay-at-home mom and breast cancer survivor who turned her lifelong dream of writing into a full-time career—fueled by coffee, stubborn determination, and a love of storytelling. She's jumped from a mischievous children's book series to two raw, laugh-out-loud nonfiction books about her cancer journey, and now she's diving into new adult romance—where heartbreak meets healing and love always gets another shot.

Her stories have just enough spice to heat things up and keep you wanting more. She writes for hopeless romantics who root for love to stumble, fall, get back up, and find their happily ever after.

When C.M. isn't writing, she's with her green flag husband or adult kids—preferably both—obsessing over their pets and chasing sunsets.

www.ingramcontent.com/pod-product-compliance
Lightning Source LLC
Chambersburg PA
CBHW020127310726
48970CB00006B/1756